ONE TO WATCH

A DETECTIVE KAY HUNTER NOVEL

RACHEL AMPHLETT

SAXON PUBLISHING

National Library of Australia Cataloguing-in-Publication entry

Creator: Amphlett, Rachel, author.

Title: One to Watch: a detective Kay Hunter crime thriller / Rachel Amphlett. ISBN: 9780994547903 (paperback)

Series: Amphlett, Rachel, Detective Kay Hunter; 3.

Subjects: Murder—Investigation—Fiction.

Detective and mystery stories.

CHAPTER ONE

Eva Shepparton cried out once, her voice swallowed by the music and loud voices that emanated from the white marquee at the top half of the garden, and flung out her hands to keep her balance.

She steadied herself, cursed the damp grass from the morning's rain shower and stood with her hands on her hips, breathing hard while she glared back up the slope towards the party.

In hindsight, she should've asked where the toilet was – or *water closet*, as Sophie's mother would have insisted – except she couldn't bring herself to approach the officious woman, or her husband.

Sophie was nowhere to be found – Eva hadn't seen her since the speeches, so instead, she'd decided that the thicket of rhododendron bushes would have to do instead.

She sighed. If it weren't for the fact that Sophie was such a good friend, she'd never have agreed to be here in the first place.

The sweet scent of freshly mown grass filled the air around her, whilst smoke from the flaming braziers set around the edges of the garden wafted over her head. She'd seen the gardeners when they had turned up that morning, followed half an hour later by the florist. Between them, they'd pruned and plucked the garden to within an inch of its life.

They'd finished moments before the marquee hire company truck had arrived. Now, the large white tent took up most of the lawn space, its timber flooring echoing the footsteps of a crowd of enthusiastic dancers.

Eva's ears still rang from the noise of the disco. The roof of the marquee swam with multi-coloured lights from a gantry set up above the DJ's booth, and she could hear him now, encouraging the older members of the group to get up and dance to a Seventies disco hit.

She held up her hand and squinted at her watch face, tilting it until the faint light from the braziers shone on the dials.

Ten o'clock.

She snorted. No wonder everyone was drunk.

'For a bunch of devout Christians, you sure do know how to knock back the drink,' she slurred, then hiccupped.

She covered her mouth and giggled.

Sophie had told her that the pastor of the small private church group she and her parents belonged to had suggested the ceremony be held at the church after hours; however, Sophie's mother had poured scorn on that idea.

She'd cast her eyes over the other parishioners before murmuring, 'I don't think that's a good idea, Duncan. I think I'd rather keep this private. It's more in keeping with my family's position in society, don't you think?'

The religious man had shuffled in his chair, blushed, and conceded the point.

The next logical step had been for Sophie's mother to offer the use of her own home.

Eva's top lip curled.

When Sophie had told her, she'd hidden her immediate reaction from her best friend, but couldn't contain her disgust when she'd returned home, venting her frustration at her mother instead.

'It's like she's always having to *prove* herself,'

she'd grumbled. 'I know she probably means well for Sophie, but since the engagement announcement, she's got worse. All because she's some distant cousin thirteen times removed from the Royal family or something.'

Now, Eva gazed up at the house, its imposing outline towering over the marquee below.

Sophie had told her the original house had been built in the Regency era, with subsequent owners adding and extending its footprint over the years.

Eva shook her head, and wondered why on earth a family with one child would want such a huge property, before she giggled again, then hiccupped.

Of course, Sophie's mother loved the prestige that came with it, and the title.

'Have the ceremony at the house,' Eva muttered, mimicking Diane's voice. 'Matthew and I can organise a party afterwards. It'll be fun.'

She sighed. The ceremony had been okay, she supposed, but *fun*?

Diane had spent most of the time holding a handkerchief to her face, dabbing at her eyes.

Sophie, of course, looked gorgeous. Her mother had arranged for a hairdresser and make-up artist to attend to her daughter's every need, although Eva strongly suspected it was more to do with Diane wanting to keep up appearances than for Sophie's benefit.

Eva had made her way down the hallway to the spare room she'd been allocated for the weekend and had spent the time before the party changing into the dress she'd bought especially for the event and doing the best she could with her thick wavy hair, which had taken on a life of its own over the summer.

When she had returned downstairs, the other party guests were starting to arrive, spilling across the hallway, through the substantial living area and out through French doors to the patio beyond.

Caterers had appeared in Eva's absence, and she'd wandered along the tables of food with Sophie, picking at canapés and clutching a glass of champagne while making small talk with the other guests.

Josh Hamilton had turned up with his parents an hour later.

Eva had to admit, he wasn't bad looking at the best of times and tonight, he shone.

Josh charmed complete strangers with the ease of someone used to being the centre of attention, shaking hands with the men and making small talk with the women, working the small crowd while his father, Blake, grinned as he draped his arm around his wife's shoulders, their American accents cutting through the gathering of well-wishers.

Eva bit her lip.

She had no idea what would happen tomorrow, once Sophie's secret was revealed.

Because it would have to be, wouldn't it?

She'd agreed.

Of course, by then it would be too late. Everything Sophie had set in motion would culminate in the events of this evening.

She wished, in hindsight, Sophie had never told her.

It would have been easier that way.

The music paused for a brief moment, and the sound of the stream at the bottom of the hill reached her ears. The urge to pee dragged Eva from her thoughts, and she tottered towards the rhododendron bushes at the bottom of the slope.

Her foot slid out from under her again, and she swore under her breath. Checking over her shoulder, she could still see the tops of some of the guests' heads, the ones who had ventured away from the marquee to smoke cigarettes, and there was no way she was peeing within sight of someone.

The ground began to level out, and Eva spotted a large rhododendron to her right.

She hiccupped, then groaned as she stepped into a large puddle left by the morning's rainfall.

'I'm having one more glass of champagne, then I'm calling it a night,' she muttered as she squatted behind the shrub.

She sighed with relief, and then straightened and tried to wipe as much of the muddy water off her sandals as she could, swearing as she recalled she hadn't even paid her credit card bill yet, and here she was with damaged shoes that she'd only purchased a week ago.

Eva sighed, and resolving to leave as soon as possible, she turned to make her way back up the slope, and stopped.

At first, she couldn't work out what she was seeing.

A form lay stretched out behind one of the other rhododendron bushes several paces away from her position. Only the legs were visible, white and unmoving.

She swallowed, and moved closer, squinting in the poor light.

It looked like a person, and as she wobbled her way towards it, she recognised the skirt of the dress.

'Sophie? That you? You pass out or something?'

Concerned, she quickened her pace.

She'd done a first aid course at school, and knew that if someone had passed out, you were meant to check their airway and then put them in the recovery position. If Sophie had passed out drunk, then she needed help.

'Soph?'

As she rounded the corner of the shrub, she gasped.

Her best friend lay motionless, a dark splattered pattern now strewn across her new dress, her body twisted at an impossible angle where she'd fallen, one leg tangled behind the other and her face turned away from where Eva stood.

'Sophie?'

She moved around her friend, fighting down the urge to panic. If her friend needed first aid, she had to keep calm.

As she stepped over Sophie's feet to crouch down next to her, she stopped.

Sophie's eyes were wide open in terror, a thick trickle of the same dark splatter covering her cheek, a gaping recess where her nose had splintered into her face.

Eva screamed.

CHAPTER TWO

Detective Sergeant Kay Hunter swung her car through the gated entrance and kept a steady distance behind Detective Inspector Devon Sharp's vehicle.

She wasn't on call that evening, but within minutes of her mobile phone ringing and taking down the address from Sharp, she'd hastily dressed and hurried out to her car.

'I'm going to need your help with this one,' he'd said. 'Uniform have three cars on site, but there are a lot of people to deal with.'

She'd driven north out of town for at least fifteen minutes before turning into a narrow lane. Sharp's vehicle had been parked over to the left in a lay-by and she'd slowed as she approached to let him pull out and take the lead. Five minutes later, they'd arrived at the property.

She knew the area – a golf course swept beyond the trees that lined the opposite side of the lane, and most of the houses were centuries old, passed down through families that suffered the expense of the upkeep rather than experience the humiliation of their family homes being sold to developers by a common property agent.

As the narrow driveway curved and widened out, she realised what Sharp had meant by the number of people.

Cars littered the gravel apron in front of the large house, while groups of men and women in formal wear milled about the space.

Kay braked next to Sharp's vehicle and grabbed her bag, then joined him next to his car and ran her eyes over the gathered partygoers.

Most wore expressions of disbelief. A distraught woman sobbed while the man accompanying her guided her to a wooden garden seat before kneeling beside her and talking to her in low tones.

Kay rubbed at her right eye, unable to conceal the sigh that escaped her lips. 'They're all drunk, aren't they?'

'Most of them, I would expect,' said Sharp. 'If

they weren't to start off with, then they will be now, given the circumstances.'

Kay groaned. Trying to collate witness statements within the first few hours of a murder investigation was imperative, before people's memories became hazy or influenced by talking to others and comparing what they'd seen. Add alcohol to the mix, and it made an already difficult job near impossible.

'Who's in charge of the guest list?'

'Gavin Piper's working with uniform – he's here, somewhere,' Sharp added, casting his eyes over the people gathered around. 'Get your bearings – I'll meet you out the back on the terrace in ten minutes, and then we'll speak to the victim's parents.'

'Okay.'

Kay wandered through the house, her eyes sweeping over the uniformed officers that had spread out amongst the rooms interviewing one guest at a time, their faces patient as they tried to coax coherent information from the intoxicated partygoers.

The statements would be analysed in the morning by the assembled team, and then the hard work of filling in the gaps would begin.

She passed by the living area, and found a side door that had been left open that led out to a paved terrace, abutted by a large white marquee.

At the outer edges of the terrace, braziers smouldered while a small team of uniformed officers guarded each one, their stance enough to put off anyone thinking of approaching the iron frames.

At first, Kay wondered what they were doing, the question quickly dying on her lips as she realised the fires had been smothered by the quick-thinking first responders, in order to preserve the remains of any murder weapon that might have been thrust into the flames.

She hoped for the sake of the uniformed guards that the tablecloths from the marquee had been used rather than water, otherwise they'd never hear the end of it from the crime scene investigators.

She lifted her gaze to the disco lights that pulsed against the plain backdrop, the speakers silent.

Kay moved across to the marquee and peered through the drawn-back flaps into the abandoned space.

Here and there, a chair had been upturned, the occupants no doubt leaving their tables in a hurry once the alarm had been raised.

She turned towards the DJ's booth as a man straightened from a crouching position, a fistful of cables protruding from his fingers.

He visibly jumped, then recovered.

'Sorry, didn't see you there,' he said.

Kay held up her warrant card. 'Detective Sergeant Kay Hunter.'

He offered his free hand. 'Tom Williams. I've already given my statement to one of your colleagues.'

'Good, thanks.' Kay's gaze travelled over the equipment laid out as he unplugged a cable from the back of one of the speakers, the PA system dying with a soft *pop*. 'How long were you here for, before the party started?'

'Got here about four o'clock,' said Williams. 'Lady Griffith wanted my van out of sight well before any of the guests started to arrive.'

'So where did you go until the disco started?'

'Same as I always do at gigs like this. Sat in the van, listened to the radio. Read the paper.' He shrugged. 'It's not very glamorous, is it?' He sniffed. 'As it is, it's going to take me all day tomorrow to try and get the smell of smoke out of the equipment from those bloody braziers out there.'

He picked up another cable and began to coil it around his hands before dropping it into a black box next to Kay's feet.

'Notice anyone hanging around or acting suspicious today?'

Williams shook his head. 'No,' he said. 'Like I told the policeman that took my statement, I didn't spot anything weird while I was setting up. I fell asleep in the van for a couple of hours before my phone alarm went off. Sorry.'

Kay handed him one of her cards, and deciding she wasn't going to learn any more, left the DJ to his packing up and walked back out to the terrace.

She noticed Sharp at the far end, talking to an older couple and a young man, their voices wafting on the breeze towards her.

She recognised the twang of an American accent and, intrigued, made her way across the terrace to them.

The elder man stood a couple of inches shorter than Sharp, but with his legs planted squarely in front of the detective inspector, his eyes earnest as he spoke in hushed tones. His hands remained clasped in front of him, as if he wouldn't waste his time with pointless gestures.

A younger version of him stood at his side, eyes downcast, a picture of misery.

Kay's eyes travelled over the wife with interest – it appeared the woman had been under the knife at least once, and her features bore little natural expression. Immaculate in appearance, she kept a protective arm around her son, and lifted her chin as she noticed Kay.

Sharp glanced over as she approached. 'Ah, Hunter – good timing,' he said. He gestured to the couple. 'This is Blake and Courtney Hamilton, and this is their son, Josh.' Sharp's tone softened. 'Josh was to be engaged to our young victim, Sophie.'

Kay shook hands with the parents, offering her condolences before she turned her attention to Josh.

'Hello, Josh. I'm DS Hunter.'

Red-rimmed eyes met her gaze, pure anguish emanating from the man before he spoke.

'You need to find who did this,' he said, his voice breaking.

Sharp stepped forward. 'We'll do everything in our power,' he said before turning back to the parents. 'We have your statements, so please – take Josh home, and we'll be in touch again tomorrow.'

'Thank you,' said Blake. He rested his hand on his son's arm. 'Come on, Josh.'

Kay watched as the small family moved away, their figures retreating to the shadows as they followed the garden path around the house and out to the assembled vehicles in the driveway.

'Poor kid must be heartbroken,' said Kay. She glanced over her shoulder at the desolate marquee.

'Some engagement party. They must be doing all right for themselves.'

Sharp cleared his throat. 'It wasn't simply an engagement party. Apparently the Hamiltons and the Whittakers – Lady Griffith and her husband – belong to a small religious group that encourage the teenage girls to take "purity pledges" until they marry. They held the ceremony here earlier today, and then had the engagement party afterwards.'

'They what?' Kay realised her jaw had dropped open, and clamped it shut. 'What's a "purity pledge"?'

Sharp's lips thinned. 'I hadn't heard of it, either. Seems to be an American trend that found its way over here a few years ago.'

'Oh.' Kay blinked, and gestured at the lavish surroundings. 'So, all of this was for a vow of chastity, huh?'

'Yes.'

'Wow.'

Sharp shoved his hands in his pockets and nodded towards the rear of the marquee where a team of crime scene investigators led by Harriet Baker was setting up a swathe of floodlights.

'The ambulance crew confirmed the death when they arrived here with uniform,' he said. 'The victim,

Sophie Whittaker, was found at the bottom of a slope just beyond those rhododendron bushes. Harriet reports the girl's been hit with a blunt object with enough force to crack her skull wide open.'

'So, we're looking for blood spatter on guests?'

Sharp nodded. 'As well as the caterers, the wait staff, the bartenders—' He broke off and ran a hand over his head.

'Where are the parents?'

'In one of the guest bedrooms with an officer in attendance – Debbie West. Two of Harriet's team are processing their own bedroom before they can be granted access.' Sharp checked his watch. 'In fact, let's go talk to them now, and then you and I can come back down here and discuss strategy.'

'Sounds like a plan.'

Kay followed him through the house and along a wide corridor with four windows that gave the residents a sweeping view over their driveway, then up a flight of carpeted stairs.

A woman met them at the top of the stairs, her grey hair tied back into a severe bun and her hands clasped in front of her.

'Can I help you?'

'Detective Inspector Devon Sharp. I'm here to speak with Mr and Mrs Whittaker. You are?'

'Grace Jamieson. I'm Lady Griffith's housekeeper.'

Kay peered around Sharp's shoulder as a door was wrenched open, and Debbie West stepped out of a room, looking harassed.

'Sir, great timing,' she breathed. 'Mr and Mrs Whittaker are getting a bit—'

'Thanks, Debbie.' Sharp brushed past Mrs Jamieson and led the way into the guest bedroom.

The housekeeper began to follow, before the young police officer held up her hand. 'You'll need to wait here with me, Mrs Jamieson.'

Kay followed Sharp, gave Debbie a quick nod, and steeled herself.

Dealing with the family of a murder victim was never easy, let alone when that victim was only sixteen years old.

The mother, Diane Whittaker, Sharp had informed her on the way from the terrace, was known as "Lady Diane Griffith", and was somehow, through a myriad of cousins, reportedly related to the Royal family.

She sat, bolt upright, on a pale green velvet ottoman, her dark hair held back from her face with what Kay realised were real tortoiseshell hair ornaments. She wore a navy-coloured dress that bared her shoulders, although she adjusted a wrap over her collarbone before raising pale blue eyes to Sharp as he stood before her and her husband.

'Mr Whittaker, Lady Griffith, I'd like to introduce you to DS Kay Hunter, who will be co-managing this investigation with me.'

Kay took the woman's hand, fought down a sudden panicked thought as to whether she should curtsey, discarded it almost immediately and returned the firm handshake.

She turned to Matthew Whittaker.

As he was taller than her by at least four inches, she had to lift her chin to make eye contact.

Dark brown irises peered out from under bushy eyebrows and the faint whiff of alcohol reached her as he introduced himself.

'Inspector, I hope you're not going to keep us from our own bedroom much longer,' he said. 'My wife is obviously upset, and it's quite outrageous that we have to be kept in here.'

'I'm sorry, Mr Whittaker,' said Sharp. 'We're working as fast as we can.'

Kay noticed that he made no mention of the Whittakers' bedroom being methodically searched by two of Harriet's team at the present time.

'Well instead of standing around here, you should at least go and speak to that despicable boy that was always hanging around here,' said Diane, her voice full of venom.

Kay spun round to face her, surprised. 'Josh Hamilton? I thought Sophie was going to get engaged to him?'

Diane rolled her eyes. 'Not Josh, for goodness' sake. The other boy that was always turning up and making a nuisance of himself.' She clicked her fingers while her eyes roamed the ceiling. 'Peter... Peter—'

'Peter Evans,' said Matthew. He turned his attention to Sharp. 'She's right. You should talk to Peter Evans. He hated the idea of Sophie marrying Josh one day.' His face darkened. 'Last time he turned up here, I had to threaten him with calling the police. The lad's a bloody nuisance. Like a lovesick puppy.'

Kay pulled out her notebook. 'What's his address? Do you know?'

Matthew rattled off the flat number and street name with the anger and precision of a machine gun.

Kay glanced at Sharp.

'Go,' he said. 'And get uniform to go with you in one of their cars. Hurry.'

Kay spun on her heel and raced from the room.

CHAPTER THREE

Kay gripped the steering wheel and concentrated on the rear lights of the patrol car in front of her.

They'd burst from the lane and onto the slightly wider B-road heading back into town five minutes ago, and were now barrelling along a dual carriageway that, fortunately at this time of night, was empty save for a lone taxi that kept in its lane, well out of their way.

The patrol car killed its siren as they entered the fringes of the sprawling suburbs, and Kay was thankful for their foresight.

There was no need to forewarn a potential suspect of their imminent arrival, nor did they need to deal with the wrath of the local populace the next day for being woken from their slumber by an over-zealous patrol.

She braked as the car in front took a left exit off a roundabout, and followed in its wake as it weaved through a maze of terraced houses before sliding to a stop outside a plain-looking three-storey end of terrace.

She yanked the handbrake and launched herself out of the driving seat.

The patrol car driver, an older constable by the name of Derek Norris, met her at the gap between their vehicles.

'With all due respect, we'll go first,' he said, his voice gruff and his meaning clear.

Kay gestured to him to lead. 'Sounds good to me, Derek. Mind how you go.'

He winked as he passed, nodded to his passenger, a young probationer whose name escaped Kay, and pushed through the rotted wooden gate that separated the property from the pavement.

'It's the basement flat,' she said.

Norris held up a hand in response.

A stubbly garden filled the first few yards between the house and the road, and then she saw it in the beam from the younger policeman's torch.

Steps, leading downwards.

She held her breath as Norris gestured for the probationer to move aside, and then descended the concrete steps to a single wooden door.

He rapped his fist against the surface, setting off a dog in one of the flats above, its yapping silenced by harsh words closely followed by a single yelp.

Kay didn't doubt the abilities of Norris or his sidekick, but she extracted the telescopic nightstick she'd brought with her from the car and held it ready.

Norris raised his fist to knock a second time, but a light came on above his head, and the door opened.

A youth in his late teens or early twenties gazed out, his expression turning from hope to stunned horror as he took in the presence of a policeman a split second before Norris coaxed him backwards and stepped over the threshold.

Kay glanced at the probationer, who wore a similar stunned expression to that of the tenant.

'Is he always like this when he first meets people?'

'Umm…'

'Stay here. Call for back up if we yell,' she said. She patted his shoulder and began to descend the stairs. 'Good boy. Stay,' she murmured under her breath.

Norris appeared at the front door as she reached the bottom step, his face stricken.

'Stay there,' he said. 'We have a problem.'

She peered round his shoulder, her eyes quickly assessing the situation.

The door opened into a simple bedsit, an unmade double bed at the rear of the room next to a threadbare two-seater sofa and a small coffee table. A small television perched on a bracket set into the wall.

Beyond, she could see the entrance to the bathroom, a single light bulb in the ceiling.

She retracted the nightstick, and glanced at Norris before turning her attention to the man sitting on the end of the bed, his elbows on his knees and his head in his hands.

'Peter Evans?'

He raised his gaze from the carpet and peered at her from under a swept-back fringe, his shoulder length hair damp and his pale blue eyes red-rimmed. 'That's me.'

'There's a packed suitcase behind this door,' said Norris.

'Going somewhere?' said Kay, directing her question at Evans.

'There are two sets of clothes in the suitcase,' said

Norris. 'Male and female.' He jutted his chin towards the bottom step, and Kay moved away from the door, Norris following. 'There's blood on the bed,' he murmured.

Kay craned her neck, but she couldn't see from where she stood. 'Any sign of injury on him?'

Norris shook his head.

'Shit,' said Kay. 'Okay, let's take him in. Lock this down as a crime scene.' She jerked her thumb over her shoulder. 'Have your friend stay here until forensics arrive. You can come back here once we've got him booked in.'

He nodded, turned on his heel and went back inside.

Kay could hear him cautioning Peter as she climbed back up the stairs.

'We're going to take him in,' she said to the young police officer. 'Don't enter the flat. We'll lock it down as a crime scene and get forensics here as soon as possible.'

She pulled out her mobile phone and hit the speed dial for Sharp's number as she walked back to her car. Unlocking it, she leaned against it while the phone rang, and noticed at least two windows bathed in light above the basement flat.

No doubt the neighbours had realised that their

house was receiving unwanted attention from the police.

Sharp answered on the fourth ring. 'What have you got?'

'We arrived five minutes ago. Peter Evans is here, with a suitcase full of clothing,' said Kay. 'There's blood on the bed linen, and he's recently showered. We're bringing him in for questioning.'

'Good work,' said Sharp. 'I'll finish up here, and meet you back at the station. Harriet's obviously going to be busy here for a while yet, so I'll let her know she needs to send another team to the flat.'

'Thanks,' said Kay. 'See you in a bit.'

She finished her call as Norris swung the gate open and gestured for Peter to walk ahead of him.

Kay opened the back seat of the car, waited until he had settled in his seat and fastened his seatbelt, then slammed the door shut and turn to Norris.

'Sharp will meet us at the station,' she said. 'Let's get this one booked in, and find out what he has to say for himself.'

CHAPTER FOUR

In the interview room, Peter Evans shuffled towards the chair DI Sharp indicated to him, the duty solicitor setting his briefcase on the floor before taking the chair next to his client.

All of Evans's clothes had been taken from him upon arrival at the custody suite in the early hours of the morning. Each item had been carefully placed in a bag and catalogued before being taken away for processing by the forensic team.

Now, he wore a regulation set of overalls that hung off his narrow shoulders, and he'd rolled the sleeves up above his elbows. A pair of soft slippers covered his feet as he scooted the chair nearer to the desk and then rested his hands in his lap.

Kay opened up her notebook, wondering what the hell was going through the young man's mind. She resisted the urge to sigh, and tuned in to Sharp's voice.

Sharp began the interview by formally cautioning Evans and then asking him to confirm his name, address and occupation. That done, the detective inspector leaned back in his seat and eyed the young suspect.

'Peter, I'll start off by saying I've dealt with a few murder cases in my time, but none as cold-blooded as this.'

'I didn't do it,' said Evans. He lifted his chin until he was staring Sharp eye to eye. 'I didn't murder Sophie.' His voice broke, and he wiped the back of his hand under his nose.

Sharp pushed a box of paper tissues across the table, and Evans plucked two from the box before blowing his nose.

'When did you last see Sophie alive?' said Sharp.

'Eight o'clock yesterday morning,' said Evans. 'I hadn't been invited to the party. I didn't go to church – never have, let alone that creepy inner sanctum of theirs.'

'Where did you meet her yesterday morning?'

'About quarter of a mile down the lane from the house. She'd snuck away while all the preparations were being made.'

'Did you try to convince her not to go ahead with the ceremony, is that it?'

'Yes.' Evans shrugged. 'It's just wrong. She has to pledge her chastity to her dad for fuck's sake. It's medieval. She's not even getting married to Josh until she's eighteen.'

'What did she say to you?'

Evans wiped at his eyes. 'She said she had to. "To keep up appearances",' he said, emphasising the words with his fingers held in the air. 'It's bollocks.'

'How old are you, Peter?'

'Nineteen.'

'And you've been sleeping with a sixteen-year-old?'

The young man's bottom lip stuck out. 'It's not illegal.'

'Were you sleeping with her before she was sixteen?'

'No.' Evans sat forward in his chair and glared at Sharp. 'I loved her. Those people – they used her.'

'Which people?'

'Her parents – and Josh's.'

'In what way?'

Evans sank back into his chair, his face a picture of misery. 'It's all about the money, isn't it? It's like, Blake Hamilton's lived here for seven years and he's obsessed with being part of that whole scene.'

'Go on.'

'Well, if Josh marries – sorry,' Evans sniffed, and wiped his nose on his sleeve, 'married Sophie when she hit eighteen, then Blake'd be linked to the English aristocracy.'

'So, what happened – you found out Sophie was going ahead with the ceremony and decided to take matters into your own hands?'

'No!'

'How do you explain the bloodstain found on the sheets at your bedsit?' said Kay.

Evans swallowed. 'We had sex.'

Sharp frowned. 'A moment ago, you said you met her a quarter of a mile from her house.'

'I had my van. We went back to my place.'

'Did you rape her?'

'No!' Evans's face turned white. 'No. Of course not. I loved her. She loved me.'

'Then explain the blood.'

Evans's face flashed to crimson in a heartbeat. 'It was only her second time. I didn't hurt her, I swear.'

'Why did you have her passport, Peter?' said Kay.

The nineteen-year-old's shoulders sagged. 'We were going to run away,' he said. 'That's why she had a suitcase full of clothes there. I bought the suitcase, and every time I met up with her for the five weeks prior to the ceremony, she gave me a bit more to pack in it.'

'Where were you going to go?'

'France,' he said. 'I speak some French, and so does Sophie – better than me, in fact.' He sighed. 'Put it down to a private education when she was younger. We were going to find work teaching English as a foreign language. Travel a bit. Oh, God.' He leaned forward, rested his elbows on the table and buried his head in his hands. 'I can't believe she's gone.'

Sharp gave the young man a few moments, then flipped open the folder on the table in front of him and resumed his questioning.

'You've stated no next of kin on your charge sheet,' he said. 'Where are your parents?'

Evans raised his head from his hands. 'They died when I was six. So did my twin brother. Car accident. I got fostered until I hit eighteen last January.'

'What was foster care like?'

Evans looked confused. 'What has that got to do with anything?'

'Just answer the question, please.'

'It was fine, I suppose. I got placed with a middle-aged couple that couldn't have kids of their own, so they fostered me.'

'We'll need their details.'

'Brendan and Marjorie Chambers.'

'And how can we contact them?'

Evans's jaw set, and then he took a deep breath. 'Good luck with that. They're buried at Maidstone Cemetery. They died six months ago in a road accident outside Sittingbourne.'

'What did you do with the murder weapon, Peter?'

'What?'

Sharp's sudden turn of questioning threw the young suspect, and Kay waited for his response with interest.

'The murder weapon you used to kill Sophie. Where is it?'

Evans shoved his chair back and stood, his hands on the table as he leaned forward. 'I didn't kill her,' he spat. He pointed at Sharp. 'And while you're sat here interviewing me, trying to get me to confess, her murderer is out there walking around!'

The duty solicitor placed a hand on Evans's arm

and coaxed him back to his seat, his eyebrows raised in Sharp's direction.

Sharp ignored him, and instead rose from his seat. 'Interview terminated at twelve twenty-seven a.m.'

CHAPTER FIVE

Kay cruised the car to a standstill in the driveway of her house and quickly switched off the engine.

The pub up the road had closed three hours ago, and the lane was silent.

She climbed from the vehicle and shut the door, catching a fleeting glimpse of a fox as it darted across the potholed asphalt. Slinging her handbag over her arm, she used the light from a waxing moon to find her house key and unlocked the front door.

After a burglary a few months before, a new lock had been fitted and Kay was grateful that it didn't squeak like the old one had. She turned and closed it behind her, careful not to let it swing shut and wake her other half, Adam.

He had left the kitchen light on – its glow pooled

down the hallway so she could see what she was doing.

It made a change for her not to come home and discover an animal of some sort. As a partner in one of the town's busier veterinary practices, Adam often brought home his work – in the literal sense. However, his time had been taken up the past few weeks looking after mares who were foaling. Although the births had gone well, it meant at the moment they hardly saw each other as he was often out the door in the early hours of the morning or working late into the night.

Thirsty, she dumped her handbag on the kitchen worktop and filled a glass from the water filter next to the sink. She drained it in four large gulps, rinsed the glass out and tipped it upside down on the draining board. Although exhausted, she knew it would take her half an hour or so for the adrenalin to subside enough for her to sleep, so she kicked off her shoes and padded through to the living room. She flicked the switch on a reading lamp and pulled the previous day's newspaper across the coffee table and began to turn the pages.

Unable to concentrate on the words before her, her mind returned to the scene of Sophie Whittaker's murder. She hadn't seen the girl's body in situ as there were already crime scene investigators processing the scene, and there was no sense in traipsing all over the place and adding to their work. Apart from the fact that there were traces of blood in Peter Evans's apartment and a suitcase full of Sophie's clothes as well as her passport, they would still need evidence to link him to the scene of the crime. Otherwise, they might not get a conviction.

She shrugged her jacket off her shoulders and untucked her blouse from the waistband of her trousers, before sinking back into the cushions with a sigh. The next morning would bring a mountain of paperwork as the team sifted through the statements uniformed officers had taken from the partygoers, as well as from the parents of both Sophie Whittaker and Josh Hamilton. She couldn't imagine what the young man was going through, to lose his fiancée.

The American family appeared to be affluent, their clothing expensive. The mother had looked as if she'd had some cosmetic surgery, and Kay couldn't work out her age. Blake, the father, appeared to be in his mid-fifties.

Intrigued to know how a rich American was linked to a minor aristocratic family, let alone one whose son was marrying into it, she pushed herself off the sofa and made her way back to the kitchen, pulling her mobile phone out of her bag before returning to the living room. She opened up the search app and typed in his name.

It didn't take long for the search engine to display its results. Hamilton Enterprises filled the first three pages on the screen. She clicked on the website for the company and scrolled through the menu until she found the page that set out the details for the executive management team.

Originally from Connecticut, Blake Hamilton had arrived in the UK three years ago, establishing a consultancy business that seemed to thrive on creating networks and lucrative connections. The business had grown rapidly, leaving its competitors in its wake.

Kay opened up the calendar on her phone and made a note to investigate the website further when she got into work. Intrigued, she then searched for Sophie's mother's name.

Lady Griffith generated fewer results, and Kay had to read through several society news articles in order to put a picture together. The woman's parents had died some years ago, her father being an earl who seemed to enjoy a busy social life, if the number of photographs were anything to go by. Lady Griffith appeared to support local charities and good causes, but the articles revealed little about her character – each one was carefully worded and full of praise.

Sophie's father, Matthew, ran his own software business. Peering closer at the information she found on the business registry website, Kay surmised that his business wasn't doing as well as Blake Hamilton's, but that he was well respected within the industry he worked. He had written several articles for IT magazines over the years, and had been photographed at society events with his wife.

She enlarged one of the photographs showing Sophie with her parents, a huge smile on her face as the photographer's flash had lit up the room, and Kay felt a familiar pull in her chest at the thought of the young girl's life being taken from her in such a brutal way.

She yawned and tossed her phone onto the coffee table, realising that if she kept surfing the search engine, she'd never get any sleep. It was tempting to start making notes, but from experience she knew she'd make a better job of it in the morning. As it was, Sharp would probably delegate the task to one of the admin staff or one of the uniformed officers that would be assigned to help the team with the investigation.

She roused herself from the sofa once more,

picked up her jacket and switched off the downstairs lights before making her way up the stairs.

She lifted her foot over the fifth tread – it had a tendency to squeak, and she didn't want to wake up Adam. Chances were that he'd be out the door before her in the morning, and he'd looked exhausted the past three days.

The door to the bedroom was ajar, and she slipped through the gap. He had left her bedside light on, and she set her alarm before quickly undressing and sliding into bed beside him.

'New murder investigation?'

'I thought you were asleep,' she hissed. 'I crept up those stairs like I was in the bloody SAS or something.'

'You were doing quite well.'

She rolled over and slapped his arm, trying not to laugh.

'Go back to sleep.'

CHAPTER SIX

Kay glanced up from her work as Sharp entered the room, closely followed by Detective Chief Inspector Angus Larch.

The more senior detective ignored her as he breezed past her desk to stand next to the whiteboard.

His glare passed over the assembled investigation team who quickly ended their conversations and turned their attention to the senior officers, before Sharp spoke to him in a low murmur and the two men began to confer about a document Sharp held out to him.

Snatching it from him, Larch pursed his lips, then glanced up and met Kay's eyes, and her heart sank. He sneered, then shoved the document back at Sharp and gestured to him to begin.

After the success of her previous investigations, she'd hoped that Larch would finally put the Professional Standards investigation he'd subjected her to behind them, but it seemed he had other plans.

Kay bit her lip.

She had plans of her own, and not ones she was willing to share with anyone else in the room.

Plans that would, hopefully, put the unfairness of her suspension behind her once and for all.

She was jerked from her thoughts by Sharp's voice cutting across the room.

'Okay, everyone. Let's make a start.'

Sharp waited until he had the group's attention before continuing.

'Right, to bring you up to speed on events from last night. Our victim is Sophie Whittaker, daughter of Lady Griffith of Crossways Hall,' he said, pinning a recent photograph of the teenager to the whiteboard against a photograph the CSI team had taken at the crime scene. 'Sixteen years old, and killed with a single blow to the face with a blunt instrument. No sign of the murder weapon at the scene. There were several people at the Whittakers' house last night, as a party was taking place. Sophie and her parents are part of an exclusive church group, an offshoot of one of the local Baptist congregations, and the party was to celebrate Sophie taking what they call a "purity pledge", as well as an engagement announcement to a Josh Hamilton. Hunter – note that down. I want you to follow up on what the hell a "purity pledge" is, and what's involved. We'll come back to that.'

'Guv.'

'We received a tip-off while we were attending the crime scene that led to the arrest of Peter Evans,' Sharp continued, 'who right now is a guest in our custody suite downstairs. When DS Hunter arrived at his residential address, Evans had a packed suitcase containing some of Sophie Whittaker's clothes, together with her passport. Blood was found on his bedclothes. He denies all knowledge of Sophie's murder, and I've placed him on suicide watch while we continue our investigation.'

Silence filled the room, save for the scratching of pens in notebooks.

'We'll be conducting a further interview with the suspect after this briefing.' Sharp checked his watch. 'DCI Larch has requested that the post mortem be fast-tracked, but it will still be at least forty-eight hours or more before we get those results. So,' he said, and turned to each member of the team, 'unless we get an extension, we work on the basis we have ninety-six hours to prove our suspect's guilt or otherwise. Larch?'

'Thank you, Sharp.' The DCI stepped forward. 'I'll be monitoring this case closely. Sophie Whittaker's godfather is the Right Honourable Richard Fremchurch, and he's going to expect a tidy investigation with a quick result.' He glared at the team. 'None of the detail about this investigation will be passed on to the media by anyone in this room other than me, is that understood?'

A murmur filled the room, as the team acknowledged their understanding.

'Right, please continue,' said Larch, and nodded at Sharp.

'Okay, tasks for today,' said Sharp. 'Carys – I'd like you to observe the first interview. We'll have a chat afterwards about your initial thoughts. Follow up with Harriet after we've interviewed Evans and see if her team have found anything else at his property.'

'Will do, guv.'

Kay smiled at the detective constable as she wrote in her notebook.

She'd worked with Carys Miles for a while now, and admired her tenacity. Her sense of duty had nearly cost her dearly in the last case they'd worked together on and the incident had calmed her ambition, but only a little.

'Gavin – you start looking into Peter Evans's background. I want to be able to corroborate as much as possible with what he tells us.'

Gavin Piper nodded, and Kay noticed his bloodshot eyes. His spiky blond hair looked more dishevelled than usual, and she realised he'd probably spent most of the night working to get the witness statements from the Whittakers' party guests gathered. She made a note to get one of the administrative staff to run out and buy him a proper coffee from their favourite café up the road once the briefing had ended.

She glanced back to the front of the room as Sharp turned his attention to her. 'Kay, I want you to interview Sophie's parents. Take Barnes with you.'

'For chrissakes, Hunter – tread carefully when you're speaking with the parents,' Larch said, pointing his finger at her. 'I will hear about it if you don't play this one by the book.'

He stalked off, leaving a trail of strong aftershave in his wake.

Sharp tapped the whiteboard marker pen against his chin as he watched the older detective depart, and then dropped it onto the shelf below the board. 'All right, that's enough for now. Let's get on with it.'

CHAPTER SEVEN

Kay scrolled her way through a backlog of emails on her phone as Barnes swung the car into the turning for the Whittakers' house.

She lowered it, and tried not to let her jaw drop at her surroundings.

In daylight, the driveway leading to the house provided a sweeping view over the North Downs, the M20 motorway and Eurostar train route carving two distinct lines through the landscape. As Barnes slowed the vehicle to follow the gravelled track around a right-hand curve towards the house, Kay craned her neck to see the tall chimneys that towered above the building. Ivy climbed the walls, reaching upwards to the topmost windows, while a wisteria embraced the ornate front porch.

'Nice work, if you can get it,' he said.

'No kidding. I can't help wondering if they'll stay here now, though.'

'Yeah. I don't know if I could.'

The driveway widened out as they approached the house and Barnes brought the car to a standstill beside a white panel van.

Kay climbed from the passenger seat, put her phone back in her bag and waited for Barnes to join her.

'How do you want to do this?'

'I think you'd be better speaking to Diane,' said Kay. She swallowed, and turned away so he couldn't see her face. 'You've got a kid, so you'll probably be better than me at it. I'll take Matthew.'

'Okay.'

As they began to walk towards the front door, it was flung open and a large man with a beer belly waddled down the front steps, his face etched with fury.

He brushed past Kay, stormed over to the van, climbed in, and pulled away with such speed that he sent gravel flying up against Barnes's pool car, chipping the paintwork.

'Did you get the registration?' said Kay.

'Got it.'

'I'm so sorry about that.'

They both turned to see Matthew Whittaker standing on the doorstep, his face stricken.

'Who was he?' asked Kay.

'The man in charge of the marquee hire. Your lot are still here, it's all taped off, and he won't waive the additional rental fee. Said it's not in their terms and conditions. Even threatened to charge more for "inconvenience" because he won't get the tent back until tomorrow.' He raised his fingers to emphasise his words, before dropping his arms to his sides, his shoulders slumped.

'If you give me his details, I'll have a word. See what I can do.'

'Thanks. Sorry. Did you want a word?'

'If we could,' said Kay.

'Morning, Detectives.' A smartly dressed woman peered out the door, then stepped to one side to let them through.

'Morning, Hazel.'

Kay hoped her voice didn't betray her relief at seeing Hazel Aldridge, one of the division's family liaison officers. As a conduit between the police investigation and Sophie's family, Hazel's role was invaluable.

'Mrs Whittaker is in the living room,' she said.

'Come through,' said Matthew, and led the way across the hallway.

He pushed open a dark coloured wooden door and stood to one side to let them pass.

Diane Whittaker rose from a mauve two-seat sofa, her eyes red.

'Good morning, Lady Griffith,' said Kay. 'I understand this is a very difficult time for you, however we'd like to ask you some initial questions to help with our investigation.'

'Of course. Please, sit down.'

Kay waited until everyone had settled before pulling out her notebook. 'When we apprehended Peter Evans last night, he had some clothes packed into a suitcase, and Sophie's passport.'

Diane gasped and sank back against the cushions, her hand over her mouth.

'How— how did he get that?' said Matthew.

'Can you tell me more about Peter's relationship with Sophie?'

'There wasn't a relationship,' Diane spat. 'Despite what they thought.'

'We'd introduced Sophie to Josh Hamilton through our church group six months ago,' said

Matthew. 'About five weeks after that, she mentioned Peter for the first time. I think she'd bumped into him in town when she was out with friends one Saturday afternoon.'

Kay flipped open her notebook and jotted down the details. 'What did she say?'

'Well, she didn't exactly mention him,' said Matthew, and coughed. 'She and Eva were talking about him when they got back here, and didn't realise Diane and I were on the terrace under Sophie's window. We overheard them talking about him.'

'That bloody girl,' muttered Diane.

'Can you elaborate?'

'Sophie asked Eva what she thought of Peter,' said Matthew. 'I think Eva knew of him prior to them meeting, possibly through another friend of hers. She told Sophie that Peter wasn't seeing anyone, and that it was rare to see him in the summer. Apparently, he spends a lot of time down in Cornwall surfing. Or travelling overseas.'

'He's good for nothing,' said Diane, her chin tilted upwards. 'No prospects.'

'So, back to my question – how did he come to have Sophie's passport in his possession?'

'Hasn't he told you?'

'I'd like to hear your thoughts.'

Diane sniffed. 'I think he probably convinced her to run away with him rather than marry Josh.'

Kay glanced at Barnes. 'Lady Griffith, would you mind showing DC Barnes where Sophie's window is in relation to the terrace?' She turned to Matthew. 'I'd like to see her bedroom, if you wouldn't mind showing me?'

Diane rose from the sofa with a sigh and beckoned to Barnes. 'This way.'

'I'll meet you back in the hallway,' said Kay as he passed her.

She caught up with Matthew and followed him up the staircase, casting her eyes over the family photographs placed on the wall as she climbed the treads.

In each, the three family members were gathered formally as the years traced Sophie's life; Matthew standing behind his seated wife in the earlier photos, his hands on her shoulders while Sophie grew from a baby in her mother's lap to a toddler. As Sophie matured, she stood next to her mother, while Matthew had placed a protective hand on each of their shoulders.

Kay paused near the top of the stairs and allowed Matthew to continue without her. She stepped closer to the final photograph and peered at the ensemble.

The girl that stared back at her held her head high with an almost defiant look in her eyes as she posed for the camera, and despite the fact she wasn't wearing heels, was only a few inches shorter than her father. In this most recent photograph, his hand was no longer placed on her shoulder, but on the upper part of her left arm.

Kay frowned as she peered at the photograph, and then glanced at Matthew. 'The same dress she was wearing last night? It looks like a communion dress.'

A sad smile crossed the man's lips. 'No, not a communion. This was taken six weeks ago. Ready for her pledge ceremony. We wanted to get some professional photographs taken before the day, in case the weather turned inclement.'

'Pledge ceremony?'

'It's growing in popularity here. Sophie was a little old for it, but—' He shrugged. 'She wanted to do it. Most girls take a pledge when they have their thirteenth birthday, or sometimes before that.'

'What does it mean?'

'She undertook to remain chaste until she was married.'

Kay's eyebrows shot upwards. 'Is it legally binding?'

He shook his head. 'That's not the point. It's binding in our Lord's eyes.'

'Oh.'

His hand shook as he reached out and traced his fingers down the glass pane, and then he sniffed. 'Her bedroom's this way. Your lot finished a few hours ago.'

He led the way along a carpeted landing, and then stopped at the last door on the right. 'This is Sophie's.'

'Thank you,' said Kay. She paused at the threshold while Matthew switched on the lights.

Spotlights in the ceiling cast a muted tone until he turned the dimmer switch, illuminating the space in a harsher light.

She frowned. 'The curtains are drawn – why?'

Anger flashed across his face. 'Bloody reporters. One of the caterers helping to clear up this morning saw a camera flash from up in the woods behind the house. Probably trying to get a photograph of your colleagues while they were working in here. We've had to close all the curtains on this side of the house.'

'I'll have a word once I'm back at the station. See if I can put a stop to that.'

'Thank you.' He hovered in the hallway. 'Look, if you don't mind, I might wait downstairs for you. All this—' He gestured at Sophie's things. 'It's just too much.'

'I understand. I won't be long.'

Whittaker nodded, and disappeared.

Kay moved into the centre of the room and turned in a circle, her eyes roaming the single bed, built-in wardrobes and nightstand.

Harriet's team had worked methodically but with empathy; the room had been tidied as best as possible once they'd completed their systematic search, yet it was plain to see that this was no longer the bedroom of a teenager.

It held the atmosphere of a life now extinct; something intangible that left a whisper on the air of a moment stopped in time, forever frozen in memories.

Kay checked over her shoulder, and then pulled on protective gloves and began to go through the drawers of the nightstand.

She didn't doubt Harriet's ability, nor that of her team, but she did want to better understand Sophie, to get an idea of what the girl's life had been like before it was taken so violently from her.

Two paperback books, both non-fiction, were shoved into the top drawer together with an eReader and a packet of headache tablets. A couple of hair elastics and a nail file were pushed to the back.

Sophie had kept an assortment of old CDs in the lower drawer, and Kay ran her eyes over the titles before pushing them to one side. A box of tissues took up the rest of the space, but she found no diary and neither had Harriet's team.

Sophie had been a keeper of secrets, that much was already evident.

Kay turned her attention to the built-in wardrobe that took up the length of one side of the bedroom, but apart from a selection of clothes hanging in order of length and a variety of shoes, she found nothing to suggest that Sophie was involved with anyone else apart from the young man she had recently been betrothed to, or Peter Evans.

A murmur of voices reached her from the bottom of the staircase and she realised Barnes had returned with Diane and was talking to Matthew.

She sighed, and stepped out of the room. Descending the stairs, she pocketed her gloves as three faces turned to her.

'Thank you for your time this morning,' she said to Diane and Matthew. 'We'll be in touch as soon as we have something to report. In the meantime, Hazel will be on hand for anything you need, so please don't hesitate to let her know.'

'Thank you, Detective,' said Matthew, and

showed them to the door. He wiped at his eyes. 'I can't believe she's gone.'

Diane shivered, and pulled her cardigan around her sides. 'The Lord knows how on earth Josh is coping. He'll be heartbroken.'

CHAPTER EIGHT

'What do you think?'

They'd travelled away from the Whittakers' house in silence until Barnes accelerated up the ramp onto the motorway and weaved around a slow-moving car in the left-hand lane.

'Diane Whittaker definitely didn't know Sophie was still seeing Peter Evans, much less planning to run away with him. I asked her how long Sophie had had her own passport, and she only got it six months ago for an art school trip to the Loire Valley in May. Sponsored, apparently, so the parents didn't have to pay.'

'They never holidayed abroad?'

Barnes shook his head and indicated left, taking a slip road off to the north of the town and moving into the lane that would put them in the right road to get back to the station. 'I got the impression they couldn't afford to.'

'With a house like that?' Kay rubbed at her eye. 'I guess stately homes take a lot of money to maintain.'

'Well, that place definitely needs some work.'

'Yeah. Some of it looked a bit worse for wear, didn't it?'

'Diane Whittaker told me they were expecting some sort of grant or payment from a foundation or something to come through shortly, to help kick off some renovations.'

'Hopefully they'll get it. It must cost a fortune to keep up with the work on a place like that. By the time you'd worked your way through it, it'd be time to start all over again.'

'Did you find anything in Sophie's room?'

'No – and Harriet and her team are still compiling their report. Sophie's bedroom was quite sparse, actually. I always remember my bedroom being a bit of a tip when I was a teenager.'

'Yeah, mine too.'

'It was strange – there weren't even any posters on the walls.'

'Antique wallpaper, maybe.'

Kay narrowed her eyes at him.

'Okay, so the house isn't a museum – yet,' he grinned. 'What did you think you'd find?'

'I thought there might have been a diary or some love letters or something hidden away that we'd missed during the formal searches, but there was nothing.' She peered out the window as they drew up to a set of traffic lights and watched as a young mother pushed a toddler on an oversized toy car along the pavement, while the child laughed and threw his head back with delight.

'Any thoughts on motive yet?'

'Jealousy, maybe?'

'So, he kills her.'

'But then why wait for us to come and pick him up?' Kay shook her head as the lights turned green and Barnes pressed the accelerator. 'Doesn't make sense. He had a passport on him, and was packed and ready to go – so, why didn't he?'

'Shock?'

Kay wrinkled her nose. 'Bit of a long shot.' She rested her hand on the clip to her seatbelt as Barnes turned into the police station car park. 'Listen, take a look into Matthew Whittaker's business. Find out if there's anything going on there we should be aware of. Same with the house and the funding for the renovations.'

'Anything in particular I should look for?'

'Something that doesn't fit. You know how it can be. We might not know what it is until we see it.'

He killed the engine and pulled on the handbrake before turning to her. 'There also might be nothing there.'

Her mouth twitched. 'Guess there's only one way to find out.'

'And what are you doing while I'm pushing paperwork?'

'I'll grab Carys and head out to the Hamiltons. Find out how much Josh knew about Sophie's relationship with Peter.'

Barnes raised an eyebrow as he opened his door.

'Now that's going to be an interesting conversation.'

CHAPTER NINE

'Nice place you have here, Mr Hamilton.'

Kay strode across the driveway towards an expensive-looking four door saloon car, Carys at her side.

Blake finished arranging the suitcases in the back of the vehicle, shut the lid and turned before placing his hands on his hips. He squinted at the sun reflecting off the water.

'Yeah, it's a nice spot. Of course, we had to pull the old place down.' He wrinkled his nose. 'Whole building was rotten. Took about a year to get the plans for this agreed by the local council, but they saw sense in the end.'

'How long have you been here?'

'About three years. I wanted somewhere easy to

commute to the office in the city, and Courtney wanted to be in the English countryside.' He spread his hands expansively and gestured to the house. 'This is perfect.'

'It's certainly a very nice house.'

Blake smiled, and then his eyes fell. 'Any other time, I'd love to give you a guided tour, but as you can see, we're on our way out.'

'We?'

'Myself and Josh.' He jerked his thumb over his shoulder. 'He only started back at university a few weeks ago, but given the circumstances, we've spoken to his lecturers and agreed with them he'll spend the rest of the semester back at home. He can study online and go back in the New Year.'

'Which university?'

'Brunel.'

'I was wondering if we might have a word with Josh, actually.'

A pained expression crossed the other man's face. 'We really need to be off,' he said. 'Traffic's a bitch in the city late afternoon.'

'I understand that, Mr Hamilton, but I'm in the middle of a murder investigation.'

He frowned. 'You've got your suspect, haven't you?'

'We do, and we'll continue with that side of our inquiry. In the meantime, I'd like to speak to Josh, please – I'd like to learn more about Sophie Whittaker.'

Blake sighed. 'Look, you can have a quick word, but we can't hang around.'

Kay plastered a smile on her face. 'That's fine. We'll go through some preliminary questions now, and come back tomorrow.'

'Right, um – okay.'

Kay and Carys followed him through the front door and into an expansive hallway, an iron and marble staircase sweeping up through an atrium to the upper level of the house while doorways led off to different rooms on the lower floor.

Baking aromas wafted through from a door beyond the staircase, and Kay was struck by the sense of normality compared to the Whittakers' house.

It was also evident that, by contrast, Blake Hamilton's business was doing well – his house retained a polished sheen whereas the ancestral home of Diane Whittaker had appeared to be falling apart.

Shabby chic, Crossways Hall was not.

She jumped as Blake yelled up the stairs.

'Josh – get a move on.'

The gangly form of the teenager appeared at the

top of the stairs, a sports bag slung over his shoulder, sunglasses pushed up on top of his blond spiky hair.

He slouched his way across the landing before descending the stairs, and stopped dead when he caught sight of Kay and Carys.

'Come on,' said Blake. 'The police want a quick word with you before we go.'

'Everything okay?'

Kay turned at the sound of Courtney Hamilton's voice. 'Morning, Mrs Hamilton.'

'What's going on?'

The woman's eyes were wide as she dried her hands on a towel.

'We wanted to ask Josh some questions about Sophie Whittaker,' said Kay, 'but I understand Mr Hamilton wants to get him up to the university as soon as possible. We won't keep you long – we can come back tomorrow.'

'Oh. Okay. I'll leave you to it.'

She disappeared back into what Kay presumed was the kitchen, humming under her breath.

'Right, so – what did you want to ask Josh?' said Blake, and placed an arm around his son's shoulders as he joined them in the hallway.

Kay realised he wasn't going to back down on his

assertion that he would be leaving imminently, and decided she didn't have time for subtlety.

'Josh, can you take me through the events of last night, in your own words?'

Blake Hamilton let out a loud sigh. 'Honestly, Detective, we really don't have time for this. Josh already provided a statement to one of the police guys last night.'

She ignored him, and nodded to Carys who had her notebook and pen ready. 'Josh?'

The teenager shrugged. 'We got to the Whittakers' house about six o'clock I suppose. The people from our church group were the only ones invited – we wanted to keep it a private ceremony. We walked around for a bit and talked with everyone, and then our pastor, Duncan, got everyone together in the marquee so Sophie could take her pledge. After that, I presented her with an engagement ring.'

Kay nodded, but said nothing and waited for him to continue.

Another shrug. 'After the ceremony had finished, we sat down for the formal meal, and then the staff cleared the tables away and the disco started.'

'What time was that?'

'About half eight, I think.'

'What did you do after the meal?'

'Mingled. Had a few beers.' He wrinkled his nose. 'One of the older women tried to get me to dance, but no way.'

'When was the last time you saw Sophie?'

His brow creased. 'About nine-fifteen, I guess.' He scratched his cheek. 'Yeah. About nine-fifteen. She was on the terrace talking to her mother, and I wandered over. I don't know what they were talking about, but Diane looked pretty pissed off about something. She seemed to get over it pretty fast though, and then left me and Sophie to it.'

'What did you talk about?'

'Oh, this and that, y'know.'

'Could you elaborate, please?'

'Hang on.' Blake held up a hand. 'What sort of question is that?'

'I'm trying to ascertain what your son and Sophie Whittaker spoke about,' said Kay. 'It might help us to gauge what her state of mind was at the time.'

'State of mind?' Blake laughed. 'I'll tell you what her state of mind was. She was drunk, like everyone else.' He patted Josh on the shoulder. 'If that's all, Detective, I'm going to get Josh to the university,' said Blake. 'Like I said, I don't want to get stuck in traffic on the way.'

Kay clenched her jaw. 'Thank you. I appreciate your time. We'll be back tomorrow.'

The American nodded, then steered Josh towards the front door to the waiting car.

Kay and Carys stood on the front steps as it pulled away.

'Would you like a coffee before you go?'

Kay turned to see Courtney in the hallway, her eyes hopeful. She glanced at Carys, then back. 'Yes, that'd be nice, thanks – as long as it's not putting you out of your way?'

'Not at all. Come on through to the kitchen.'

They followed her along the hallway and through wide double doors into a space that Kay felt sure was twice the size of her garage.

Airy and light, the room showed the worktops glittering under the gleam from strategically-placed spotlights in the ceiling.

Courtney noticed her gaze. 'Marble,' she grinned. 'Blake had it shipped from Italy especially for me.' She ran her hand over the surface nearest to her. 'It's gorgeous, isn't?'

'Lovely,' said Carys, and raised an eyebrow at Kay once the other woman's back was turned.

A fresh aroma of vanilla and cinnamon filled the whole room and Kay hoped her stomach wouldn't rumble loudly like it always did when she hadn't eaten for longer than four hours.

'Smells great in here,' she said.

'Oh, we usually have a housekeeper that does all the cooking for me,' said Courtney, 'but, y'know, baking helps to calm me, so I just asked her to get me the ingredients and leave me to it.'

She busied herself with making coffee, and then handed them the resulting brew in bone china mugs.

'Josh must be devastated,' said Kay.

'Or relieved.' The woman clamped her hand over her mouth, and blushed.

'Relieved?'

'Well,' said Courtney, and flapped her hand. 'They're both so young, really, aren't they? I mean, were, I suppose.' She fell silent for a moment, and then shook her head if to compose herself. 'I'd rather Josh see the world before he settles down. He's got plenty of time before he has to worry about getting married and taking over Blake's business.'

'Whose idea was the purity pledge ceremony?' asked Carys.

Courtney's eyebrows puckered, her smooth forehead refusing to crease. 'Matthew's, I think.' She paused. 'Or was it Sophie?' She shrugged. 'Doesn't matter. I know they both started talking about it after

Blake mentioned it during one of our private church gatherings one evening.'

She turned, slipped heat-proof mitts over her hands, and opened the oven door, extracting two trays before turning them around and shoving them back inside.

'The private worship gatherings – how did that start?' said Kay, and tried to ignore the aroma of the cookies emerging from the oven.

Courtney closed the door and tweaked the timer before removing the mitts and returning to her bar stool. 'Blake suggested it a couple of years ago, and Duncan agreed.' She pursed her lips. 'It's okay mingling with others from the village, I suppose, but there are some things that we just like to keep from people that wouldn't, well, they wouldn't understand, y'know?' She caught Kay's stare, and forced a small smile. 'Nothing out of the ordinary, I can assure you, but perhaps things they needn't worry themselves with.' Her nose lifted in the air a little. 'We're quite a way removed from their little problems and issues,' she added, gesturing around the expansive kitchen.

Kay forced down the retort that rose to her lips. 'So, are these private gatherings held on a regular basis?'

'Oh, yes – every Tuesday night.'

'Where?'

'At the church. Duncan's ever so accommodating,' Courtney gushed. 'He's got such an open mind when it comes to how one should be allowed to celebrate one's faith.'

Carys cleared her throat.

Kay glanced across the worktop at her, but the young detective had her head bowed over her notebook and refused to meet her eye. She was glad; she didn't think she could keep a straight face if Carys chose to look up at that point.

She turned her attention back to Courtney. 'So, back to the purity pledge. That's an American thing, isn't it?'

The woman narrowed her eyes and twisted the wedding band on her finger. 'I guess.'

'It's just that I've never heard of it before. Can you tell me a bit about it?'

Courtney's eyes lit up. 'Oh, right, yeah. Well, it originated out of the Baptist movement in Connecticut years ago – that's where Blake's family are from – but it's really taking off in other states, too. It's very popular amongst teenage girls who want to honour God and remain chaste until their wedding night.'

'And they sign a contract?'

'Yeah,' said Courtney. 'The girls look so gorgeous – you should've seen the dress Sophie was—'

Kay waited, content to let the woman squirm.

'I mean, I guess, you did,' said Courtney, her face crimson. She placed her fingertips against her cheeks for a moment. 'Anyway,' she said eventually, 'the girls dress in white, and they and their fathers take a pledge – the girls to remain chaste, and the fathers undertake to protect their daughter's chastity.'

'The fathers swear to protect their daughters?'

'Yes.'

Kay met Carys's gaze this time as the young detective's head snapped up, eyes wide.

'Interesting,' she said.

CHAPTER TEN

'Right, pay attention.'

The hubbub of noise dwindled at Sharp's voice, and the team turned their attention to the front of the room as the DI paced the carpet in front of the whiteboard.

'We're twenty-four hours into this case, and we need to get cracking. Let's start with Gavin – what has Lucas reported so far?'

'His preliminary findings indicate a blunt trauma wound to the face – Lucas says the blow was hard enough to break her top teeth and splintered her face, which pierced her brain. Death was instantaneous,' said the young police officer. 'Lucas has been able to bring in an extra pathologist to help with the workload after that motorway crash at the weekend, and said he's hoping to get his full report to you tomorrow.'

'Good. Let me know the minute it's through. Who's got an update from Harriet?'

'Me, guv.' Carys stuck her pen up in the air, and then lowered her gaze to her notebook. 'No murder weapon found at the crime scene, but whatever was used, it made one hell of a mess – she said there was blood on the nearby rhododendron leaves, and across the grass next to the body. Unfortunately, Eva Shepparton traipsed through that, and spread it back towards the slope that leads up to where the marquee is. We obviously need to ascertain whether she saw or heard anything. She stated she couldn't remember, but hopefully sobriety will help her recall.'

'Good work, Carys. Kay – did you and Barnes glean anything from Sophie's parents?'

'They had no idea Sophie had still been seeing Peter Evans, let alone sleeping with him,' she said. She glanced at Barnes. 'In fact, they both came across as being shocked that they didn't know about it, didn't they?'

'Yeah, and when I was talking with Diane Whittaker, all she was going on about was that she couldn't understand why Sophie would do that – sleep with Peter when she was about to be engaged to

Josh Hamilton,' said Barnes. 'From a due diligence perspective, I've started going through Matthew Whittaker's business accounts, and Diane mentioned that they were waiting on some sort of funding or grant to help with renovations of their house, so I'll keep working on that.'

'How was Blake Hamilton?' said Sharp.

'Unhelpful,' said Kay. 'More interested in getting Josh to his university in London to pick up his stuff than help find out why Sophie was murdered. His wife, Courtney, was more talkative, but seems to be oblivious to the fact we're trying to run a murder inquiry.'

'In what way?'

'She seemed to be relieved that Josh wouldn't be getting married any time soon. Said both of them were too young for that sort of thing – she was keen for him to travel once he finishes university, and didn't sound like she was enamoured about the whole engagement business at all.'

'You'll speak to them again?'

'Yes – tomorrow.'

'Where are we on getting copies of Sophie's school reports?'

'Here,' said Debbie West. 'Nothing out of the ordinary. No truancy, no detentions in the past two years. Couple of awards for tennis.' She tossed the pages back onto her desk. 'Model pupil, by the look of it.'

'What were the parents' thoughts about Peter Evans?'

'They certainly gave the impression that they felt he was beneath having a relationship with Sophie,' said Kay. 'Diane had no time for him at all, and they were both taken aback when I told them Sophie's passport was found at Peter's flat.'

'All right. Keep up the good work, everyone. DCI Larch and I will be interviewing Evans again in half an hour. Anything else?'

'When we spoke to Matthew Whittaker earlier, he didn't mention the fact that he took a pledge as well,' said Kay. 'Apparently, his part of the deal is to protect his daughter until such time as she marries.'

'Failed there, then,' Barnes mumbled. 'Seems she was stringing them all along.'

'I was wondering though, maybe if Matthew found out Sophie was sleeping with Peter, would that be motive enough for him to harm her?'

A hush filled the incident room, broken only when Gavin's pen rolled across his open notebook and fell to the floor.

Sharp rubbed his chin. 'You think he took his pledge that seriously?'

'Perhaps. I think it's worth having another word with him.'

'Do it, but tread carefully.'

'Understood.'

'Okay, tasks for tomorrow. Barnes and Piper – sort out another interview with Eva Shepparton. When you speak to her again, find out what she knew about Sophie's relationship with Peter.'

'Guv.'

'Hunter, first thing in the morning head over and speak to the pastor, Duncan Saddleworth. Get a feel for his relationship with the parents, and find out from him whose idea it was for Sophie to take this "purity pledge". Then take Carys with you and speak to Matthew Whittaker again – find out how seriously he was taking his end of the bargain.'

'Will do.' She tapped her pen against the side of her notebook. 'You think maybe Sophie was having second thoughts?'

'Or, she was determined to go ahead, and either Peter Evans or Matthew Whittaker didn't like the idea.'

CHAPTER ELEVEN

A mustiness filled Kay's senses the next morning as she shook out her umbrella and placed it in a cast-iron stand in the church porch, grateful for the shelter from the brief summer rain shower.

As she straightened, she ran her eyes over the various messages pinned to the noticeboard, and reached out to lift the corners to read the calls to arms from the different groups that used the church for meetings, bell-ringing practice, and flower arranging.

She frowned at a rectangular space at the left-hand lower corner of the noticeboard, a red and a blue tack pinned in the middle of it.

Her eyes drifted to the collection box set on top of a narrow shelf above an old pew, and the metal loop on one side that was attached to the wooden wall of the porch by a solid chain.

Kay placed her hand on the centuries-old latch and eased open the wooden door.

She blinked as she pushed the door back into place and her eyes adjusted to the gloom.

Lights hung from long cords set high into the ceiling, while spotlights picked out the altar and pulpit.

Murmured voices carried through the large space and her gaze fell upon two older women and a man on the far side of the space. The two women held cloths and aerosol spray cans as they moved between the rows of pews, the sweet aroma of furniture polish wafting on the air.

They fell silent at the sight of Kay.

The man, dressed in a plain black shirt and matching jacket and trousers, turned towards her, a white collar at his neck. He spoke to the two women, one of them giggled and nodded, and then he threaded his way through the pews.

He swaggered towards Kay, an easy smile breaking through his fashionably trimmed beard.

She realised he probably managed to charm all the ladies in the congregation, and smiled before holding up her warrant card as the religious man joined her, his brow creasing.

'Duncan Saddleworth?' she said, her voice echoing in the space between them.

'Yes?'

'I'm DS Kay Hunter from Kent Police,' she said. 'Is there somewhere we can talk?'

'About?' He ran his hand over light brown hair, his expression wary.

'Sophie Whittaker.'

He glanced over his shoulder at the two women trying their best not to stare while they worked, and back to Kay. 'Um, okay, well I suppose we could use the vestry.'

'Lead the way.'

Saddleworth turned left and moved towards the back of the church.

Kay raised her gaze to the gallery, the pipes from the church organ vaulting up into the shadows of the ceiling, a spotlight above the organist's chair casting a soft yellow hue over the rows of keys and buttons.

The lines of pews ended and as Kay passed a large stone font, the plain flagstones gave way to a thin carpet. A flight of steps behind an ornate wooden screen led up to the gallery, and then Saddleworth opened a door and held it so Kay could enter before him.

'Give me a moment,' he said as he followed her in and closed the door behind them, 'I'll clear one of these chairs for you.'

As he began lifting what looked like Sunday school textbooks from a chair next to the door, Kay ran her eyes over a small desk covered in various pages from a notebook, a large bible opened three-quarters of the way through, and a small printer. An ancient computer sat to one side, its keyboard gathering dust – either from lack of use or the cleaners being banned from the room, she supposed.

'Here, please – have a seat,' said Saddleworth.

'Thank you.'

Kay lowered herself into the wooden chair, put her bag on the floor at her feet and extracted her notebook and a pen.

She waited while Saddleworth fussed over the pages on his desk before he clipped them together, tossed them onto the open bible and sat down, his hands clasped in front of him.

'Now, Detective, how can I help? I gave my statement to the police last night.'

'I understand,' said Kay. 'As I'll be co-managing the investigation, however, I like to speak to people myself wherever possible. What time did you arrive at the Whittakers' house?'

'Just after five o'clock,' said Saddleworth. 'Sophie was getting a bad case of stage fright, I think.' He smiled benevolently. 'Diane phoned me an hour before and said Sophie wanted to go through her lines one more time before the ceremony.' A wistful expression crossed his face. 'She needn't have worried – she was perfect.'

'I'll come back to that in a moment,' said Kay. 'Can you tell me a bit about yourself?' She gestured around the room. 'How did you end up here? I can hear a trace of an American accent, can't I?'

Saddleworth smiled, and leaned back in his chair. 'I was a bit of a nomad before I came here,' he said. 'When I graduated from Oxford, I volunteered to work abroad with a charity – I ended up in South America for a couple of years, and then ended up in Connecticut.'

'How come? Seems an odd choice.'

'I met some people while I was serving in Ecuador who were from Bridgeport, and their volunteering stint ended at the same time as mine, so they invited me to go back to the States with them.' He sighed. 'After being away from England for so long, I knew I'd have to work hard once I got back here, so I figured a short stay in the USA on the way home would give me a kind of a break first.'

'How long were you there for?'

'About a year.'

'That's a long holiday.'

'I ended up helping out in one of the local churches. I only came back here because my visa was due to expire.'

'And this was when?'

'Six years ago,' he said. 'I came to Maidstone two years ago.'

Kay leaned forward on the chair to try and stop her backside going numb while ignoring the ominous creak from the dilapidated furniture. 'This "purity pledge" that Sophie took yesterday. What's all that about? I've never heard of it before.'

'It's become very popular in the past fifteen to twenty years amongst the more conservative church organisations—'

'Like the one you worked with in Connecticut?'

He nodded. 'The purity movement started in Connecticut,' he said. 'And grew in popularity as more and more girls chose to take a pledge. In short, a girl can be any age to take it, but it's typically done between the ages of twelve to sixteen.'

'About the time they'd start taking an interest in boys, then?'

'Yes.'

'Go on.'

'The girl, Sophie in this case, undertakes to remain chaste until her wedding day, and to serve God. The father, Matthew in this case, makes an oath to help his daughter maintain that pledge.'

'What about boys?'

Saddleworth shook his head. 'No. Boys aren't required to take the oath. Upon marriage, any woman that has taken a purity pledge in her youth forgives her future husband for any indiscretions he may have committed.'

Kay lowered her gaze and drove her pen nib into her notebook. She made herself count to ten before speaking.

'Surely this "purity movement" as you call it is simply based on hysteria formed out of the notion that a girl could be damned by her God if she doesn't take the pledge, or if she breaks it?' said Kay, her brow furrowed. 'It's just a way of controlling a potentially wayward teenager, isn't it?'

She resisted the urge to throw her pen at Saddleworth as a patient smile formed on his lips.

Here we go, she thought. *Here comes the lecture.*

'Not at all,' he said, and steepled his fingers in front of his chin. 'As I said, the girls are never forced or coerced into taking the pledge. It's their choice.'

'How did Sophie find out about it then?'

He dropped his hands to the table and lowered his eyes. 'I may have mentioned it to her.'

'When?'

He shrugged, and his eyes shifted to the window. 'Maybe about six months ago? I can't remember exactly.'

'How many times did you "mention" it to her before she chose to take the pledge?'

He sighed, and refocused his gaze on her. 'I didn't force her into it,' he said, his voice taking on a slightly defensive tone. 'She asked what work I'd done in the States, so I told her. I explained that the church encouraged the teenage girls in the congregation to take a purity pledge. At some point, I don't know – maybe, a couple of weeks after that – Sophie came to me and said she'd been doing some research online about it, and wanted to take the pledge. I discussed the ceremony with her parents, and we went from there.'

'And that went quite a bit further than making a pledge to have no sex until she was married, didn't it?'

Saddleworth's Adam's apple bobbed in his throat. 'I'm sorry, what do you mean?'

Kay flipped through her notebook. 'Sophie's pledge specifically stated that she'd remain chaste until she married Josh Hamilton. They got engaged immediately after she'd taken her pledge.' She flipped the pages back into place. 'Is it normal for a girl to name her future husband when taking her pledge?'

Saddleworth coughed, his face turning crimson. 'It is, er, slightly unusual.'

'What was behind her including that wording?'

'You'd have to ask Matthew and Blake about that.'

'You mentioned Diane Whittaker phoned you and asked you to arrive early, and you said you thought Sophie might be getting "stage fright". Was she given the option to change her mind?'

'Change her mind?'

'Yes. Was she counselled in any way so she knew she could call it off?'

He sat back in his chair, shock on his face. 'Why on earth would she want to call it off? She and Josh were perfect together.'

Kay narrowed her eyes. 'Does the diocese know about these ceremonies?'

Duncan cleared his throat. 'Er, no.' He fidgeted in

his seat, then re-crossed his legs and picked an imaginary piece of lint off his knee. 'Sophie's pledge was the first.'

'What about the rest of your congregation? What do they think about the idea of a purity pledge?'

'They don't know,' he mumbled.

'I beg your pardon?'

'They don't know,' he said, his voice clearer. 'The Hamiltons and the Whittakers were part of a group of people that preferred to worship separately to the main congregation.' He regained some of his composure, his voice taking on an air of authority once more. 'The purity pledge ceremony idea was restricted to that group.'

'I see.'

Kay closed her notebook and recapped her pen before dropping both into her bag and standing. She held out her hand. 'Well, Mr Saddleworth, thank you for your time,' she said. 'It's been *enlightening*.'

He took her hand, and she noted his palms were noticeably warmer than when she'd first met him out in the nave.

'I'll see you out,' he said, and scurried out from behind his desk.

As he pushed open the doors to the church and

Kay passed by him into the porch and retrieved her umbrella, she pointed at the noticeboard.

'There's a notice missing. What was that for?'

He glanced to where she indicated, and frowned. 'Oh. I'm not sure.' He gave her an apologetic smile. 'We get so many.'

She held his gaze. 'Think. Was it something to do with Sophie?'

'I, er—'

'Go on.'

'I put a notice up before I left to go to the Whittakers' house yesterday,' he said, his shoulders sagging. 'I thought that given the interest amongst our more private members in the purity pledge, that our main congregation might be keen to get involved so I advertised a meeting to discuss it next week.' He reached out and straightened an errant flyer above the space before turning back to Kay. 'After what happened, I thought it would be a good idea to postpone it.'

'Postpone, or call the whole thing off altogether?'

The pastor had the decency to lower his eyes. 'I don't know,' he mumbled. 'It'll be up to the Hamiltons and the Whittakers now.'

CHAPTER TWELVE

Duncan Saddleworth closed the door behind the police detective, and then leaned forward until his forehead rested against the medieval framework and closed his eyes.

'Focus,' he murmured.

He straightened, before hurrying towards the vestry, tugging the white collar at his throat as he passed row upon row of pews.

The figure on the brass crucifix on the altar burned its eyes at his retreat, and Duncan wiped a bead of sweat from his forehead as he resisted the urge to turn back and prostrate himself at its feet.

Instead, he slammed the door to the vestry shut.

He ran his hand under his collar, loosened the top

button at the neck of the black shirt and ripped the white collar loose, throwing it across the paper-strewn desk with a low snarl.

Next, he removed the jacket from his shoulders, and crossed the room to a wardrobe next to a plain frosted window. He tugged the curtains across the panes, then hung the jacket on a coat hanger and undid his suit trousers.

He redressed quickly in jeans and a grey sweatshirt, ran his hand through his hair in the absence of a comb, and shut the wardrobe door. He glanced at his reflection in the mirror, and was taken aback at how scared he looked.

Sunlight now streamed through the stained-glass window that overlooked his desk. The glasswork was a modern design compared to the rest of the church, added along with the vestry extension in the late eighteenth century and ugly, in his opinion. It jarred his sentimental longing for something more traditional, but those days were long gone. His own exploration of the faith while at university had led him across Europe, soaking up the history and architecture before he'd immersed himself in the role that now saw him here, in this fractured parish.

A bookcase lined the wall opposite him, the

shelves taken up by photo albums that he hadn't opened in years, books he had no intention of reading ever again, and framed photographs that pinched at his heart if he dared to look at them too closely.

He groaned and leaned forward, clutching the edge of the desk, his knuckles white.

A persistent dragging sound filled his ears, and had done for the past week, as if his memories were trying to pull him downwards with them.

'No,' he groaned, and closed his eyes.

He'd been so careful.

He exhaled, then straightened and squared his shoulders. He'd been tested before, and his faith had triumphed.

He'd acted on the information to hand, his actions justified and true in the eyes of his god, as far as he was concerned.

He slumped into the cracked leather chair behind his desk, waited until his heart rate had calmed, and then pulled a mobile phone from his pocket. He dialled a number from memory and fought down the panic.

The call was answered on the third ring.

'What do you want?'

Duncan cleared his throat. 'The police were here.'

'Do they suspect anything about us?'

'No.'

'Are you sure?'

'Yes.' Duncan dabbed at his brow once more. 'She was asking questions about Sophie.'

'She?'

'Detective Sergeant Kay Hunter.'

'Interesting.'

Duncan held his breath while the silence dragged out, until he could bear it no more. 'What should I do?'

'Nothing,' came the reply. 'Carry on as normal. Don't draw attention to yourself. It'll be fine.'

'Okay.'

The line went dead, and Duncan erased the call log before tossing the phone onto the desk.

He swallowed, and checked his watch.

Carry on as normal.

'Jesus,' he swore, then quickly raised his eyes to the ceiling and apologised.

Sweeping up the phone and a set of car keys from his desk, he locked the vestry door and hurried outside.

A warm breeze brushed his face as he exited the porch, the morning rain shower lending a renewed freshness to the day, before a whirling dervish of leaves spun across the car park and chased at his ankles as he hurried to his vehicle. He peered over his shoulder as he pointed the key fob at the door.

He'd invested too much of his life into the church, but now it seemed he was losing control.

He couldn't let that happen.

CHAPTER THIRTEEN

When Kay and Carys entered the main sitting room, the family liaison officer was sitting on a sofa opposite Sophie's father, an earnest expression on her face while she spoke to him in muted tones.

A surprised expression crossed Matthew's face on seeing Kay, before he recovered. 'Have you charged him yet?'

'We're still interviewing Peter Evans, and waiting for some of the forensic results,' said Kay. She gestured to the sofa. 'May we join you?'

He nodded, and slid across the cushions to make room.

Kay waited until Carys had settled and pulled out her notebook. 'I wanted to ask you a bit more about the "purity pledge" that Sophie took. I understand about her side of the pledge, but I didn't know that you also made a commitment. What did that entail?'

Matthew cleared his throat. 'It's something all fathers do as part of the "purity pledge". We undertake to protect our daughter's chastity, and provide spiritual guidance if required.'

'How long have you and Diane attended the private church gatherings?'

The man's eyes drifted to the patio windows. Beyond, Kay could see his wife talking to what appeared to be a gardener. The man had to be in his seventies at least, his features crinkled by years spent outdoors, and his pose relaxed as he leaned on a garden fork and listened to Diane.

She wore a wide brimmed hat and held secateurs in her hand, her free hand gesturing towards the flowerbed before them. She turned from the gardener and proceeded to snip away at a nearby rosebush while he returned to digging. After a moment, she stopped what she was doing and stood with her hands on her hips, watching him.

Kay bit back a smile. It appeared that Lady Griffith preferred to do "at" gardening, rather than actively participate. She cleared her throat, and Matthew turned back to face her.

'Sorry, what was the question?'

'I was asking about the private church gatherings. How long have you been going to those?'

'About eighteen months.'

'I understand from Duncan Saddleworth that there was quite a lot of preparation for Sophie leading up to taking her purity pledge. Was it the same for you?'

'I suppose. I had a couple of meetings with Duncan when Sophie first spoke about it.' His gaze dropped to his hands in his lap. 'To be honest, Diane was more interested in the whole thing than me. Obviously, I'd have supported Sophie in whatever decision she made, which is why I made an effort to read all the pamphlets Duncan gave us. Diane was determined that the whole ceremony would go off without a hitch – whether that was for Sophie's benefit, or her own, you'll have to ask her.'

Kay noticed the note of bitterness in his voice, but pressed on.

'How did you meet your wife?'

'It was when I was working in London. I'd started up my first software business and it was doing really well – money wasn't a problem, and so I was socialising every night, going out to parties and attending all sorts of events. Diane was doing some modelling work here and there. Tame stuff – nothing dodgy. Things like those magazine "true stories posed by models" – that sort of thing. I don't know how she managed to persuade her parents to let her do it, but she even enrolled in a part-time acting course at one of the theatres for a time. Said it made her look more realistic in front of the cameras.'

Kay resisted the urge to roll her eyes. 'How seriously did you take your responsibilities regarding the purity pledge?'

'What you mean?'

'You said yourself that you had ordered Peter Evans to stop hanging around the house, and that you didn't want him to see Sophie. Was that because of the purity pledge?'

He frowned. 'I didn't want him hanging around with my daughter. Diane will tell you – he's just a labourer. Sophie could have done so much better than that, I mean – she was. She was engaged to Josh Hamilton, after all.'

'Bearing in mind the nature of Sophie's pledge, was she accompanied by yourself or your wife when meeting Josh?'

'Of course not,' he spluttered. 'This is the twenty-first century. The purity pledge isn't some sort of Victorian way of controlling teenage girls. It was Sophie's decision to take it. Josh respected that – he's always been the perfect gentleman towards my daughter.'

'Can you recall why Sophie decided she wanted to take the pledge?'

'I think she'd been talking to Duncan about the church group he'd worked with in Connecticut. She spent quite a bit of time with him after school on some days. She seemed interested in the pledge, so he gave her some brochures about it. A few weeks later, we were having dinner and Diane asked her if she was thinking of taking the pledge. She seemed surprised at the question, and then Diane mentioned that she had heard from Blake that Josh was really quite taken with Sophie. By then, they had been seeing each other for six months.' He smiled at the memory. 'You could see her blossom at that news – I think she hoped that Josh was serious, you know what teenage girls are like. No confidence. She announced then that she'd like to take the pledge and that if Josh was serious, she didn't want anyone else.'

'When did Josh propose to her?'

'About a week later, at a garden party at the Hamiltons. Sophie was beside herself with excitement all week after hearing what Diane had to say. The three of us swore ourselves to secrecy that we didn't know he was going to propose because we didn't want to spoil the occasion for him. In the end, it was perfect,' he said, his eyes wistful. 'He's a nice lad.'

'I'm surprised at her getting engaged at sixteen,' said Kay. 'You didn't have a problem with that?'

'No, not at all. After all, they weren't going to marry until Sophie was eighteen. I think in a world as cynical as ours has become, it's rather nice to think that some youngsters are quite old-fashioned.'

Kay noticed movement out the corner of her eye and saw Diane making her way up the garden towards the house. 'Thank you for your time, Mr Whittaker. We'll be in touch when we have an update for you.'

She led Carys from the room, almost bumping into the housekeeper in the hallway.

The woman jerked backwards, recovering quickly before gesturing to the front door.

'I'll see you out, Detective.'

Kay smiled to herself as she followed the woman to the front door. Evidently, the housekeeper was desperate for gossip and Kay made a mental note to speak to her in private at some point.

It would be interesting to learn what else the woman had overheard.

CHAPTER FOURTEEN

Kay was about to suggest to Carys that they try the back door to the Hamiltons' house, when the front door was wrenched open.

Blake Hamilton glared out at them. 'Detectives?'

Kay forced her sweetest smile onto her face. 'Good morning, Mr Hamilton. We'd like to speak with Josh, please.'

The man sighed. 'This is bordering on harassment, DS Hunter.'

'I'm investigating the murder of your son's fiancée, Mr Hamilton.' Kay's smile disappeared.

He raised his hand. 'Sorry. Of course. Come this way.'

He led the way through to the living room leaving

Carys to close the front door, and gestured to a pair of armchairs.

Josh and his mother sat on a sofa next to one another, the young man's face miserable.

Kay waited until Carys was ready, notebook and pen in hand, before she began.

'I hope everything went as well as it could with the university yesterday?'

'It's fine.' He shrugged. 'I'll go back in the New Year.'

'It's better this way,' said Blake. 'The dean advised yesterday that he'd already received two phone calls from national newspapers.' He held out his hands as if to say *what can you do?* 'Unfortunately, when you're top of your business game, your family has to cope with being under the microscope as well. It wouldn't have been fair on Josh to have to deal with that sort of scrutiny.'

Kay's eyes moved from the father to the son, who withered under her gaze.

'Have you any idea why Peter Evans would want to harm Sophie, Josh?' She glared at Blake as she phrased the question, keen to stop him answering on his son's behalf.

He shook his head. 'I didn't know him. I didn't

know Sophie knew him.' He glanced at his hands, then raised a finger to his lips and chewed at a nail.

'Josh, hands,' said Courtney.

The young man dropped his hand into his lap and sighed. 'I'm sorry. I really can't help you.' He wiped at his eyes. 'I can't believe she's dead.'

He burst into tears, and Courtney rose from her chair. 'Detectives, if you wouldn't mind, I'd like you to stop questioning Josh now.'

Kay bit back the retort that formed on her lips, and instead nodded. 'I'll come back tomorrow, Josh. I'd like to find out more about Sophie. It'll be of enormous help, okay?'

He nodded, and then traipsed after his mother out of the room.

Kay waited until she heard Courtney's voice from some distance away, comforting her son, and then turned her attention back to Blake.

'How did Josh meet Sophie?'

'Her parents were invited to join a select group of worshippers with myself and Courtney through our local church.'

'Did you know Lady Griffith and her husband before that?'

'Only in passing. Did you know Diane's family

have been linked to royalty in England since the sixteenth century?'

'I didn't, no. How did you find out?'

'Oh, I like to study history, so when we moved out this way, I made a point of finding out about the stately homes around here and the land they're on. Lots of Roman and Norman history in Kent, of course. Diane's house has been passed through the generations since the mid-1700s – did you know?'

'No. How did the engagement between Josh and Sophie come about?'

Blake smiled. 'Like a dream,' he said. 'Those two – well, let's just say fate shone upon them. A rich American heir to a business empire and a titled lady's daughter?' He lowered his gaze before pinching the bridge of his nose. 'Sorry. I still can't believe she's gone.'

'Take your time, Mr Hamilton. It's okay.'

He nodded, his eyes closed, and then took a deep breath before speaking once more.

'They were perfect for each other,' he said. 'You should've seen them. Last night. Before—' He gulped. 'Sorry. They were such a beautiful couple.'

Kay waited for him to compose himself, then nodded at Carys and rose from her seat.

'Thank you for your time today, Mr Hamilton.

We'll be in touch about speaking to Josh again. We'll see ourselves out.'

———

Kay overtook a slow-moving moped and aimed the car for the lane that led back to police station.

At the last minute, she indicated and swerved into a side street that widened before depositing them in the town centre.

'Coffee?'

'Yeah. I could do with something stronger after that conversation, but coffee'll have to do.'

Kay reversed the vehicle into a parking space, then climbed out and led the way across the street and up a flight of concrete stairs to the shopping precinct, before turning right and following the paved pedestrian area until a favourite café of theirs came into sight.

'Grab a table. You want something to eat?'

'That'd be great, thanks. Bacon butty, please?'

'Coming right up.'

Kay left Carys at a table bathed in sunlight outside the window of the café and pushed the door open, the bitter tang of freshly ground coffee filling her senses as she approached the counter and placed their order.

The owner handed her a table number on a metal stalk along with her change, and she hurried back to the table, her stomach rumbling.

'Did you forget to eat this morning?' Carys grinned.

'I don't really do breakfast. I will at weekends if we're both home, but that usually ends up being brunch or something.'

'God, I couldn't manage to get out the door without my bowl of porridge first thing.'

Kay eyed the other woman's figure. 'I honestly have no idea where you put it.'

Carys laughed. 'I run. That helps.'

They looked up as the door to the café swung outwards and a waitress appeared bearing a tray with their drinks and food.

'Thanks.' Kay poured milk from a small jug and pushed the jug towards Carys before picking up her spoon and stirring her coffee.

Carys stirred a sugar sachet into her coffee cup and frowned. 'I wonder how desperate Blake Hamilton was to get Josh married into the English aristocracy?'

Kay leaned back on the bench, squinting in the bright sunshine. 'But why kill Sophie? That'd defeat the object of his plans, right?'

The younger detective shrugged. 'I don't know, but this whole thing seems to be related to an elitist church group, of which he's a founding member, a business of his that's doing great in the city, and the fact he wanted to get his son married into the English aristocracy.'

'You think he'd do anything for a whiff of a title?'

'Maybe he found out something about Sophie he didn't like, and decided he didn't want his son involved with her.' Carys bit into her bacon butty, a glob of ketchup splashing over her fingers. 'The only time he's mentioned Sophie he's sounded like she was some sort of prized brood mare, anyway.'

Kay placed her coffee cup on the table between them and ripped off the side of her croissant before stuffing it in her mouth. She swallowed, her hand hovering over the pastry. 'It does seem extreme, but then these things sometimes are, aren't they?' She shrugged. 'I suppose we shouldn't rule it out.'

'Whatever. He's still a creep.'

Kay grinned, and put another piece of croissant in her mouth. 'You got that right.'

CHAPTER FIFTEEN

Kay dumped her notes on her desk and swivelled her chair round as Sharp entered the room to lead the afternoon debrief.

He frowned as he passed her. 'Where's Barnes and Piper?'

'They're not back yet from interviewing Eva Shepparton,' said Debbie. 'Should be back soon.'

Sharp checked his watch. 'All right, well let's make a start and they can catch up when they get here.' He wandered over to the whiteboard and called over his shoulder. 'West – you first. What have we got so far about the companies run by Blake Hamilton and Matthew Whittaker?'

'A tale of two contrasts,' said Debbie. 'On one hand, you've got Blake Hamilton running a very successful business, with his financial statements showing a year-on-year profit well into seven figures. On the other, Matthew Whitaker's business is failing, to be honest. I'm surprised he hasn't given up.'

'Does Matthew Whitaker owe a lot of money?'

'Yes, and it looks like those debts will be called in within the next few weeks. I don't think he's going to have any other option than to declare himself bankrupt.'

'Keep an eye on them.'

'Will do, guv.'

'Kay? What did the pastor have to say for himself?'

'He confirmed that the Hamiltons and the Whittakers are part of an exclusive group of worshippers out of his congregation,' she said. 'There are six other couples, all of whom were present at the ceremony and the party afterwards, so after this I'll catch up with Gavin regarding the statements that uniform took down. I'll get Carys and Gavin to re-interview those over the next day or so.' She sighed. 'It appears that the group saw themselves as being elite from the rest of the churchgoers, and Duncan Saddleworth was happy to oblige them. He admitted he told Sophie Whittaker about the purity pledge ceremony after she'd asked him about the work he did in the States six years ago before he returned here. I had a quick look online, and it seems to have emerged out of the conservative Christian movement in Connecticut, where Duncan Saddleworth was based.'

'Was she forced into it?' said Debbie.

'He says it was her idea. He pointed her in the direction of the information, and she came to him a few weeks afterwards and said she wanted to take the pledge.' She frowned. 'However, what *is* noticeable is that none of the template pledges online or provided by Duncan to Sophie included anything about being betrothed to one particular person. She added in the wording that she would remain chaste until she married Josh Hamilton.'

'Interesting,' said Sharp. 'We'll need to speak to the families again, to see what gave her that idea.'

Kay jotted down a reminder in her notebook. 'Will do.'

'I think it's wrong they can marry off their daughter like that,' said Carys, shaking her head. 'That sort of thing usually happens in other cultures, for goodness' sake. That's why the council spends so much money trying to stop arranged marriages and educate communities around here.'

'Well, it's a bit different from those scenarios,' said Debbie. 'For a start, at sixteen Sophie was already old enough to marry whoever she wanted, as long as she had her parents' consent.'

'Besides,' said Kay, 'it's worked well for the English aristocracy for years. All those upper-class families, marrying off their kids to protect their wealth and standing in society. Keeps the lineage going, doesn't it?'

Sharp wrinkled his nose. 'You'll be telling me you're a Jane Austen fan next. All that "Ooh, Mr Darcy" rubbish.'

Kay burst out laughing. 'Not me.'

'It is a bit creepy though, isn't it?' said Debbie.

Kay turned in her seat as Barnes and Gavin hurried into the incident room and apologised to Sharp for their lateness. She noticed the air of excitement between them.

'What happened?' said Sharp.

'Sophie Whittaker was pregnant,' said Gavin.

A stunned hush filled the room.

'Pregnant?' said Kay eventually. 'Is Eva sure?'

'Apparently, Sophie confided in her the day of the ceremony.'

'Is Peter the father?' said Sharp.

'Eva said Sophie didn't tell her who the father was,' said Barnes. 'They were outside, next to the conservatory when Sophie told her and she clammed up when the gardener appeared. Eva didn't get the chance to ask her about it again because everyone was so busy getting ready for the ceremony.'

'Do you think she's telling the truth about not knowing who the father is? Perhaps to protect that person?'

'We wondered that,' said Gavin. 'She did seem to be holding something back from us.'

'I'll get on to Lucas and ask him if he can hurry up with the full post mortem report so we can confirm it,' said Kay. 'We'll obviously ask for a paternity test as well, in the circumstances.'

'Christ,' said Sharp, and rubbed his chin. 'What a mess. Did Eva give any indication as to Sophie's state of mind when she told her?'

'Frightened,' said Gavin. He flipped open his notebook. 'Her exact words to Eva were, "they'll kill me if they find out. What am I going to do?" – Eva said she managed to calm Sophie down, and they'd agreed to talk again the day after the ceremony once they could get some time to themselves.'

'Did Sophie tell anyone else?' asked Carys.

'She told Eva that she hadn't,' said Gavin, 'and Eva says she hadn't told anyone else either – she was still in shock.'

'How did Sophie find out?' said Kay. 'Missed period, or did she do a pregnancy test?'

'Both. Missed her period four weeks ago,' said Barnes. 'Eva said Sophie told her she'd eventually bought a pregnancy test in a chemist in the Fremlin Walk shopping centre, and used the public toilets there to do the test. She found out the day before she told Eva.'

Sharp perched on top of the desk nearest the whiteboard. 'Well, we're not going to have the post mortem results for a while yet, even if you do chase up Lucas this afternoon,' he said. 'Not after that bus crash on the M20 over the weekend. In the meantime, we'll follow this up with Peter Evans. Find out if he knew his girlfriend was pregnant.'

'You think he panicked, guv?' said Barnes.

'Maybe,' said Sharp.

'I'll phone the duty solicitor and ask him to get here as soon as possible,' said Kay.

'Thanks,' said Sharp. 'I'll clear my diary for the rest of tomorrow as well. Let's see what transpires out of this interview, and go from there.'

'I'll continue to research this purity pledge business, too,' said Kay. 'And I want to find out more about Duncan Saddleworth's background. I got the impression he wasn't telling me something, so I'll look into where he was based before he came to Maidstone, and whether anything cropped up while he was at university in Oxford.'

'Right.' Sharp recapped the pen and tossed it onto the shelf under the whiteboard. 'We'll have another briefing at eight o'clock tomorrow morning. Barnes, let's go have a chat with Peter Evans and see what he's got to say for himself.'

CHAPTER SIXTEEN

Kay sipped her wine as Adam stood at the stove, stirring a Thai green curry that had been simmering away for twenty minutes.

He seemed tired, reticent. Usually, by now he'd have asked her about her day even though he knew she wouldn't be able to tell him too much about the current investigation. Instead, he appeared to be preoccupied, lost in thought.

'Everything okay?'

His shoulders sagged and he put the spoon to one side before turning down the heat on the stove and moving to where she sat.

'I went up to the cemetery this afternoon. I took some fresh flowers – the heat over the past few days had withered the ones we left last time.'

She reached out for his hand and gave his fingers a squeeze. 'If you'd waited until the weekend, I might've been able come with you. You didn't have to go alone.'

'I know. I happened to pass it on the way out to a farm this morning, so I thought I'd drop in on my way home. It was a spur of the moment thing. It did me good to sit there for a while.'

Kay squeezed his hand once more, and then let go.

He didn't often show his emotions about her miscarriage the previous year, and guilt washed over her that she hadn't thought of asking how he was doing more often.

As if picking up on her thoughts, he walked around the worktop to where she sat and pulled her into his arms. He kissed her hair.

'We can go up there at the weekend again if you like.'

She twisted round on her bar stool to face him, and placed her hand against his cheek. 'That's okay. I imagine Sharp will have us working overtime this week. I think it's nice you went there.'

'You don't mind?'

'Of course not.'

'I tidied up a bit while I was there,' he said, moving back to the stove and picking up the wooden spoon. 'There were weeds growing all around. Can't have that.'

Kay eased herself off the stool and grabbed the bottle of wine off the worktop before topping up his glass. 'I thought perhaps we could donate those boxes of clothes upstairs to one of the local charities sometime.'

He clinked his glass against hers. 'I think that's a great idea.'

'I'm going to keep the blue bear, though.'

He smiled. 'Thought you might. I saw he's taken up prime position next to your new computer.'

'He's guarding it.'

'That so?'

'True story. He'll take your hand off if you go anywhere near him.'

'I'll *bear* that in mind.'

Kay groaned, and moved away to grab the plates from the cupboard.

As Adam spoke to Kay about his day while they ate, she was struck as always by how much she loved him.

He had a habit of telling stories with his hands, so

as he described the farm he had visited that morning and the animals he had attended to, she found herself putting down her utensils and covering her mouth as she dissolved into laughter at his impressions of the hapless farmer he had to deal with.

It never ceased to amaze her how much information he had to recall about all the animals he looked after on a day-to-day basis. She knew he often spent the evenings she was working with his head bowed above an open textbook on the kitchen worktop, or flicking through the latest edition of a veterinary journal, always making sure his knowledge was up to date.

Since their house had been burgled, Kay hadn't brought up the subject of her own investigation into who had tried to end her career by implicating her in a case where vital evidence had gone missing, and a subsequent Professional Standards investigation had been lodged against her.

She'd survived the ordeal, but not unscathed. Not only had the ensuing suspension from duty resulted in a devastating miscarriage, but her ambition to become a detective inspector had been quashed by her superior officer, DCI Larch. Only DI Devon Sharp had fought her corner for her and remained one of the few from the top floor she felt she could trust.

Embittered and vowing justice on those who had wronged her, Adam had suggested she conduct her own investigation into who it was and why she had been set up.

Neither of them could have foreseen the consequences of her actions. The burglary had been shocking enough; the attack on her colleague, DC Gavin Piper – a police constable at the time – had frightened them both, and Adam had pleaded with her to stop.

She'd agreed, and had ceased to spend her evenings at her computer in the spare bedroom above, but her natural curiosity continued to keep her mind busy as she tried to work out why she had been targeted. She'd been too busy at work the past few months to have time to carry out any research, yet the temptation proved too much.

'I was thinking,' she said, swirling her wine. 'Things have gone quiet recently. I might take a look at that case again.'

Adam froze, his wineglass halfway to his mouth. He blinked, and lowered it to the worktop before speaking.

'Are you sure?'

She nodded. 'I need to know, Adam. I can't let them get away with it.' She leaned forward and reached out for his hand. 'Since they hauled me over the coals about the missing evidence, it's like no-one is going after Jozef Demiri anymore. It's almost as if they're too scared to. Nothing's happening. I checked the database earlier today, and there's no-one investigating him.'

'For good reason, Kay.' He frowned. 'Who do *you* think burgled our house? His lot, or one of yours?'

She sat back on her stool. 'I'm not sure. But,' she added, holding up her hand to stop him interrupting, 'if it *is* someone I work with, then I want to know who – and why.'

He sighed, squeezed her hand. 'I wondered how long you'd be able to stay away from it.'

She bit her lip. 'Sorry. I'll be careful, I promise.'

Her mobile phone buzzed next to her elbow, and she glanced down at the number before frowning.

'Guv?'

Adam began to clear their plates away while she listened to DI Sharp's voice, her heart sinking as the impact of what he was saying hit her.

'I'll be right there.'

Adam automatically grabbed her takeaway coffee cup from the worktop and flipped the kettle on as she put her phone away.

'You on your way out?'

'Yes. Sharp's at the hospital. I've got to go. Peter Evans attempted suicide.'

CHAPTER SEVENTEEN

Kay pulled the handbrake on the car and leapt from the vehicle, swinging her bag over her shoulder as she aimed her key fob over her shoulder and heard the deep *thunk* of the locking mechanism.

Hurrying across the car park, she pushed her hair away from her face as a light breeze tickled her skin, and a bright moon appeared from behind a cloud, its glow muted by the orange of the sodium lights above her head.

Kay swept into the hospital through the main visitor entrance and then turned right and along a familiar corridor.

She realised her hand was clenched into a fist, and forced herself to relax her grip on her handbag strap, before pressing the button for the elevator.

As it rose through the building, she stared at her feet and rubbed at her right eye, refusing to glance at her reflection in the mirrored walls to her left and right.

Exiting the elevator, she pushed through the double doors of the reception area to the ward and flashed her badge at the nurse standing at the desk with a phone to her ear.

'Peter Evans?'

The woman nodded and placed her hand over the receiver. 'Through there,' she said, and pointed to a corridor off to her left.

Kay held up her hand in thanks and took off down the corridor, fighting down a familiar sense of panic that had nothing to do with Peter Evans. Her head jerked up at the sound of murmured voices.

Sharp emerged through a door off to the right, then looked over his shoulder and stopped to speak to someone who was still in the room.

From her position outside, Kay glimpsed a uniformed police officer sitting on a chair pushed against the wall. Another stood with his hands clasped beside a small cabinet set to one side of the bed, and she realised Sharp would have organised round-the-clock surveillance to ensure Peter Evans didn't try to take his life once more.

A doctor appeared and ushered Sharp from the room, then pulled the door closed behind him.

'Your officers understand my patient has to rest?' he said.

'They do,' said Sharp. 'We can't question him without his solicitor being present anyway, and I'm sure that's not going to be happening tonight, is it?'

The doctor shook his head, and held out his hand. 'I must be off,' he said. 'I'll let you know if anything happens, but otherwise I'll talk to you in the morning.'

'Thanks.'

The doctor nodded at Kay as he passed, then disappeared down the corridor, his shoes squeaking on the polished floor with every step.

'How is he?' said Kay once the doctor was out of earshot.

'He'll live,' said Sharp, his eyes weary.

'What happened?'

He jerked his chin towards the exit. 'Let's find somewhere to have a coffee, and I'll bring you up to speed.'

Kay fell into step beside him as he led the way from the ward and along the main corridor of the hospital. He ignored the elevators and instead pushed through double glass doors that led to a staircase. As they descended, he sighed.

'You okay?'

'Yeah,' he said. 'Long day.'

He opened the door at the next level to let her through, and they followed the signs to a small cafeteria.

Their footsteps echoed off the walls, the space abandoned, and only one set of lights shone above a glass counter and till, both of which were unmanned. Kay withdrew her purse and headed for the vending machine, selected two coffees and joined Sharp at a table he'd chosen towards the back of the empty café, his back to the wall, facing the exit.

Kay placed the two plastic cups on the table between them and lowered her bag to the floor before sliding into the seat opposite him.

'What happened?'

Sharp leaned back in his seat and swept imaginary crumbs from the table. 'He somehow loosened a screw from the cot in the cell, hid it in his sleeve or somewhere, and used it to slash his wrists.'

'Oh, shit,' she breathed.

'His solicitor was meeting with him in a side room off to the custody suite. When they'd finished, the solicitor went to find the custody sergeant to let him know Peter could be taken back to his cell. By the time they returned, Peter had collapsed.'

'Jesus – didn't the solicitor think to go back to the room and wait with him?'

Sharp shook his head. 'It seems he thought it was more important to remonstrate with the custody sergeant about how long it was taking to process other suspects – there was a fight at one of the bars in town and uniform had brought three men in. It wasn't until those had been processed that they got around to returning to Peter. They managed to bandage him up and stem the flow by laying him down and keeping his arms elevated before the ambulance arrived, but he still needed a transfusion as soon as he got here. The scars are going to be horrendous.'

Kay picked up her coffee and forced herself to take a sip while her mind ran through all the different scenarios they would be faced with over the coming days.

The implications for the case would be extensive. There would be an immediate investigation, of course. Accusations would fly, policies and procedures would be scrutinised, and in the midst of all of it, the team would still be expected to deliver a result to convict Sophie's killer.

'It's my mistake,' said Sharp. 'I organised the

suicide watch for when he was in his cell. I should've insisted on him being under constant observation.'

'You could never have foreseen this,' said Kay. 'No-one could. If he was that determined to commit suicide, then we'd have needed eyes in the back of our head to stop him.'

Sharp ran a hand over tired eyes. 'Maybe.' He reached out for the coffee, and then changed his mind.

'You couldn't have known he was going to react this way.'

'Yeah,' he sighed.

'What happens next?'

'I've spoken to Larch. We've got a meeting with the Chief Superintendent and the media advisor at seven o'clock tomorrow—' He broke off and checked his watch. '*This* morning. We'll have the usual team briefing at eight o'clock and I'll bring you all up to speed then. Can you phone everyone first thing to make sure they get there at least twenty minutes beforehand? I don't want any stragglers.'

'Will do.' Kay dug out her mobile phone and set the alarm on it for five o'clock, which would give her time to have a quick shower then phone the team and get them to spread the word amongst the administrative support staff as well. 'Peter Evans stated he had no immediately family – is there anyone at all we can call?'

Sharp shook his head, and took a sip of his coffee before replying. 'He says not, even when the doctor asked him.'

'What about his solicitor?'

'I phoned his boss before I called you to let him know their client survived. The partner of the firm who I spoke to will take on Peter's case now. On the basis that he didn't want to spend every waking hour in his client's room here while he recovers, he's agreed to us having uniform there. They're under strict instructions not to question him about the case, and if he does attempt to converse with them, they call us immediately but provide no response to him in the interim.'

Kay pushed her coffee to one side, unable to face another sip of the burnt foul-tasting liquid.

'When do we tell Sophie's parents?'

'Before any media statement – and that'll be done early tomorrow as well, to avoid the local press catching wind of this and coming to its own conclusions.'

Kay dropped her phone back into her bag before raising her gaze to Sharp. 'Do *you* think his actions are an admission of guilt?'

He yawned and stretched his arms over his head. 'Maybe.'

'Come on. Neither of us is going to be thinking straight at this time of night.'

'You're right,' he said, and stood. 'Let's get out of here. I'll see you back at the station in a few hours.'

CHAPTER EIGHTEEN

Kay took one of the steaming cups of coffee from the tray Gavin held out, and inhaled the aroma.

'Perfect timing, Gavin – thanks.'

'No problem. Figured we're going to need this,' he said, and made his way over to where Barnes and Carys sat.

'You're not wrong there,' she murmured.

She fought down the urge to yawn, and turned her attention to the pile of paperwork on her desk. Aside from Sophie Whittaker's murder, she was still juggling two burglary cases and a suspected arson attack on a corner shop near Maidstone West train station.

Sophie's murder would take precedence, but she worked her way through her voicemail messages while she prioritised what she could fit around the major investigation.

She hung up the phone and spun her seat around at the sound of voices approaching the incident room and took a sip of her drink as Sharp appeared, followed by DCI Larch.

She couldn't help but wonder if Sharp had taken his own advice and got some sleep before arriving at the station that morning, or whether he'd spent the past few hours preparing for his early meeting with DCI Larch and the Chief Superintendent.

Either way, he wore dark circles under his eyes and she suspected he'd made use of the change of shirt and tie he kept on a hook on the back of the door to his office.

She resolved to send one of the admin staff out to get him a sandwich after the briefing, otherwise he'd be running on empty.

His murmured conversation with Larch stopped as they passed the desks, and the room fell silent.

'Cheers, Gavin,' he said as he took the last two coffees and passed one to Larch. He took a sip, and then put his cup down. 'Right, we've had an update from the hospital, and Peter Evans is now in a stable condition and should be released within the next couple of days,' he said. 'We've met with the Chief

Superintendent this morning and our media advisor, and a statement will be issued to the press at nine o'clock. In the meantime, you are all requested to refrain from giving out any information to callers regarding the matter, and to provide all journalists with the number for the press office. The reception desk officers have been ordered to do the same. Guv?'

'Thanks, Sharp.' Larch turned his attention to the team. 'Obviously, a suspect attempting suicide while in custody is a worrying occurrence and a formal investigation will take place immediately. There will be an internal review as to why Peter Evans was left alone considering he was placed on suicide watch, and why he wasn't considered a risk. We'll be interviewing his solicitor, too.' He glared at the team. 'The investigation will also focus on how it happened.'

He turned to Sharp. 'Right, I've got another meeting upstairs before the media briefing. I'll leave you to it.'

Kay waited until he'd stalked from the room, the door slamming shut in his wake.

'Never mind *how* it happened,' she said, and frowned. 'Shouldn't we be asking *why*?'

'Guilt,' said Barnes. 'We found out what his

motive was.'

Kay bit her lip. 'Is that it? What if he isn't the killer? Eva Shepparton only had Sophie's word she hadn't told anyone else she was pregnant.'

Sharp stood, ran a hand over his close-cropped hair and uncapped a marker pen, adding a note to the whiteboard. 'Okay, then. Who else would have cause to kill Sophie if they found out she was pregnant?'

'Josh Hamilton, if he's not the father,' said Kay. 'Considering Sophie's purity pledge was all about her remaining chaste until they got married in a couple of years' time.'

'Or his parents,' said Carys. 'There are a few statements that mention Blake Hamilton was pretty determined to marry his son into English aristocracy – however tenuous the link might be.'

Sharp added the names to the board. 'We also need to consider Sophie's parents,' he said, before turning back to the team. 'Uncomfortable as it is, we know these sorts of murders are often committed by someone close to the victim.'

'Surely if Sophie loved him, she would have told Peter she was pregnant?' said Kay. 'Or was she going to tell him once they'd run away?'

'Maybe she was worried he'd change his mind

about running away with her if she was pregnant?' said Gavin.

Sharp finished updating the notes on the board. 'All right. This morning's tasks. Barnes – you and Debbie investigate the Whittakers. Tread carefully, but find out if she was seeing someone else – maybe it was affecting her schoolwork, or her teachers knew something her friends and family didn't. We already know about Peter and Josh – was there anyone else involved? Carys – you and Gavin work on the background for the Hamiltons, including a greater focus on Blake's business. We'll regroup here at eleven o'clock.'

He drained his coffee and tossed the empty cup in the bin next to him.

'Hunter, let's go have a chat with Peter Evans,' he said. 'Phone the solicitor and have him meet us there.'

CHAPTER NINETEEN

The duty solicitor had arrived before Sharp and Kay, and was standing outside Peter's room with the doctor from the previous night.

The doctor looked as tired as Sharp did, and Kay wondered how long the man's shifts were, and when he was due a break. She suspected it would be some time before the man would get some rest.

Both men turned at the sound of their footsteps.

The duty solicitor was an older man who Kay had dealt with before. Brian Sutherland was a partner in one of the bigger local legal firms and wore a dark grey suit that accentuated his snow-white hair that he wore slightly longer than most men his age. Keen blue eyes held her gaze as they shook hands, before his brow creased.

'This isn't good, Detectives,' he said. 'I hope a full investigation is underway.'

'It is,' said Sharp. 'You heard the media statement earlier?'

'Yes. Thanks for keeping my client's name private.'

Sharp acknowledged the remark with a small shrug. 'Standard practice.' He turned his attention to the doctor. 'How's he doing?'

'Better than I'd hoped, considering the mess he made of his wrists.'

'Can we talk to him now?'

The doctor checked his watch. 'I've got another appointment for the next half an hour, so you can talk to him until I get back. He's still very weak, mind. If he shows any sign of tiredness, I want you to stop.' He eyed both Sharp and Kay carefully. 'Is that understood? He lost a lot of blood last night, and needs to rest.'

'Understood,' said Sharp and handed a bag to Kay before gesturing to the duty solicitor. 'Lead the way, Mr Sutherland.'

The solicitor opened the door and held it open for Sharp, who dismissed the two new uniformed officers that had taken over the observation role for the day.

Kay stood to one side to let them pass, then entered the room.

Peter Evans looked like a ghost.

As Sutherland moved closer to the bed and helped his client reach the remote control to raise the back of the bed until Peter was in a sitting position, Kay bit her lip.

She'd noticed when she'd first met Peter that his skin was pale – almost alabaster – but since losing so much blood, he was almost translucent. It was the first time she'd noticed how thin he was as well.

She caught Sharp's gaze and realised he was as shocked as she.

If the custody team hadn't raised the alarm when they did, the situation would have been much worse.

They certainly wouldn't be interviewing their main suspect this morning.

She refocused, moved to one of the vacated chairs and sat before reaching into the bag Sharp had handed to her while Sutherland spoke in a low murmur with his client. Sharp hovered nearby until Sutherland glanced over his shoulder and nodded.

Sharp moved closer and shoved his hands in his pockets. 'How are you doing, Peter?'

'I'm okay,' he said. He held up his two bandaged wrists. 'I guess.'

'All right. This is what we're going to do. We need to talk to you, but we're still under an obligation to caution you and treat this conversation as a formal interview. DS Hunter here will operate a portable recorder, and then the interview will be copied onto CDs and stored as evidence.'

Sharp waited while she set up the equipment, then formally cautioned Evans and began his questioning.

'What happened?'

Peter wiped angrily at his eyes with the back of his hand. 'I'm not going to prison for something I didn't do,' he choked. 'I loved her. I had no idea she was pregnant, I swear.' He sniffed and raised his eyes to Sharp. 'And if I did, I would've stayed with her. I'd have done anything for Sophie.'

Sharp wandered round the foot of the bed, ignored Kay and leaned against the opposite wall. 'Peter, you have no alibi for the night of the party. You told us you saw Sophie that morning.' He sighed. 'If you two were so keen to run away, why didn't you go then? Why wait? Did she change her mind? Is that what happened? Did she change her mind, so you decided to stop her?'

'Detective Sharp!' The duty solicitor shot him a warning look.

'No!' Peter jerked upright, and then winced. He

fell back onto the pillows. 'It was Sophie's idea. She insisted she go through with the whole ceremony. I think—' He broke off and sniffed again. 'I think she felt guilty that her parents had spent all that money on the marquee and the caterers and everything, and she didn't want to let them down.'

'What did you say to her when she told you she was going to proceed with the ceremony? Did it make you feel angry?'

Peter's brow furrowed. 'No,' he said. 'Frustrated, yes. But not angry.'

Sharp pushed himself away from the wall. 'How did you two meet?'

A sad smile twitched at the corner of Peter's mouth, and his gaze fell to the bandages on his wrists. He picked absently at a loose thread on the blanket. 'I help out a local handyman,' he said. 'I was pretty good at carpentry at school, and I can do some basic plumbing stuff, too. There was a gutter that needed replacing at the church she and her family went to, but the only time we could do it was late on a Tuesday afternoon. By the time we were finished, it was getting dark. Some people started turning up at the church, and I remember being surprised because I didn't know there was anything on that day.'

The smile disappeared and a frown creased his

features. 'Of course, now I know it was that creepy group her parents belonged to. Including Josh and his family.'

'Go on,' said Sharp.

'I was carrying a ladder back to my van,' said Peter, his face wistful. 'She smiled at me, and – I don't know. I can't remember the last time I felt like that about someone. They all went into the church and about five minutes later – I was packing up my tools – she came out again. I think she'd told her parents she'd left something or other in the car. She gave me her phone number, and then went back inside.'

'How long ago was this?'

'Five months ago.'

'Did you know then that she was going to get engaged to Josh?'

'No.'

Sharp glanced over his shoulder to where Kay sat, and she gave him a small nod before writing a reminder for herself on a fresh page of her notebook. They would have to check the timeline of events prior to the purity pledge ceremony, to see if Duncan Saddleworth and Peter's recollection tallied.

'Whose idea was the purity pledge?' said Sharp. 'Did Sophie tell you?'

'Hers. It was her idea.'

'Seems strange to me, Peter, that on one hand you're adamant Sophie loved you, but on the other she's making plans to remain chaste until her wedding to someone else entirely.'

The young man shrugged, but said nothing, and turned his head so he couldn't see Sharp.

Kay turned at a knock on the door, and the doctor appeared.

Sharp glanced at his watch, then at the duty solicitor.

'That'll have to do for today. We'll come back tomorrow.'

He ended the formal interview, waited while Kay packed up the recording equipment, and then led the way out the room, waiting to thank Brian Sutherland and the doctor before they left.

Kay fell into step beside him, and waited until they were next to their car before she spoke.

'What do you think?'

'If he'd been going out with Sophie for the past five months, and knew she was going to do this purity pledge and get engaged to Josh Hamilton, then he's had plenty of time to plan something, hasn't he?' said Sharp.

'But if Sophie loved Peter, why the charade?' Kay watched Brian Sutherland's car leave the hospital grounds and turn onto the main road back to Maidstone.

'That's something we'll have to ask the parents,' said Sharp. 'I'm starting to get the impression there's more going on here than a young woman changing her mind about a religious pledge.'

————

'If Sophie loved Peter, why go through with the purity pledge and her engagement announcement?' said Kay.

The thought had burrowed its way into her mind after interviewing Peter Evans, and troubled her constantly once she was back at the incident room and re-listening to the recording she'd made.

Barnes rummaged in the bag of sweets on the desk and pulled out a lemon sherbet.

'Maybe she wasn't sure about Peter. Maybe she was playing them both along until she decided which one was the best option,' he said, and popped the sweet in his mouth.

'And perhaps the pregnancy put paid to that idea.' Kay leaned back in her chair and stared at the ceiling. 'So, we've got a few possibilities to consider. Peter didn't like the idea of her being pregnant, and killed her—'

'Which we think is unlikely, given his reaction to the news.'

'Right, so then maybe Josh found out, and killed her.'

'Except he says he didn't know Peter, and didn't know that Sophie knew him either.'

'His parents were with him when you asked him that though, weren't they? Maybe he's hiding something from them.'

'True. We also have to add Blake Hamilton to the list. He seemed more upset than his son, but purely from the angle that Josh wasn't going to get the chance to marry into English aristocracy. Honestly, Ian, you saw the state of the Whittakers' house – why on earth would you want to take on that as a dowry?'

Barnes coughed on his sweet. 'Tax deduction?'

'Very funny.'

CHAPTER TWENTY

Kay cursed under her breath as a tractor passed perilously near to the right wing of the car before it powered away and roared up the narrow lane behind her. She accelerated away from the grass verge and chuckled as Carys exhaled loudly. 'Yeah, he was a bit too close.'

'I spent some time online last night looking up about those purity pledges,' said Carys as the car increased speed.

'Anything interesting?'

'Well, it seems that unplanned pregnancies amongst teenagers that have taken a purity pledge is higher than those that don't.'

'Really? So much for remaining chaste, eh?'

'Might go some way to explain how Sophie

ended up pregnant, though. Apparently neither the parents nor the churches involved ever think to educate their daughters about safe sex. They seem to think that once the girls take the pledge, they can forget about having to have that conversation. Like it's swept under the carpet.' Carys looked out of the window at the fields passing by in a blur. 'It's almost as if they're washing their hands of the responsibility.'

'That certainly ties in with this case by the look of it.'

'Although Peter maintains he used a condom both times.'

Kay shrugged. 'Accidents happen, I guess.'

'I think it stinks that it's only the girls that take the pledge,' said Carys, warming to her subject. 'Apparently, the boys don't, and can sleep with who they like. The women are expected to forgive the men for any indiscretions up to the day they marry someone. The divorce rate is disproportionately high, too among those groups. It's sad, really.'

'It is,' said Kay. 'Mind you, I can't help feeling it's just another way for religion to control women.'

Carys turned in her seat. 'You're not a religious person, are you?'

Kay shook her head. 'No. My parents had me

christened as a kid but neither of them was particularly religious. You?'

'I don't know. I was christened as well, but I've never really thought about it much until now. This business with Sophie and all these people using her to further their own agendas kind of makes me think I don't want to be, though.'

They fell into silence as the gates to Crossways Hall appeared, and Kay slowed to make the turn into the gravel-covered driveway.

The family liaison officer's car had been parked off to one side of the house and had been boxed in by three more vehicles – all were top of the range, and gleaming.

'Visitors?'

'Looks that way.' Kay pulled the keys from the ignition. 'Let's find out, shall we?'

As they drew closer to the front door, it was opened and the woman Kay recalled as being the housekeeper peered out.

She put a finger to her lips, and then beckoned them over the threshold.

'Good morning, Detectives.'

'Good morning. We'd like to speak to Mr and Mrs Whittaker, please.'

The housekeeper arched an eyebrow. '*Lady*

Griffith and Mr Whittaker are not available at the present time.'

'Who do all the cars outside belong to?'

'They currently have guests.'

'Mrs – Jamieson, isn't it?'

The housekeeper nodded.

'I'm currently investigating the murder of Lady Griffith's daughter. Perhaps that has slipped your memory.'

The woman took a step back. 'Well—'

'In the circumstances, I'd appreciate it if you would go and let them know that we're here, and wish to talk to them.'

'I-I can't right now. You'll have to wait.' She gestured to a thinly-padded two-seater chair beside the front door.

'Why?'

The woman wrung her hands. 'You must wait. Until they've finished their prayers.'

'Prayers?'

'The church group is here. To lend spiritual support at this difficult time.'

Kay glared at her.

'Please, have a seat. They won't be long.'

Kay took one look at the seat the housekeeper indicated and shook her head. 'We'll stand, thanks.

Actually, while we're waiting, I'd like to ask you a few questions.'

'Me?'

'Yes.' Kay lowered her voice. 'You must overhear a lot of the conversations that take place around here.'

'Well, I—'

'So, what did you think of Sophie's relationship with Josh Hamilton?'

Jamieson's shoulders slumped. 'It's so sad. They were perfect for each other. He was such a gentleman to everyone. A pleasure to have here as a guest.'

'Oh? Did you spend much time with him?'

'Of course. I'm responsible for the running of this house, and one day he'd be my employer. He showed a keen interest in the history of the place.' She beamed. 'Like his father – very interested in Lady Griffith's family.'

'Did he and Sophie ever argue?'

The housekeeper pulled her cardigan around her chest and folded her arms. 'Not that I ever recall, no. Like I said, he was a gentleman.'

'What about Peter Evans?'

'A good for nothing,' said Jamieson. 'Mr Whittaker had to have strong words with him the last time he showed up here. I'm not surprised he murdered our beautiful girl. I always said there was something not quite right about him.'

A bell sounded, and Jamieson's head cocked to one side. 'I must go. That's Lady Griffith signalling her guests will require tea shortly. Wait here.'

The housekeeper disappeared through another doorway leading out of the hallway, and Carys began to pace the floor, her chin tilted upwards as she gazed at the various paintings on the walls.

A large grandfather clock kept a steady beat from its position next to the wall at the bottom of the stairs, and Kay scowled at it. She could never bear the sound of a ticking clock – to her, it was as annoying as a dripping tap.

She fought down her frustration at having to wait.

Sophie's parents were grieving, after all, and she knew that with Larch watching her every move, she'd have to tread carefully.

Carys moved closer. 'How much do you think these paintings are worth?'

Kay turned and stepped back, craning her neck to take in the thick oils that coated each canvas, the colours mottled over the years.

She wrinkled her nose. 'Some of them are mouldy, look.' She jutted her chin towards the lower corner of one of the frames. 'If these are family members, I guess it'd depend on who painted them. I can't imagine you'd get much for them otherwise.'

She shivered and pulled her jacket closer around her middle, crossing her arms. 'This place is freezing. Can you imagine what it'd be like in winter?'

'I'd take my tiny two-bedroom place any time over this,' agreed Carys.

They both turned at the sound of the door behind them opening, and a small group of people emerged, talking in low voices.

Matthew Whittaker followed an elderly man into the hallway, and patted his arm. 'It was good of you to come, Richard. And thanks for joining in our prayers. It was appreciated.'

'Least I could do.'

Kay swore under her breath, tugged Carys by the sleeve and pulled her towards the foot of the staircase out of the way as two older women bustled past, heading towards the kitchen.

'That's the Right Honourable Richard Fremchurch,' she hissed.

'DCI Larch's friend?'

Kay nodded and pursed her lips.

'Awkward.'

Kay said nothing, but had to agree with the young detective constable.

The conversation she'd planned to have with Matthew and Diane was going to be difficult enough, without having to worry about Larch's threats to keep the investigation low-key and maintain the family's privacy.

'Excuse me?'

Kay jumped at the voice behind her, and spun round to see Mrs Jamieson beckoning to her.

'Lady Griffith is in the sunroom, off the terrace, if you'd like to speak in private with her?'

Kay managed a small smile, thankful for the woman's resourcefulness. In her haste to keep the police away from the guests, the housekeeper had also saved Kay from having to come face to face with the politician.

'Thanks. We'll need Mr Whittaker as well.'

'I'll ask him to join you as soon as possible.'

Kay thanked her, and then led Carys along the hallway. They emerged into the living area that had been littered with shocked guests only three nights ago. Now, the room seemed abandoned, as if it didn't get much use between functions.

'You can almost feel the dust waiting to pounce,' whispered Carys.

Kay bit down on her bottom lip and glared at her.

She was right, though – now that she was seeing

the place for the first time without party guests or crime scene investigators poring all over it, the house seemed neglected as if it was slowly retreating in on itself.

'Grace said you wanted to talk to Diane and me?'

She turned at the sound of Matthew's voice behind her, and was relieved to see he'd left his guests elsewhere.

'Good morning, Mr Whittaker. Yes, we would. We were told your wife was waiting for us in the sunroom.'

'Through here.'

Kay stepped to one side to let him pass, then followed him through double oak doors and into a glass-panelled room that had been added on to one side of the house several years ago. Despite the bright sunlight outside however, the angle of the extension on the building left it in shade, and Kay noticed that spotlights had been set into the ceiling at some point over the years.

'Late twentieth century addition.'

Kay tore her eyes away from the patches of damp and peeling paint in the far corners of the room and made her way over to where Diane sat in a wicker armchair, a tray containing two china cups and a teapot in front of her on a small matching table.

Matthew hovered near one of the windows that overlooked a walled garden, and folded his arms across his chest.

'What did you want to talk to us about?'

Kay gestured to the seat next to Diane's. 'Perhaps you'd like to sit?'

'I'll stand,' he said and glared at her. 'What's taking so long with this investigation? Surely the mongrel should have been in front of a magistrate by now?'

Fine, thought Kay.

'Peter Evans attempted suicide last night while in police custody.'

Diane gasped and rocked back in her chair.

Matthew's eyes narrowed. 'Attempted?'

'He's currently recuperating in hospital, having undergone emergency surgery overnight.'

'More's the pity he survived.'

'Mr Whittaker—'

'Well, that's it, isn't it? Obviously, the guilt got to him and he couldn't live with himself.'

'How well did you know Peter?'

'We didn't. He turned up here a few times, like I've already told you. I had a word, told him to stay away, and we haven't seen him since.'

'Did Sophie ever stay away from home overnight?'

Matthew's brow creased, and he glanced across to where Diane sat, her face white.

'Sometimes,' he said, 'but she always told us where she was going, and we know her friends' parents, so it was never a problem.'

Kay checked her notes. 'She was studying part-time, wasn't she?'

Diane withdrew a lace handkerchief and dabbed at her eyes, then nodded. 'Art school. Four days a week.'

'No school for one day a week?'

'No, that's right. It's to give the students a chance to build up their portfolios. Sophie would often paint in here, or take a sketchbook into town and find somewhere to sit and draw.'

'What on earth has this all got to do with Peter Evans?' demanded Matthew.

Kay took a deep breath. 'We're trying to build up a picture of Sophie's life these past few weeks. Peter Evans attempted suicide after discovering Sophie was pregnant when she was killed.'

'Oh, my Lord,' whimpered Diane.

Matthew staggered, and reached out for the back

of the chair, his knuckles white. 'Where the hell did he get that idea from?'

'We received the information yesterday. At which point, Peter Evans was re-interviewed and asked if he had slept with Sophie.'

Diane emitted a wail, and Matthew rushed to her side, crouching next to her and taking her hands in his.

He turned and glared at Kay.

'Peter Evans confirmed that he had slept with Sophie recently,' she said softly. 'It seems the method of contraception they used didn't work. The post mortem results are still awaited, at which point we'll be seeking a paternity test as well.'

'I'm going to be sick.'

Diane launched herself from the chair and rushed from the room.

Matthew straightened, his face distraught.

'I'm sorry, Mr Whittaker. We had to let you know. You had no idea?'

'No.' He ran a hand over his face, and then pointed towards the door. 'I'd like you to leave now.'

CHAPTER TWENTY-ONE

A hush descended on the incident room the next morning as Kay let the door close behind her, as if she'd interrupted a private conversation.

She checked her watch, but the morning debrief was still twenty minutes away.

She ran her eyes over her colleagues as she passed them, but none would look up and meet her gaze.

Instead, they seemed intent on staring at their computer screens, or taking phone calls. A couple of the administrative staff appeared from the corner where the photocopier was, chatting happily until one of them saw Kay, and lowered her voice before nudging her colleague. Blushing, they scurried back to their desks and sat down, studiously ignoring her.

Before she could sit at her desk, Sharp peered out of his office and beckoned to her.

'Got a minute?'

Perplexed, she dumped her bag on the desk and followed him.

He shut the door behind her and gestured to the chairs opposite his desk.

'Have a seat,' he said and pulled the blinds down.

'I'd prefer to stand, thanks. What's going on?'

He moved past her, then perched on the corner of the desk and folded his arms across his chest.

Kay raised an eyebrow. Sharp had never seemed the nervous sort to her, especially with his military background, but right now he looked like he'd prefer to be anywhere other than talking to her.

Afghanistan, perhaps.

'Guv?'

'There's – ah – there's a rumour circulating that your health might not have been all that good these past few months, Kay.'

She narrowed her eyes. 'In what way?'

He dropped his gaze and ran a hand over his hair. 'Is it true you've had a miscarriage?'

The air left her lungs so fast, Kay staggered and reached out for the back of one of the chairs to steady herself.

Her vision blurred, the corners of her eyes darkening before filling with pinpricks of light, and her stomach heaved.

'Who—'

'I don't know how the rumour started. No-one seems to know who heard it first, but you know what it's like – one moment it was business as usual out there, and the next everyone's talking about it.'

'Everyone?'

He rose from the desk and placed a hand on her shoulder. 'I'm sorry. Sit down.'

'I don't want—'

'Sit.'

He pushed her gently into one of the seats and then lowered himself into the other and leaned forward, his elbows on his knees.

'I'm guessing from your reaction that it's true?'

She nodded, unable to speak, her thoughts tumbling over as she tried not to panic.

'Should you be here?'

'What?'

'Should you be at work? You know, if you're—'

'It happened ten months ago, guv.'

He straightened, confusion spreading across his features. 'But that's when—'

'Larch threw the Professional Standards

investigation at me. Yeah, I know. The doctors think the stress of that caused my miscarriage.'

He ran a hand over his mouth, hurt in his eyes. 'You should've told me, Kay.'

She snorted. 'Why? You had enough to deal with, trying not to believe one of your officers was corrupt.'

'That's not fair, Kay. I stood by you. The least you could do is trust me.'

She blinked, and rose from her seat, trying to ignore the stinging sensation at the corners of her eyes.

Beyond the closed confines of the office, the incident room remained silent as if everyone was holding their breath, waiting.

'It was none of your business,' she said, her back to him. 'I was already suspended from duty. Nobody had to find out.'

'Still, Kay. How long have I known you? And Adam? Have you told anyone at all?'

She shook her head. 'Adam's parents live in Canada, and I'm not close to my family. We decided it was better to keep it to ourselves.'

Except, she thought, there was only one other person who knew, who had found out by accident, and had been sworn to secrecy.

Someone who she thought she could trust.

'I'm sorry it got out like this,' said Sharp. 'You know how I feel about office gossip.'

She nodded and bit her lip before glancing over her shoulder at the door.

'Guess I'd better get back out there, huh? Can't stay hiding in here forever, can I?'

'Are you going to be all right?' He rose, and placed his hand on the doorknob, his eyes not leaving hers.

'This is probably going to be the shittiest day I've had for a while, but I'll live.'

He sighed and opened the door for her. 'Next time, try talking to me, okay?'

She didn't reply and instead concentrated on leaving his office with her head held high and made her way across the room to where she'd left her bag on the desk.

Flinging the strap over her shoulder, she checked her security pass was clipped to the waistband of her trousers and stalked out of the room, ignoring the embarrassed glances from her colleagues.

'Kay, wait!'

She paused halfway along the corridor and stared at the faded blue carpet while footsteps approached, before turning around at the last moment.

Carys held up her hands and lowered her voice, her face stricken. 'It wasn't me, Kay. You have to believe me. Whoever started this rumour – it wasn't me.'

Kay pursed her lips. 'No-one else knew, Carys. No-one.'

She spun on her heel and hurried down the stairwell, ignoring the strangled cry her colleague emitted in her wake.

CHAPTER TWENTY-TWO

Kay turned down the radio and indicated left into the car park behind the three-storey building that housed the county's forensic science services.

She'd spent most of the journey swearing under her breath, cursing Carys and everyone else who had gossiped about her miscarriage.

Her initial horror about her private life being laid open had led to embarrassment, and then anger. She'd kept her foot pressed to the accelerator along the motorway, weaving in between traffic and cursing slower drivers that hogged the overtaking lane.

She exhaled as she steered the car into one of the few remaining parking spaces and dropped her hands from the wheel.

It wouldn't do to walk into Harriet's office in the

mood she was in. She needed to calm down, to be objective if she was to understand why Sophie had been murdered, and getting emotional wasn't going to help anyone.

She'd deal with her colleague's treachery when she returned to the incident room.

She climbed from the car and slammed the door before making her way through the door to the building and taking the stairs to the floor where Harriet was based.

By the time she reached the woman's office, her mind was refocused and she managed a smile as she greeted the crime scene investigator.

'Good to see you, Kay. Have a seat.'

Kay dropped her bag to the floor next to one of the visitor chairs opposite Harriet's desk and sank into it. 'How are things progressing?'

'Slowly.' Harriet shuffled paperwork into a folder at her elbow before sliding it out of the way and selecting another from a tray on the corner of her desk. She opened it, and then spun it round so Kay could see the contents.

'Lucas Anderson conducted the post mortem late yesterday and emailed it to Sharp and me, so I'm guessing you haven't heard Sophie Whittaker *was* pregnant when she was murdered.'

Kay didn't tell the crime scene investigator that she hadn't hung around for the morning briefing. Instead, she cleared her throat. 'So, her friend Eva was telling the truth.'

'Right. Lucas gave me some samples, which we've expedited this morning, given the circumstances. The paternity results came back inconclusive. I've asked them to run them again.'

'Is that normal?'

'It can happen. Nothing to worry about. We'll have an answer for you as soon as possible.'

'But we can't say for sure at the moment that Peter Evans is the father?'

'Not yet. Not definitely, no.'

Kay flipped open her notebook and wrote a reminder for herself before continuing. 'What about other findings at the scene – anything to tie Sophie's murder to Evans?'

Harriet flipped the documents over until she found the one she sought. 'We've been struggling, to be honest. By the time the first responders were called, several people had traipsed all over the crime scene – we've got traces from both of Sophie's parents, two of the men from the same church congregation, and her friend of course.'

Kay grimaced. Trying to establish a crime scene

and maintain it was hard at the best of times; when it involved a party and several people that would all have been panicking and drunk, the result was disastrous for the likes of Harriet and her team.

'We've taken hair samples, clothing, footprint casts, the lot,' Harriet continued. 'It's going to take us a while to work through all of it.'

Kay knew there was no sense in grumbling – Harriet's department had been affected by ongoing government budget cuts, and the woman could only demand so much from her team. If they rushed, there was more likelihood they'd miss something.

Instead, she flipped the pages until she came to Harriet's copy of the post mortem report. A sequence of photographs depicting the blow to Sophie's face had been included, and her lips thinned.

'Any more thoughts about this?'

Harriet sighed and leaned back in her chair. 'We're still working through the evidence Lucas passed to us. It appears the weapon was wooden in nature; at least, the part that impacted with Sophie's skull was. You saw he found splinters in the wound?'

'Yeah.'

'We're going through the contents of what was left in the braziers at the moment, in case our murderer tried to burn the evidence. We've got the added problem of some of the partygoers treating the fires as rubbish bins, so each brazier is being processed separately to ensure we don't miss anything. It's a mess, Kay – not to mention the problems caused by the mud at the bottom of that slope.'

Kay spun the photos back to face Harriet, who leaned forward and traced her fingers over the images.

'This was driven by hate, wasn't it?' she said.

Kay leaned down and picked up her bag. 'I think so, yes.'

'That was one strike to the face. Poor kid didn't stand a chance.' Harriet raised her gaze to meet Kay's. 'I'm short-staffed, Kay, but I'll do everything I can to help you bring her killer to justice.'

'Thanks, Harriet. I know you will.'

CHAPTER TWENTY-THREE

'What's the angle we're going with here?'

Kay glanced up from her notebook as Barnes slowed the car to a standstill on the driveway outside the Hamiltons' extensive property and turned to face her.

They hadn't spoken during the drive over from Maidstone. Kay had returned from Harriet's office mid-morning and studiously ignored the atmosphere in the incident room around her while checking her emails and phone messages.

Carys had passed her desk a couple of times, but hadn't raised her head and had scuttled past, her face red.

Eventually, Kay was satisfied she'd caught up with her workload enough to keep any impending emergencies at bay and had asked Barnes to accompany her to the Hamiltons'. She'd stalked from the room, ignoring the hurt expression on Carys's face.

'The paternity results have come back inconclusive,' she said now. 'So, we don't know for sure yet that Peter Evans was the father of Sophie's baby.'

'Well, he obviously thinks he is – that's why he tried to kill himself, right?'

'Maybe. Or, maybe he realised he wasn't and that someone else is.'

She followed Barnes to the front door and hovered on the step while he rang the bell, the peals sounding through the house.

She rubbed at her right eye. She hadn't told Barnes or Sharp what she intended to discuss with the Hamiltons. Barnes, to his credit, hadn't asked.

At least one member of the team still trusted her.

She hoped.

Blake Hamilton answered the door, his eyes failing to mask his displeasure at seeing them again.

'Detectives. What do you want?'

'A quick word with Josh, please,' said Kay, stepping over the threshold before he had time to react.

'He's studying.'

'This won't take long.'

Blake sighed, slammed the door behind Barnes, and then led the way through to the living room. 'I'll go get him.'

The teenager appeared moments later, closely followed by Blake and his wife.

Kay waited until Courtney had stopped fussing over who should sit where, and then leaned forward. She wasn't in the mood to waste time with niceties.

'Josh, I have to ask a very personal question. Were you and Sophie having sex?'

'What the hell?' Blake leapt from his armchair. 'What sort of question is that? How dare you!'

Kay ignored him, and kept her eyes on Josh. 'Answer the question, please.'

'I— er, no. I didn't. I mean— we weren't, no.'

The teenager blushed.

Kay waited a heartbeat. 'If there's something you need to tell me, we can discuss this in private,' she said.

'No you damn well won't.'

Hamilton strode across the carpet towards her, and Barnes raised himself from the sofa, putting his bulk between Hamilton and Kay.

'Mr Hamilton, sit down please. This isn't helping.'

'Get out of my way.'

'Sit down, Mr Hamilton.' Barnes's voice was low, but Kay could hear the unspoken threat. 'If you continue to act unreasonably, then we'll have no choice but to question Josh at the station. Without you. Is that what you want?'

Out the corner of her eye, Kay could see Hamilton clench his fists, and held her breath, waiting for the explosion.

It didn't happen.

He swore under his breath and spun away from Barnes, muttering as he stalked away.

She waited until he reached the window, then turned her attention back to Josh. 'Is there anything you'd like to tell me?'

The teenager blinked, and then dropped his gaze to his hands. 'No. No, there isn't,' he said. 'I never had sex with Sophie.'

'What's going on?' asked Courtney. 'What's this all about?'

Kay stood, straightened out an imaginary crease in her jacket, and lowered her gaze to where Josh sat, his eyes wide.

'Sophie Whittaker was pregnant when she was murdered,' she said.

Josh paled.

Courtney gasped and clamped a hand over her mouth.

'Like I said, Josh, if there's something you need to tell me in private, you can call me any time.'

Kay held out one of her business cards, and wasn't surprised when Blake snatched it from her before Josh had a chance to take it.

She glared at him, and then stood. 'Come on, Barnes. I think we're done here.'

'Damn right, you are.'

Blake stormed across the room and held open the door through to the hallway, and made no attempt to hide his impatience as they made their way to the front door.

'Get out of my house,' he snarled. 'I'll be speaking to your superiors about this.'

Kay bit her lip as the door slammed shut in their wake.

'Did you see Josh's face when you told him Sophie was pregnant?' said Barnes, before steering the car away from the house.

'Yeah. He definitely didn't have a clue about that,

did he? I think he's lying about not having sex with her, too.'

'Interesting. I wonder why Blake Hamilton didn't want us to talk to him in private?'

'Something else going on there, you think?'

'Maybe. I want to go back and speak to Courtney Hamilton when Josh and Blake aren't around. I got the impression she was bored out of her mind last time Carys and I spoke with her. She might be a bit more open to having a conversation.'

'I don't think we'll be talking to the Hamiltons any time soon, if Blake carries out his threat and reports us.'

'Why?'

When Barnes didn't answer, Kay bit her lip, and then groaned. 'Do you mean to say Blake Hamilton is also friends with the Right Honourable Richard Fremchurch?'

'Yes.' Barnes slowed as the car approached a T-junction. 'I looked him up online before we came out here, to see if he'd been in the news recently. Looks like he's quite a big donor to Fremchurch's charitable trust.'

'Larch is going to kick our arses.'

CHAPTER TWENTY-FOUR

'Shut the door, Hunter.'

Kay pushed the door into its frame, closed her eyes for a split second, and took a deep breath.

Sharp was present, at least.

She had a feeling she was going to need someone to fight her corner with her.

She turned back to the detective chief inspector, who leaned back in his chair, straightened his tie, and then clasped his hands together on the desk.

He didn't offer her or Sharp a seat.

At least he'd waited until after the afternoon debrief.

At least no-one else would hear what was going to be said.

'What part of "low-key" didn't you understand, Hunter?'

'Sir?'

'When we opened this investigation, I specifically ordered you to keep your enquiries respectful. There's a lot at stake here, Hunter.'

'Yes, sir. I understand. We have a dead sixteen-year-old girl, a suspect in custody who's attempted suicide, and several other leads we now have to follow up.'

Larch's fist hit the desk so hard, his computer screen wobbled. 'That's not what I meant, Hunter, so don't take the piss.'

'Sir.'

He stabbed a forefinger at her. 'You may have redeemed yourself in your colleagues' eyes, Detective, but you've still got a long way to go before you convince me you take your career seriously. If you honestly thought you stood a chance in hell of becoming Detective Inspector, you'd understand that.'

Kay swallowed, but refused to lower her gaze. Her throat constricted, her eyes stinging, but she wouldn't let him see her reaction. She couldn't let him know how his words frustrated her. She clenched her fist so her nails dug into her palms.

Sharp shifted his weight from one foot to the other beside her, his arms behind his back, but he remained silent.

She was suddenly reminded of the fact he came from a military background; his whole stance reflected a soldier standing at ease, but within Larch's office it carried almost an air of defiance.

She took strength from it, knowing that he too had to tread carefully. If he attempted to rebuff Larch's accusations, it could earmark him for problems, too. And she would never forgive herself if that happened.

Larch leaned forward and opened a file in front of him, swept his reading glasses from the desk surface, and perched them on the bridge of his nose.

He picked up a page and ran his eyes over it before tossing it to one side. 'Blake Hamilton has lodged an official complaint about your line of questioning in relation to his son and Sophie Whittaker,' he said. He peered over his glasses. 'Care to elaborate?'

'It's the twenty-first century. Sir.'

'These people have standards, Hunter! You have to learn to be more diplomatic!'

'Sir, my sole focus is finding out who killed Sophie Whittaker. If that's Peter Evans, so be it. But I can't rest until I've exhausted every angle of this investigation. It would be unprofessional of me.'

'Stay away from the Hamiltons, Hunter. That's an order.' He turned to Sharp. 'In future, you handle all interactions with that family, is that understood?'

'Sir.'

'In the meantime, get on to the CPS about charging Peter Evans with the murder of Sophie Whittaker.'

'Sir, with all due respect – and given the other leads we're continuing to follow up – that could be hasty.'

'Do it, Sharp.' Larch slapped the folder shut. 'Dismissed.'

Kay spun and wrenched the office door open, furious. She strode along the corridor back to the incident room muttering under her breath, cursing Larch for his narrowmindedness.

'Kay? Kay!'

She stopped, and turned.

'Don't let him get to you, Hunter.' Sharp moved closer. 'Hang in there.'

She blinked, hugged her jacket to her sides, and raised her chin until she was looking at the ceiling tiles. She blinked again, and tried to fight down the urge to completely lose control of her emotions, before she took a shaking breath.

'I'm just trying to do my job,' she said through gritted teeth.

'I know. We all know.'

'So why—'

'I don't know. I'm doing what I can. You have to trust me.'

'Thanks, guv.'

He nodded, and walked a few paces past her before he stopped and turned.

'You're a good detective, Kay. Don't ever forget that.'

CHAPTER TWENTY-FIVE

Matthew Whittaker tracked the mouse across the screen and began to type the numbers into the squares in the spreadsheet, his hand shaking.

It was worse than he thought.

Especially now, after having to pay for the caterers, marquee hire and everything else for a ceremony that had proved to be pointless.

And, soon, a funeral.

He eyed the spirit bottles in the mahogany cabinet, and then refocused on the screen.

He didn't dare start drinking yet. He didn't know if he'd be able to stop.

His vision blurred as tears stung at his eyelids, and he clenched his fist.

I'd have been a grandfather.

He shoved the pile of receipts to one side and rested his elbows on the desk, his head in his hands. He couldn't comprehend how everything had gone so wrong.

He'd agreed with Diane that the private church group would be a good thing for them to do as a family. After all, it ensured that they could worship with their peers, not the usual rabble that filled the pews on a Sunday morning out of duty rather than a need to prove their devotion. Those other people seemed to treat the whole business of worship as an excuse to catch up with one another and gossip, not celebrate their belief.

In addition, it meant that Sophie could mingle with others her age that offered her the support and friendship her position in society demanded. Both he and Diane agreed it balanced out the fact she had to attend school with the likes of Eva Shepparton. Neither of them wanted to admit that private school fees were beyond their means.

Not even to each other.

No, the private group was much better, and Diane had been pleased when the Hamiltons had suggested it to them after a particularly rowdy Sunday morning service. It meant she and Matthew were seen as important members of their community, which of course they were.

Diane's family had lived in the area for hundreds of years – this house had been in their possession since the eighteenth century, and prior to that her family name had resurfaced time and time again in historical records for the county.

A few weeks after first meeting Diane, he'd been introduced to her parents at a Chamber of Commerce function, the Earl peeling off from the rest of the crowd to take Matthew to one side and interrogate him about his intentions for his daughter. Matthew had explained that he owned a software business that was sky-rocketing in value, and the old man had warmed to him instantly.

The wedding had taken place twelve months later.

Twelve months after that, the dot-com bubble burst.

He'd managed to find work – eventually. He might have lost his business, but his computer skills were still in demand in the aftermath of the stock market crash. He had little choice – Sophie had been born two months prior to him finally admitting his business was no more, and Diane was beginning to worry about the state of the house.

The Earl and his wife had died a week after seeing

their first grandchild – the Earl from a severe stroke, and his wife from what their doctor could only describe as "a broken heart". Matthew hadn't thought it possible, but when the will had been read out – in this very room – it transpired that the Earl's gambling debts ensured that Diane received a pittance of an inheritance, and a family home that could, at best, be described as dilapidated.

The surveyor who attended the property in Diane's absence from the house one morning when she had been at a hospital check-up for her and Sophie, had turned to Matthew and shaken his head.

'This is the problem with these old properties,' he'd said. 'Once you let them fall into disrepair, you have to spend a fortune to restore them.'

Somehow, Matthew had managed to find a role a couple of miles out of London, an easy commute that meant he could scrimp and save the money they needed over the years to fix the major issues – a new roof; rising damp in the back bedrooms; a refitted kitchen – but it wasn't enough, even when he'd set out on his own with a new consultancy business.

He'd been delighted when Sophie had struck up a friendship with Josh Hamilton at their church group several months ago.

The Hamiltons were influential within certain

circles of the community, and Blake Hamilton carried a formidable reputation as a businessman.

Matthew couldn't remember when the business of Sophie and Josh's engagement was first mentioned, but he did recall the relief that his daughter's future would be secure.

But now—

He still felt the shock that had coursed through his body upon hearing the news that Peter Evans had been arrested on suspicion of Sophie's murder.

He'd had to threaten the boy to get him to leave Sophie alone, to stop turning up at the house, to stop phoning her.

When he'd questioned his daughter, she'd admitted that she'd met Peter through school friends – he was the same age as Josh, but from an entirely different background.

'Working class,' Diane had said, her nose wrinkling.

And Sophie – pregnant?

He raised his head as the door to the office opened, and Diane appeared, a tray in her hands.

'I asked Grace to make tea,' she said. 'I thought you might like some.'

She placed the tray on the desk in front of him and began to pour the brown steaming liquid into two ornate cups, then added milk and held out one of the cups to him.

She frowned when he slopped tea over the side and into the saucer, his hand unsteady. Her gaze found his, her eyes questioning.

He gestured to the screen.

'We're going to have to let George go,' he said.

Diane's face fell. 'But he's been here since Mother and Father were alive! How am I going to manage the garden on my own?'

'I'm sorry. I'll organise someone to come around once a month to take care of the big jobs for you, but we've got to start saving money where we can.' He held up his hand to stop her interrupting. 'It's either that, or—'

Diane sank into the velvet upholstery of the two-seater sofa in the middle of the room, her face pale.

'We're going to lose the house, aren't we? After all this, we're going to lose the house.'

CHAPTER TWENTY-SIX

Duncan Saddleworth tipped the dregs of his lukewarm tea into the kitchen sink the following morning before leaning against the draining board and peering outside.

Beyond the kitchen window, a narrow patio gave way to a neat lawn bordered by flowerbeds, a small wooden shed against the back fence.

Tall shrubs and trees lent privacy to the back garden and, not for the first time, he wondered if a neighbour who could see his face peering out would think him as sick as he felt.

Four chubby house sparrows hopped and fluttered around the cheap patio furniture he'd bought from the local garden centre two years ago, their chirping and bickering filtering through the glass as they fought over the seeds he'd put out an hour ago.

When he'd arrived in the parish two years ago, he thought the house was perfect. Rather than the grand old vicarages favoured by the Church of England, his superiors believed in a more frugal housing arrangement – one that better reflected the homes of parishioners.

He'd spent several weekends in between his church duties dashing between the hardware store and the garden nursery, gradually coaxing life back into the end-of-terrace house. His love of interior decorating paid off – the house was now bright and welcoming, and he liked nothing more than to come home of an evening and curl up with a book in the front living room, his long legs dangling off the end of the sofa as he sipped red wine and listened to his collection of vinyl records.

He'd adored the location – it was quiet and peaceful, and he got on well with the neighbours. In between invitations for evening meals or afternoon tea, he'd also found himself the go-to person for the occasional cat-sitting requirement and secretly enjoyed the responsibility.

Only four months ago, he and his neighbours had

met late one Saturday afternoon at the Smiths' four doors up to discuss whether they should club together and obtain some chickens so they'd all have fresh eggs.

He wiped angrily at his eyes.

He'd been happy here, once.

He blinked, and his focus changed from the garden to his reflection.

He gasped, and leaned a little closer.

He'd been struggling to sleep for weeks, and had managed to avoid a mirror except when shaving, keeping his eyes trained on the track of the razor and not the haunted look he knew would stare back at him.

Now, even in the pockmarked reflection, he could see how *old* he looked.

Was this the face that had greeted the police detective three days ago?

Would she simply think his appearance was caused by grief?

Or would she suspect something else?

He leaned back, and wondered whether he would have to leave.

The church wouldn't suspect anything, he felt sure – in fact, he struggled to recall the last time he'd heard from anyone at the diocese's headquarters.

With the teenager out of the way, could he relax? Pretend nothing had happened?

He exhaled and ignored a skip in his heart rate.

It would be cruel of him to revel in another's death, and it certainly went against everything he believed in. Yet there was a perverse sense of hope. Deep down. Buried and clawing its way to the surface bit by bit.

A clatter from the hallway shook him from his thoughts, and a shiver clutched at his spine as the letterbox fell back into place.

He checked his watch. The post was usually delivered mid-morning, not at seven o'clock.

He dragged himself away from the window and hurried through to the hallway.

He froze as the front door came into view.

A single white envelope lay on the mat.

He launched himself at the door, flipped back the brass lock, and wrenched it open before running out onto the path in his bare feet.

The sound of a car accelerating away down the lane reached his ears and he barrelled through the garden gate and onto the grass verge.

He was too late.

The lane was deserted, with only a faint whiff of exhaust fumes hanging in the air.

Duncan sloped back to the house, picked up the envelope from the mat, and pushed the door shut.

He moved to the stairs and sat on the second step, his legs shaking. Running a trembling hand over his mouth, he exhaled and tried to control his racing heart rate.

He turned the envelope in his hands and ran his thumb under the seal, tearing the paper apart.

A single sheet had been tucked inside, six by four inches of white lined paper that had been torn from a notebook and trimmed to fit, the tiny perforations from a wire spine still attached to the left-hand side.

'Please, no,' he murmured.

He swallowed, and then pulled the page from its flimsy housing and read the words that had been cut from a computer print-out and then glued to the notepaper.

Five words.

'No!'

He leapt to his feet, the page fluttering to the carpet as he paced the hallway and ran his hand through his hair.

Sweat dripped from his armpits, pooling into the soft cotton of his shirt, and he groaned as his gut clenched.

In the split second before he dashed upstairs to the toilet, his eyes caught the words spread across the page once more.

I know what you did.

CHAPTER TWENTY-SEVEN

'How old do you think she is?' Barnes manhandled another fistful of peanuts into his mouth and stared through the windscreen.

'Hard to tell with all the plastic.'

There was a loud splutter from the seat beside her, and Kay grinned as Barnes coughed and fought to keep the food in his mouth before he beat his chest with his hand.

'Not fair,' he gasped, his eyes watering.

'You asked for it.'

They settled into a companionable silence once more, the engine emitting a steady tick as it cooled.

'You realise Larch will have us demoted in a heartbeat if we get this wrong?' Barnes said, voicing the thought that had been going around in Kay's mind for the past twenty minutes.

'Yeah,' she murmured. 'Want out?'

'No.'

'You can, you know.'

'Yeah, I know.'

'I wouldn't take it personally.'

'Yes, you would.'

'I wouldn't. I've been thinking about what you'd look like back in a uniform for a while.'

'That's what all the girls say.'

Kay snorted.

They'd left the incident room separately an hour ago after Kay had sent Barnes a text message to meet her in the car park.

He'd risen from his desk, ignored her as he walked past hers, and five minutes later she'd joined him, dangling the keys to her own small car from her forefinger.

Barnes had raised an eyebrow. 'Like that, is it?'

She'd nodded, and he'd remained silent until they were on the move, pushing their way through the afternoon school traffic.

'Are we going where I think we're going?'

'Yeah.'

She'd pulled up into a lay-by overlooking the fence line to the Hamiltons' property away from the main road forty minutes later, and killed the engine before pushing Barnes's knees to one side and extracting a pair of binoculars from the glove compartment.

'Covert ops!' Barnes had said, feigning a look of excitement on his face.

'Grow up.' She'd rolled her eyes, then stepped from the car and walked towards the fence. Keeping low, she'd trained the binoculars on the front of the house.

'His car's still there. We wait.'

Now, she sat forward in her seat as a flash of silver appeared in front of them.

'Down!'

She knew the chances of Hamilton turning to look up the narrow lane as he passed by were remote, but she wasn't prepared to take the risk.

The rush of tyres on asphalt passed by, and she peered out the windscreen.

'Give it a minute.'

'I will.'

The next sixty seconds passed too slowly for comfort, and the moment the second hand on her watch passed the zenith, she started the engine and steered the vehicle out of the lay-by.

She slammed the brakes on as a second car passed the junction at the end of the lane, travelling in the same direction as Blake Hamilton's.

'Wasn't that Diane Whittaker?'

'Yeah,' said Kay.

'Follow her, or speak with Courtney Hamilton?'

Kay bit her lip. After a moment, she shoved the car into gear and turned right. 'Stick with the plan. Speak to Courtney.'

Within ninety seconds, she was braking to a halt outside the Hamiltons' front door.

Courtney opened it the moment Kay rang the bell. 'I saw a car coming up the driveway,' she said, tucking her hair behind her ear. 'I wondered who it was.'

'Can we come in?'

Courtney's eyes moved from Kay to Barnes, then back. She bit her lip. 'He'll be back in a couple of hours. He said he had to drop something off to the church and have a chat to Duncan.'

'That's okay. I wanted to speak to you alone. We'll be gone before he gets back.'

'You'd better be.'

She stood to one side and let them pass, and Kay noticed how she peered through the gap in the door as she closed it, as if checking that her husband's car hadn't returned while they were talking.

'Come through to the kitchen.'

Kay followed, Barnes at her heels, and moved towards the central worktop.

A magazine lay open on the surface, an empty mug next to it alongside a mobile phone and a laptop computer.

Courtney leaned over and closed the laptop, a fleeting look of apology crossing her features. 'Shopping. I thought I'd redecorate Josh's room.'

'Courtney, I won't waste your time or ours. After all, you said yourself that Blake would be back soon. What isn't Josh telling us about him and Sophie Whittaker?'

The other woman's mouth dropped open. 'I have no idea what you're talking about.'

'I don't believe you. Both you and Josh were holding back something when we spoke yesterday. Blake doesn't know, does he?'

Courtney sat down on the stool, and rested her elbows on the worktop, her face in her hands. 'He'd kill him if he found out.' She jerked upright. 'I mean – of course, he won't. I mean, he didn't.'

Kay held her breath and waited.

'Josh came to me about three months ago. He – he asked me to buy him some condoms.'

'He couldn't buy them himself?'

Courtney shook her head. 'You don't understand. Blake watches him constantly. If Blake can't do it himself, he bribes others. He thinks money sorts out everything.'

'What happened?'

'I bought the condoms.'

'So, he was sleeping with Sophie?'

'Yeah. I guess.'

'And Blake doesn't suspect anything?'

'No. And he mustn't.'

'What was Diane Whittaker doing here?'

'She wanted to know if they could hold Sophie's wake here after the memorial service. I don't think she could face having it at home, not after...'

'Did Josh know Peter Evans?'

'No – we already told you that.'

'Yes, but you also withheld the information that Josh was sleeping with Sophie. So, did Josh know Peter Evans?'

'I don't think so, no. I kind of feel sorry for Peter, to be honest.'

'In what way?'

'Oh, you know. I think he did love Sophie. Must've been one hell of a shock to find out she was pregnant, though.' Courtney folded her arms across her chest and sighed. 'Mind you, if she was inclined to sleep around like that, I'm glad Josh didn't marry her, that's for sure.'

Barnes cleared his throat. 'Sorry, Mrs Hamilton. Would you mind if I used the bathroom?'

'Sure. Through there, down the hallway. Second door on the right.'

'Thanks.'

Kay waited until she had Courtney's attention once more. 'I understand from our conversation when we first spoke with you that Josh would have been able to use Sophie's aristocratic connections to further his father's business interests. How would that have worked?'

'Oh, I have no idea. Blake's always doing deals for different people. It's not like he manufactures anything. He networks, puts people in touch with each other that have a common interest or goal, and takes a commission.'

'He seems to be doing very well from it.'

'He's got good contacts.' Courtney stretched, and checked her watch.

'It's okay. We'll be leaving in a minute—'

'Boss?'

Kay spun round. 'What's wrong?'

Barnes's eyes flickered to Courtney, and then back to her, his excitement palpable.

'I think you better call Harriet. And DI Sharp.'

CHAPTER TWENTY-EIGHT

Diane reversed her car into the last remaining space outside the restaurant, turned off the engine and sat for a moment to gather her thoughts.

She'd been surprised when Blake Hamilton had agreed so easily to meet with her at short notice. Relief had coursed through her body, too. The trauma of the past few days had left her exhausted, and it was only now that she was away from the house that she realised she'd spent most of the time holding her breath, as if waiting for something.

She climbed out the car and straightened the short skirt she'd managed to squeeze into. She tried not to think about the state of the petrol station toilet she'd used to get changed into her new outfit, and adjusted her blouse. She couldn't let Matthew know she'd been spending money behind his back, at least not the amounts that had passed through her fingers of late.

Slamming the door shut, she took a deep breath and stepped towards the front portico of the restaurant.

Part of a chain of hotels that had purchased then renovated old buildings around the country to an exquisite standard, the restaurant was popular at weekends and in the evenings. As she entered the reception area and turned right into a lounge area, she was pleased to see that at lunchtime, it was quiet. In fact, aside from two old men – from their conversation, likely two partners in one of the solicitors' firms that were dotted along the High Street – the bar was empty.

'Gin and tonic,' she said to the bartender, and then moved across to a table and two chairs next to the window, sunlight dappling the green velvet upholstery.

She checked her watch as the bartender brought her drink across, nodded her thanks, and took a sip.

She reminded herself not to gulp; she'd need her wits about her for this meeting.

For a fleeting moment, she wondered whether she

should have left it another week before approaching him – after all, some might think her callous given that her daughter had been found murdered only hours ago. She pushed the thought away. Right now, her own survival had to take priority, especially as it was evident Matthew's finances were worse than she first thought.

She heard Blake before she saw him, his sonorous tone carrying from the lounge area, his mobile phone pressed to his ear.

He entered the bar in a hurry, nodded at her before he turned away to finish his call at the same time as ordering a large glass of white wine, and then tucked his phone into his jacket pocket.

'Diane,' he said as he approached the table.

She stretched up towards him, offering her cheek.

His lips breezed past her jawline, and then he straightened, held up his glass in a toast, and took a sip. 'Have you ordered yet?'

'No. Here.'

He took one of the menus from her and placed his wineglass on the table while he ran his eyes over the food on offer.

'Thanks for seeing me in private.'

'No problem. Are you ready to order?'

'Yes. I'll have the steak, please. Rare.' She

crossed her legs, and let the short skirt ride up her thigh.

Blake ignored her, glanced over his shoulder and held the menu up to the bartender. 'One Dover sole, and the fillet steak, rare.'

'Sir.'

He hovered next to her, then pulled out one of the soft chairs and lowered his bulk into it. 'I didn't get to ask you at the house, because Courtney was talking so much. How are you holding up?'

Diane took another sip of her drink, and realised her hands were shaking. She concentrated on putting the glass on the table before answering.

'It's a nightmare. Matthew's gone over the figures again, but it's impossible – especially now that German retailer pulled out after the Brexit fiasco. The business simply hasn't recovered.'

'I meant about Sophie's murder.'

'Oh.' She blushed. 'Oh, yes. It hasn't really sunk in that she's gone, to be honest.'

'Jesus, Diane.' He shook his head, and glanced over his shoulder as a waiter in black trousers and crisp white shirt approached them.

'If you'd both like to follow me through to the dining room and I'll show you to your table?'

Diane drained her drink, picked up her bag and

allowed Blake to lead her back through the dining area.

They turned right at the reception desk and then through a large archway and into a spacious room that overlooked landscaped gardens through French doors.

The waiter fussed over them, placing napkins in their laps, poured water into their glasses, and then left with a promise that their food would be with them soon.

'I'm truly sorry about what happened to Sophie,' said Blake. He rested his arms on the table. 'Have the police charged him yet?'

'I don't believe so, no. They came to see you?'

He nodded. 'Yesterday. Accused Josh of sleeping with her.'

Diane gasped. 'What did he say?'

'"No", of course.' He frowned. 'What the hell did you think he'd say?'

'Sorry. I just thought—'

She broke off as the waiter reappeared, two steaming plates of food in his hands.

By the time he wandered off once more, she'd recovered from Blake's outburst.

He pushed his knife to one side, used the fork to carve a chunk of the fish apart and shovelled it into his mouth.

'Did you know she was pregnant?'

She swallowed. 'No.'

'Christ, what a mess.'

'I had no idea, Blake. As far as we were concerned, she was betrothed to Josh.'

'Yeah, well, in the circumstances, you can forget all about our business arrangement.'

'You can't do that!'

His eyes blazed. 'Keep your voice down,' he hissed.

She glanced over her shoulder.

There was only one other group in the restaurant, a couple and an elderly woman who seemed oblivious to anyone else around them as they clinked glasses and laughed with the waiter as he moved around their table, rearranging plates and exchanging light-hearted conversation.

She turned back to the American. 'Please, Blake – you have to help us!'

He pointed his fork at her. 'You should've had a contingency plan, Diane. Every business needs one. That's where you English aristocracy have always gone wrong. No back-up plan. You're all dying out—'

Diane glared at him, her eyes stinging.

'Sorry. That came out wrong.'

She watched as he drained the glass and waved the waiter over.

'Get me another one of these. D'you want another gin and tonic?'

She shook her head.

'Fine – just the wine, then.'

Diane picked at her food as the waiter disappeared, her appetite gone.

'I am not going to be responsible for selling the house,' she said. 'It's been part of my family for nearly three hundred years.'

'Well, what do you think's going to happen when you die? There's nobody left, Diane – sell the damn house, and get a life for chrissakes. Give that poor husband of yours a break.'

'Surely you can take a look at the numbers again. Suggest to Matthew you buy in as a shareholder?'

'Buy into what? The company's worthless.' He shrugged, put down his fork and picked up his water glass. He finished chewing. 'No. I was only going to use the house as a tax loss, anyway.'

'We had a deal.'

'No daughter-in-law, no deal, Diane.' He took a sip of water before replacing the glass on the table. 'I'm sure you understand.'

She dropped her cutlery, the silverware hitting the plate in front of her with a clatter, and then plucked her bag from the floor next to her and rose.

'Enjoy your fish, Blake. Be careful you don't choke on a bone.'

CHAPTER TWENTY-NINE

'What is it? What's going on?'

Kay pulled the living room door shut after assuring Courtney Hamilton they wouldn't keep her waiting, and noticed that Barnes seemed agitated.

'I used the downstairs toilet, okay?'

'Yes?'

For a fleeting moment, Kay wondered if the older detective was about to embarrass them both, but he shook his head.

'As I closed the door, I noticed another one open in front of me. Some sort of utility room – y'know, for when you've been out in the garden or whatever. They've got a washing machine and tumble dryer in there, and there's a bag of golf clubs standing next to another door leading outside.' He lowered his voice. 'One of the golf clubs is covered in blood.'

Kay clenched her jaw, checked the living room door was shut before turning back to him. 'Show me.'

He led the way across the hallway, towards the back of the house. 'The downstairs toilet is there,' he pointed. 'And this is the utility room.'

'Did you go in?'

'Yes. I haven't touched anything. I don't have any gloves on me – do you?'

'No, they're in the car.'

He stayed on the threshold while Kay moved into the room, casting her eyes around the room.

A worktop took up the length of one wall to her right, and she realised the wall abutted the kitchen, with the sink and taps mirroring the plumbing arrangement from the other room. In front of her, the back door resembled a traditional stable door – split in half, with locks and bolts for each section.

To her right, a row of coat hooks had been fixed to the wall, all of them overstuffed with waxed jackets, hats, scarves and a row of boots in varying styles and sizes laid out on the floor below them.

The tiled floor looked well-worn, and not as polished as the rest of the ground floor. Evidently, it was a room that saw a lot of foot traffic, and was used in accordance with its intended design.

The bag of golf clubs to which Barnes had referred stood next to the back door, in a gap formed between the doorframe and the worktop.

Kay moved closer, and crossed her arms to avoid the temptation of touching anything.

As she drew near to the clubs, she noticed that one, a "wood" she recalled from memory, was stained dark red, and whereas most modern clubs were made of metal, this one looked old – and the end was misshapen.

She swallowed.

'Barnes? Call this in. Lock down this room, and the rest of the house. Get Sharp on the phone and tell him we've got ourselves a crime scene.' She pulled out her phone and headed back towards the living room.

'In the meantime, I'll find out where the hell Blake and Josh Hamilton have disappeared to.'

———

'Good work, Barnes,' said Sharp as they entered the incident room. 'Is Harriet still at the scene?'

'Yes,' said Kay. 'She's got a team of four working

with her – she says they've done a preliminary search of the house, concentrating on the utility room where Barnes found the golf club, and they'll start a more in-depth search once they've finished downstairs.'

'Good. Are Josh and his father both booked in?'

'We had to wait for them to get back home as Courtney didn't know where they were – Blake said he'd been to a business lunch while he'd left Josh at the library to study.'

'We've split them up,' Barnes added. 'Josh is in interview room one. Blake is in room three.'

'Right, we'll start with Blake then,' said Sharp. 'How do they look?'

'Josh looks sick, very pale. The senior Hamilton looks arrogant.' Kay shrugged. 'As usual.'

'What were you doing at the Hamiltons' house after Larch's specific instructions not to go there?'

'I wanted the opportunity to speak to Courtney Hamilton without her husband being present. He's the only one that has an issue with me. To date, Courtney has spoken to us freely and candidly. I wanted to gauge her thoughts about Josh's relationship with Sophie,' said Kay. 'She told us that he had been sleeping with her – she'd even bought him condoms and kept it secret from her husband. We were getting on well, and then Barnes found the golf club.'

'Speaking of which, where is it now?'

'We dropped it off to one of Harriet's technical assistants on the way here – Harriet was too busy to leave the scene. I've asked him to expedite the testing of the blood to see if it's a match to Sophie's.'

Regardless of the find, the team would only have twenty-four hours to question Blake and Josh Hamilton. Without conclusive evidence that linked the golf club to one of them, and in turn finding an answer as to why it was covered in blood, they couldn't press charges – or expect an extension to the interviewing process given Larch had already instructed them to request the Crown Prosecution Service charge Peter Evans with the girl's murder.

They would have to wait for Harriet and her team to report their findings.

'Harriet said there's hair and skin mixed in with the blood on the end of it,' said Kay. 'Certainly consistent with it being used as a weapon.'

'You've updated the evidence log?'

Kay held his stare. 'Yes, I did. Barnes witnessed everything.'

'I did,' Barnes confirmed. 'It's all above board.'

'Good.' Sharp swallowed, and then gave Kay an apologetic shrug. 'I had to ask.'

Gavin Piper hurried over from his desk. 'I've just

had DCI Larch on the phone. He'd like to see you both. He said "immediately".'

'Right, well that's not a surprise. Barnes, get on to Harriet's office and have them contact you as soon as he has something for us. Kay – you're with me.'

Barnes walked away, humming a well-known villain's theme tune from a sci-fi film.

'Very funny,' said Kay, and glared at his retreating figure.

'Lead the way, Hunter.'

Sharp waited until they were out of the incident room and hurrying along the corridor towards their superior's office. 'Don't worry. I've got your back.'

'I'm glad someone has,' she muttered.

———

Larch glared at Kay as Sharp gave him a summarised version of the afternoon's events.

'I'm not sure I'm clear, Hunter. What were you doing at the Hamiltons after I specifically requested that you stay away from them?'

'I was passing by the house, sir, and it occurred to me that we hadn't asked Courtney Hamilton about Peter Evans. It was my intention to only ask about that, but she invited us in. It seemed a good opportunity to seek more insight into the Hamiltons' relationship with the Whittakers while Mr Hamilton was absent. During the questioning, DC Barnes requested use of the bathroom; Mrs Hamilton advised him where to find it, and moments later he reported to me that he had found a bloodied golf club. The state of the golf club led us both to believe that the best course of action was to declare a crime scene.'

Larch's eyes blazed, but to Kay's relief he turned his attention to Sharp. 'Sharp? Please tell me this is under control and the media haven't caught wind of it.'

'It's been kept very low-key, guv.' Sharp's voice maintained his usual steady tone, despite the tension in the room. 'No-one from the media has contacted us.'

'Where are Blake and Josh Hamilton now?'

'In interview rooms one and three respectively.' Sharp glanced at Kay. 'Hunter and I were about to start the formal interviews.'

'Not a chance in hell,' said Larch. 'Given the political ramifications this case could have, I'll conduct the interviews with you.'

Kay's heart sank.

Larch tugged at his tie, loosened it, and then threw it on his desk before heaving himself out of his chair.

'All right. We'll start with the father – who's the solicitor on this one?'

'They've got their own family lawyer on hand,' said Kay. 'Giles Fordingham.'

The DCI stopped midway to the door, and spun on his heel. 'Did you say Fordingham?'

'Yes, sir.'

'Is there a problem, guv?'

Larch glared at Kay, and then at Sharp. 'Only that he's the Right Honourable Richard Fremchurch's brother-in-law, Detectives. Did neither of you do your homework?'

CHAPTER THIRTY

Kay wedged herself into a semi-comfortable position by propping her feet up on the desk that held the screens and slouching in her chair.

She plucked at a piece of fluff on her trouser leg and fought down the urge to yawn. Right now, she just wanted to curl up and observe the interview, but she knew from experience that a constant stream of interruptions could be expected, given that Harriet's investigation team were still processing the Hamiltons' house for additional evidence.

Blake Hamilton had offered no explanation about the bloodied golf club when his car had been pulled over by uniform within half a mile of the house.

Instead, the uniformed officers reported that he'd seemed meek, and certainly surprised that he and his son were now considered prime suspects in the murder of Sophie Whittaker.

She'd wanted to conduct the interviews herself, especially after a second uniformed patrol had brought Josh Hamilton into the custody suite, his face taut.

Instead, after Larch had insisted on taking her place, Sharp had called to Kay over his shoulder as the two senior detectives left the incident room.

'Hunter, get yourself to the observation suite. I'd appreciate your thoughts on what the Hamiltons have to say.'

She'd grabbed her notebook and phone and had hurried after them, silently thanking Sharp as he'd turned and winked at her before pushing open the door to the room that held Blake Hamilton and his solicitor.

Despite Hamilton's attempts to insist on being present while his son was interviewed, Larch had stated quite firmly that as Josh was over eighteen years of age, the police were under no obligation to let him, especially as each were being interviewed as potential suspects.

Kay snorted as she watched Blake squirm at being put in his place by the DCI, but her heart sank as she realised it would give Larch yet another reason to make her life uncomfortable, given the man's political ambitions.

'Mr Hamilton, can you start by explaining what a bloodied golf club is doing in your possession?'

'I have no idea.'

Sharp's sigh was audible. 'Can you confirm the golf club belongs to you?'

'It does.'

'And why is there blood on it?'

'I have no idea. Look, I didn't kill Sophie Whittaker. Neither did Josh. Why would we?'

The interview continued for another forty minutes, Larch letting Sharp take the lead with the questioning, interjecting occasionally, and appearing uncomfortable during the whole process.

In the end, they'd brought the interview to a close and informed Blake Hamilton he'd be transferred to the cells.

'What?' He pushed his chair back, towering over the two detectives. 'Are you out of your minds?'

His solicitor placed a warning hand on his forearm and pushed him back into his seat before glaring at Sharp.

'Is that necessary?'

'We're conducting a murder investigation,' said Sharp. 'I'd say that it was necessary, wouldn't you?'

Kay exhaled, lowered her feet from the desk and cricked her neck while the CCTV cameras showed Larch and Sharp as they left the interview room and entered the one next door containing Josh Hamilton.

The teenager had been slumped in his chair, ignoring the solicitor next to him but lifted his head when Sharp and Larch entered the room and leaned forward.

'I didn't kill Sophie,' he blurted out.

Sharp held up a hand, waited until Larch had sat down, and then formally began the interview once they were recording.

'Tell me about the golf club we found at your house,' he said. 'Did you use it to kill Sophie?'

'No! You've got to believe me – I never hurt her. I loved her.'

'Then why is there blood on it?'

Josh ran a hand through his hair. 'Look, two days ago I found a rabbit outside the back door. It had that myxomatosis disease. It was starving, blind. I wanted to put it out of its misery, so I hit it over the head with the golf club.' His gaze dropped to his hands. 'I didn't want to kill it, but I couldn't stand it being in so much pain.'

'And you expect us to believe that?'

'It's the truth.'

'What did you do with the body of the rabbit?'

'I put it in the bin.'

'Convenient, Josh. The bins get emptied out your way on a Monday, don't they? So we can't corroborate your story.'

'I'm not lying.'

'We'll see.' Sharp terminated the interview, nodded at Larch, and the two men left the room.

Kay switched off the computer monitors and scrambled from her seat, wrenching open the door as the two senior officers passed.

'Get Harriet to process that golf club as soon as possible,' said Sharp. 'I want to know by the morning if we have Sophie Whittaker's killer in custody, or a teenager that has a knack for killing sick rabbits.'

CHAPTER THIRTY-ONE

Matthew looked up from his computer as Diane pushed the door to the study open, a couple of glasses of red wine in her hands.

'I thought you might like a drink,' she said, her stockinged feet silent on the parquet floor.

'Where've you been all day?'

'I went over to see Blake and Courtney.'

'But you didn't stay there, did you?'

She shook her head, and then frowned. 'How did you—'

'Courtney phoned here, looking for you. Said she couldn't reach you on your mobile.'

'Oh. I was shopping in Tunbridge Wells. The battery had gone dead.' She put the wineglass on the desk before wandering over to a leather armchair, curled her feet up under her, and took a sip of her own drink.

Matthew leaned back in his chair and reached out for his wine. 'I didn't hear you come back.' He rubbed his hand over his eyes before gesturing to the paperwork strewn across the desk. 'I must've been lost in my own world with all this.'

'How long have we got?'

'Two months, maximum. I'm so sorry, Diane. I've tried everything. I don't know what else to do.'

She turned her wineglass in her hands, and then raised her eyes to his. 'I thought I had it all worked out. How to save the house.'

He snorted, and held up a page. 'Have you seen these figures?' He tossed the document to one side. 'Unless you're able to perform miracles.'

She sighed. 'Almost.'

'Really? What exactly did you have "all worked out"?'

'Josh and Sophie,' she said, and shrugged. 'The purity pledge and their engagement.'

'Diane? What are you going on about? What's that got to do with the house?'

She bit her lip, her eyes darting to one side, avoiding his gaze. 'I made an arrangement with Blake

Hamilton that if I convinced Sophie to marry Josh, he'd pay us a dowry. More than enough to cover all that.' She waved her hand at the accounts. 'Josh would marry into English aristocracy – which suited Blake and his business interests – and I wouldn't lose the house.'

Matthew's wineglass hit the surface of the desk with a thud, his hand gripping the stem, his knuckles white. 'You did what?'

'It was for the best, Matthew.'

'Don't take on that whining tone with me. It won't work.' He pushed back his chair and began to pace the floor. 'What exactly did Blake Hamilton offer?'

'To clear all your business debts with the first half of the payment, which we'd have got one month after the engagement party, and then a stipend every year once Sophie and Josh were married.' She wiped at her eyes. 'There was even a bonus payment once they produced a grandchild.'

'Produced? Have you listened to yourself, Diane? You're talking about our daughter like she was a bloody commodity to be bought and sold, for chrissakes!'

She brought a shaking hand up to her throat. 'I didn't mean—'

'Yes, you did.' He stopped pacing, and tried to

fight down the fury that was seething through his body. Anger clenched in his chest, his heart beat painful. 'Who else knew about this arrangement?'

'I – I don't know. Only Blake and I were—'

'Are you sure?'

Her eyes narrowed. 'Come to think of it, no.' She tapped her fingernails against her wineglass, before she jerked her chin up to him. 'Peter Evans must've found out – that's why he killed her!'

Matthew clenched his jaw, and fought down the urge to grab her shoulders and shake her.

'You have no idea, do you?'

Confusion spread across her features. 'About what?'

He shook his head. 'The police are investigating the Hamiltons. What's really going on, Diane?'

Her mouth open and closed, her eyes wide, and then she found her voice. 'Investigating the Hamiltons?'

'That's why Courtney was trying to phone you earlier. To tell you Blake and Josh have been taken in for questioning by the police this afternoon.'

'What for?'

He raised his gaze until he met hers, and tried to recall why he'd found her so attractive all those years ago. He knew she was shrewd and calculating, qualities which once had endeared her to him as the business had grown with her input, but that had been tainted by her obsession over retaining a title that had little of the power she pretended it had, and a house that was falling down around her ears.

'Courtney said the police found the suspected murder weapon in Blake's possession.'

Diane emitted a gasp, and paled. 'What?'

He turned to the computer, reached out to switch it off, and then gathered together the documentation that covered his desk. He pulled over the wastepaper bin, before he started to tear up the pages.

'I think you should call your solicitor tomorrow, Diane.'

'What for?'

'I'll be seeking a divorce.'

'Matthew – no, please!'

'It's quite evident to me that you've been using me and my business enterprises to simply prop up this dilapidated building,' he said, his voice breaking. 'And when you'd sucked me dry, you turned to your daughter.'

'It wasn't like that.'

'You tried to sell your daughter to keep your damn house.'

'Please, Matthew – I didn't mean it like that. I'll work something out, I promise.'

'Forget it. I knew you were cold-hearted, Diane, but that was low – even for you.'

'I was trying to save my home!'

'Get out of my sight.'

CHAPTER THIRTY-TWO

Kay sat at the worktop spinning the stem of her wineglass in a pool of condensation, her chin in her hand.

The back door was open, a warm summer breeze on the air carrying the scent of freshly cut grass from their neighbour's property. Adam appeared, his hands full of small tomatoes that he had plucked from the plants they had been growing at the bottom of the garden.

He took one look at her face, dumped the tomatoes on the draining board and wiped his hands down his shorts, before grabbing a cold beer from the fridge and sitting down opposite her.

'You've got a face like thunder. What happened at work?'

'I didn't get a chance to tell you. They know about my miscarriage. I don't know how although I've got my suspicions, but it seems my secret is out.'

Adam rocked back on his bar stool, his face stricken. 'Who else knew?'

Kay took a sip of her wine before responding. 'The only person who knew was Carys. When we were burgled, she saw the baby clothes. She promised me she wouldn't tell anyone.'

'And you think it was her?'

'Who else could it be?'

'I thought you said Carys wasn't the sort of person to gossip.'

'I thought she wasn't.'

'Then maybe it wasn't her. Have you tried talking to her about it?'

'Not really. It was awful. Everyone in the incident room was staring at me when I got into work and then Sharp called me into his office. He asked if I should be there, as if it had only just happened. He seemed quite surprised that it happened months ago. I think he was annoyed with me that I didn't tell him at the time, but I pointed out to him he was still dealing with the aftermath of the Professional Standards investigation into my conduct – it wasn't exactly a good time to bring it up.'

Adam grunted in response and took a swig from his beer before setting the bottle on the worktop. 'If Carys doesn't normally have a reputation for gossip, then I'd be surprised if she started this.'

Kay didn't say anything, but she was inclined to agree with him. The young detective constable was too ambitious to let rumours and office gossip ruin her reputation, and had become firm friends with Kay and Adam over the past few months. They had had a couple of barbecues in the garden since the beginning of summer, and the rest of the team had often been in attendance. Carys had never brought up the issue of Kay's miscarriage then, so it didn't make sense for her to start now.

'If it's not Carys, then I can't think who it could have been.'

'Maybe have a word with Carys – patch things up with her, and see if she's got any ideas as to how it started.'

'Yeah.'

He leaned across and wrapped his fingers around her forearm. 'Are you going to be okay? I don't know about you, but if gossip starts at our place, it usually stops after couple of days when people find something else to talk about.'

'I think so. It's more the shock than anything else.'

Her mobile phone began to vibrate on the worktop and Adam withdrew his hand after giving her arm a quick squeeze.

'Best answer that. I'll make the salad.'

She smiled and reached out for her phone, a familiar name displayed on the screen.

'Hey. What's up?'

'I found some interesting information about Blake Hamilton,' said Barnes. 'According to the initial information we've received from his bank, he made a sizeable cash withdrawal in the past four weeks.'

'Why would Blake Hamilton be dealing in cash? His business has no need for it. It's all mergers and acquisitions, and I got the impression he earned his money from gaining shares in companies.'

'Exactly, and I'm going to speak to Sharp in the morning to draw his attention to it. It'd be worth our while asking Hamilton about it, because it's so out of character. All the other transactions on the statements seem pretty straightforward.'

'I'd have thought someone in his line of business wouldn't be able to withdraw large sums of money without having to declare what it was for. How much are we talking?'

'Six thousand pounds.'

Kay emitted a low whistle. 'Is there any way of telling where it went?'

'Not from the statements.'

'All right. Well, as you say, have a word with Sharp first thing so he can question Hamilton about it. Regardless of whether it has a bearing on Sophie's murder or not, we should still investigate it.'

'Will do. See you in the morning.'

Kay ended the call and slid the phone across the worktop

'Everything okay?'

Kay sighed, and drained her glass. 'The plot thickens,' she said. 'And nothing in this case is straightforward.'

CHAPTER THIRTY-THREE

When Kay got to work the next morning, traffic had backed up along College Road and, realising she was going to be late for the briefing, she gave up any hope of reaching the police station in time and instead parked close to the Bishop's Palace before walking the rest of the way.

Exhaust fumes hung in the air as impatient drivers honked car horns and tried to change lanes in an attempt to manoeuvre their way around the ring road.

As she crossed the road, the dark brickwork of the police station came into view and her jaw dropped as she saw the cause of the delays.

Two television vans were parked opposite the police station, the crews' cameras aimed at the front steps of the building while at the same time capturing the excited reports from the journalists standing in front of them. Beside them, a huddle of reporters stood with smart phones poised ready to take photographs and record the comings and goings of uniformed personnel.

Confused, she tried to recall whether she'd seen a notice or an email to say the Chief Superintendent was due to make a media statement, as it was rare to see such a large gathering of reporters at the police station. Normally, they could be found hanging around police headquarters looking for a story, but not here.

She kept her head down and hurried round the side of the building, swiping her card against the security panel and hurrying through the security gate as it opened rather than trying to push past the reporters on the front steps.

She swiped her card again to enter the building from the side door and made her way up to a subdued incident room. Faces turned as she entered, and her heart ratcheted up the beat as she sensed the change in tone.

She held her breath and slipped her handbag under her desk wondering what had happened, but afraid to ask.

She didn't have to wait long.

DCI Larch appeared from Sharp's office. 'Get in here, Hunter. Immediately.'

She locked eyes with Barnes as she passed his desk, but he shook his head.

'I'll meet you outside afterwards,' he murmured. 'We need to talk.'

As she entered Sharp's office, Larch slammed the door.

Sharp leaned against the wall, his hands in his pockets, his face grey.

'What's going on?'

Larch pointed at one of the visitor chairs next to the desk. 'Sit.'

Larch stalked past her, snatched up a newspaper from Sharp's desk and thrust it under her nose.

Her heart sank as she read the headline.

Eminent local businessman linked to high society murder.

'Care to explain yourself, Hunter?'

'Nothing to explain, sir. This didn't come from me.'

He sneered at her. 'Read the fourth paragraph.'

She swallowed, her eyes skimming over the words.

Detective Sergeant Kay Hunter confirmed that police were investigating a large cash withdrawal made by Blake Hamilton in the weeks leading up to Sophie Whittaker's death.

'I've never spoken to the press,' she said, and tried to stop her voice shaking. 'We have policies and procedures that set out very clearly how the media will be kept informed during the murder investigation. And you, sir, have made it very clear how important it is that this case remain out of the press given the parties involved.'

'Then how do you explain this, Hunter?'

'I can't. There's obviously a leak here, but it isn't me. Someone's trying to set me up.'

Larch flung the newspaper back onto the desk and spun on his heel to face her once more.

'I have a meeting with the Chief Superintendent in five minutes. I would be very surprised if you don't find yourself facing another Professional Standards investigation over this.'

He moved to the door and wrenched it open, slamming it shut in his wake, the frosted glass panel in the middle of it shaking with the force.

Sharp eased himself away from the wall at last, and crossed the room to the desk before sinking into the chair next to Kay.

'I'm not the source of the leak.'

'I believe you, but someone was and they're

determined to make it look like you were. Have you got any idea who it could be?'

Kay fought down the panic, her thoughts turning to Barnes's cryptic words before she'd entered the office.

Was he the source of the leak?

Or was somebody trying to tear the team apart, forcing her to question who she could trust?

And why?

'No, I haven't,' she said eventually. 'I can't believe anybody out in that incident room would do this to us, to me.'

'I'll make some phone calls. I'll speak to the reporter who authored this article, and see if I can find out who she spoke to. If it wasn't you, and somebody has contacted the newspaper impersonating a police officer, I want it investigated.'

CHAPTER THIRTY-FOUR

Kay's mobile phone vibrated as she closed the door to Sharp's office.

She glanced down and saw it was Barnes's number, and then opened the text message he'd sent her.

We're in the cafe up the road. Get here as soon as you can. Coffee ordered.

Kay grabbed her bag and hurried from the incident room before one of the admin team could waylay her. She left the building via the back door and skirted around the side of it before crossing the road in a break in the traffic, and made her way up Gabriel's Hill.

It took her five minutes to reach the café the team frequented, and as she pushed the door open she spotted Barnes sitting with Gavin and Carys at a table near the back. Gavin turned as she closed the door behind her and pointed at a mug of coffee in front of the empty seat next to him.

'Thanks,' said Kay as she put her bag on the floor and sat down. 'What's going on?'

'We were going to ask you the same thing.' Barnes jerked his chin towards the door. 'We all know you're not responsible for the vultures being out there this morning, and I certainly wasn't.'

Kay managed a small smile. She turned to Carys. 'I need to apologise to you. I realise it wasn't you who spread the rumours about my miscarriage. I should have known better.'

Relief flashed across Carys's features before she frowned. 'Who on earth *is* spreading these rumours about you, then? Who broke the story about the Hamiltons to the media?'

'I don't know. But whoever it is, he or she seems determined to make life difficult for me, don't they?' She took a sip of her coffee while the team digested her words.

'I'll bet it's Larch,' said Gavin. 'Ever since I joined this team, he's had it in for you. Of course, I heard about the Professional Standards investigation involving you, but you've been cleared of any wrongdoing. I've never seen you acting anything but professional.' He shook his head. 'I really don't understand what his problem is.'

'I guess the question is, what do we do about it?' said Carys.

'We stick together,' said Barnes. 'For some reason, someone doesn't want this team to be working together. Anyone have any ideas why?'

Kay took another sip of her coffee so she didn't have to answer.

She couldn't help recall her conversation with Adam a few nights ago, when she told him that she intended to pursue her own enquiries into Demiri once more. Was it possible she had somehow triggered the events that had affected the team since?

And if so, how did her enemies know? How were they getting that information to the incident room and to the media?

'I have no idea,' she said eventually.

———

Kay glanced up from her desk as the door to the incident room was pushed open, and Harriet Baker strode in.

'What are you doing here? I thought you were going to email your report over.'

In reply, Harriet held aloft a briefcase in her right hand, and then pointed towards Sharp's office. 'I wanted to deliver this personally. You might want to listen in.'

Kay pushed back her chair and followed her across the room.

Sharp was already opening the door to his office when they approached. 'What's going on?'

'I've got the results of the testing of the blood sample on the golf club,' said Harriet. 'It's not a match to Sophie's.'

Sharp ushered them both into his office, and closed the door. He gestured to the two seats in front of his desk, and waited while Harriet placed her briefcase on the desk, opened it, and retrieved a folder.

She withdrew three sets of documents from it, and passed one each to Sharp and Kay. 'You can read the whole report at your leisure. Turn to page three, and I'll walk you through it.' She waited while they caught up. 'We took samples from the head of the golf club, and ran a comparison against a blood sample taken from Sophie's body. The results came back, and confirmed there's no DNA match.'

'So, whose blood is it?' said Kay.

'It's mammalian in nature. I'd suggest a small animal – maybe a rat or a rabbit.'

'Damn,' said Sharp. 'Josh was telling the truth. We're back to square one.'

'Not quite,' said Harriet. She picked up a different report and stabbed her finger on a paragraph towards the end. 'Those braziers the first responders had the sense to smother? We found the remnants of a rolling pin shoved into the side of one of them. It must've been placed there moments before Eva Shepparton stumbled across Sophie's body because it was only partially destroyed.'

'The murder weapon?'

'Yes. There wasn't much to work with, but we've got a trace of Sophie's blood on the end that wasn't in the flames – caused by splatter from the impact to her face.'

Kay wrinkled her nose as she flicked through the report. 'Fingerprints?'

'No, sorry. We did find some burnt material in the same brazier – it's tested positive as wool.'

'Clothing? So, the murderer did get blood on themselves but tried to discard the evidence.'

'That's what I'm thinking.'

Sharp pinched the bridge of his nose and closed

his eyes. 'One thing at a time. Hunter – arrange the paperwork to release Blake and Josh Hamilton from custody. I'll go and break the news to Larch that we're letting them go given the new evidence regarding the golf club. We'll continue our enquiries regarding what Harriet and her team found in the brazier.'

'There's one more thing, Devon,' said Harriet. 'We found a partial footprint under one of the rhododendron bushes. It's too small to put Peter Evans at the scene, and it's not Eva Shepparton's.'

'Could be one of the guests or the parents that rushed down there before uniform arrived.'

'Larch isn't going to like that,' said Kay. 'Peter was his prime suspect.'

'But we still have Sophie's blood and her clothes at his flat,' said Sharp, 'so let's not write him off yet.'

'There's something else,' said Harriet. 'We've run some more tests and simulations using the blood traces found on the rolling pin, and we're certain that whoever your suspect is, he's left-handed. It's the way the weapon was used to strike Sophie.'

Sharp frowned. 'Both Blake and Josh Hamilton are right-handed. I noticed when they signed in with the custody sergeant yesterday.'

'Could the killer have masked his identity by using a different hand?' said Kay.

Harriet shook her head. 'I did wonder that, but I'm not convinced. Lucas confirms in his post mortem report that it only took one blow to the face to kill Sophie. The killer would've had to act fast. I don't think he would have had time to consider changing hands to mask his identity.'

Sharp scratched his chin. 'I've had Barnes and Carys going through the witness statements from the party this morning. No-one can recall seeing someone walking around with a weapon of any kind.'

'What if the killer hid the rolling pin in the rhododendron bushes beforehand? And then lured Sophie down there somehow, in order to kill her?' said Kay.

'That would make sense.' Harriet pushed her hair out of her eyes, and blinked. 'We didn't find any clothing fibres on the bushes around the area where Sophie was found. It had been raining the night before, so that might've made the branches more pliable.'

'I didn't notice any scratches on either Blake or Josh Hamilton's arms, either,' said Sharp. He wrote in his notebook, and then tossed the pen to one side. 'I'd best go and break the news to Larch.'

CHAPTER THIRTY-FIVE

Kay chewed the edge of a fingernail and stared at the computer monitor.

In the interview room, Sharp had placed a notepad and pen on the table in front of him.

Opposite, Blake Hamilton sat with his solicitor, a look of pure contempt on his features.

He'd argued, Sharp had reported the day before, at the news he'd be kept in the cells overnight and had tried to use the threat of his solicitor's personal connections to sway the police to put him and his son in a hotel room overnight instead.

The suggestion had been met with scorn, and now the American appeared to be sulking after a night on a cell bunk.

Larch didn't wait for Sharp to settle into his seat

before breaking the news to Hamilton that he was being released.

Blake blinked. 'Pardon?'

'You're free to go, pending further enquiries,' said Sharp. 'We will, however, request that you be accompanied back to your house with police officers and hand over both yours and Josh's passports to them.'

'What? Do you mean to tell me that I spent a night in the cells for nothing?' He glared at Larch. 'Well?'

'We received new information this morning that has altered the course of our enquiries,' said the DCI. He turned his attention to Giles Fordingham. 'I'm sure you understand?'

'Hey, don't look at him. He's not the one that spent the night here,' said Blake. 'And why the hell do you need our—' Realisation crossed his face. 'Oh, for crying out loud. You really think we're going to make a run for it? I run a successful business, and as I've told you repeatedly, I'm not guilty. Nor is my son.' He spun in his chair to face Fordingham. 'This is ridiculous.'

Fordingham gave a slight shake of his head, and then cleared his throat. 'Detective Chief Inspector, are you sure this is necessary? My client is a pillar of his local church, has never been in trouble with the law before, and as he says, runs a successful business that requires him to travel to the Continent on a regular basis.'

Kay held her breath.

'I'm sorry, Mr Fordingham,' said Larch. 'Mr Hamilton, we will require your passports until such time as this investigation is concluded.'

'Well, how long is that going to be?'

'I'm afraid I can't answer that.'

Blake flung his arms up and snorted. 'Bloody great. How the hell am I supposed to run my business if I can't meet with international clients?'

'There are such things as video conference call facilities in most offices,' said Sharp. 'Or Skype.'

In the observation suite, Kay snorted coffee up her nose and, spluttering, reached across the desk to a box of tissues, her eyes watering.

'Are we done here?'

'We are.'

Blake slid his chair away from the table and waited until Sharp had opened the door for him. 'You haven't heard the end of this, Detective.'

Larch shook hands with Giles Fordingham, each of them dropping their hands to their sides as quickly as possible, and then they followed Blake from the room.

Kay leaned forward and switched off the monitor.

Outside in the corridor, Blake Hamilton's voice echoed off the walls as he complained loudly to his solicitor about the way he and his son had been treated.

Eventually, the voices faded, and she peered out the door.

Sharp leaned against the opposite wall, his hands in his pockets.

'We're not going to hear the end of this, are we?' she said.

'I wouldn't worry about it. I don't think Blake Hamilton is going to risk his business reputation to phone the Right Honourable Richard Fremchurch and tell him he's spent the night in police custody. And his solicitor is bound by client confidentiality, so although he's the brother-in-law of Larch's esteemed contacts, he won't say anything.'

Kay relaxed her shoulders and stepped out into the corridor, pulled the door closed behind her and followed him as he began to walk back to the incident room. 'What's next?'

'Harriet and Lucas have confirmed all their tests are concluded; they're waiting for the results now.'

He paused at the door. 'I'll call Lucas and ask him to release Sophie's body to her family.'

'Do you want me to arrange to meet them there?'

'Yes, probably best you go once Debbie's sorted everything out at this end.'

'Okay.'

'You might want to go home and get changed first, though.'

'Pardon?'

He raised an eyebrow at her, and tapped his finger on a spot on his chest. 'You have coffee on your blouse.'

'You told Hamilton to use Skype.'

CHAPTER THIRTY-SIX

Kay leaned against the wall of the waiting room and swallowed, fighting down the urge to flee.

She'd arrived only five minutes ago, driving a circuitous route that guaranteed she wouldn't be late, and wouldn't be too early.

Debbie West had taken a call from a local Maidstone funeral director that morning after the briefing. The man had informed her that the Whittakers had been informed the coroner had completed his reports into Sophie's death, and her parents wished to arrange to have their only child released from the morgue for burial.

Now, Kay wished she'd delegated the task to someone like Gavin.

She knew only too well how hard it would be for the Whittakers to say goodbye to their daughter.

After parking the car as far away from the hospital buildings as she reasonably could, Kay took her time making her way towards the entrance doors. She had opted to take the stairs rather than the lift to the second floor where the mortuary was situated.

Anything to delay the moment she had to push through the doors and enter the small office where the coroner's officers worked.

She introduced herself, declined the offer of a seat and cast her eyes around the room as the two women answered phone calls and processed the myriad of paperwork involved in running the administrative side of Her Majesty's coroner for the county of Kent.

As well as having a caseload from Kent police, the coroner was also required to provide his services to the hospital whenever the cause of death was unknown, or when a death happened suddenly with no apparent reason.

From experience, Kay knew that the mortuary room itself was cramped and limited for space, especially in the winter months. She hoped for the sake of the coroner and his assistants that they were currently experiencing quieter times. There had been occasions when she had attended post mortems at the site when even the temporary refrigerators had been crammed full.

She glanced up at voices from the corridor outside.

The glass door to her left swung open and Matthew Whittaker stood to one side to let his wife pass first.

The woman's face was bleached of colour, and as Kay straightened her jacket and crossed the reception area towards her, she noticed Matthew's features were equally pale.

'Thanks for coming, Detective,' he said as he shook her hand. 'We appreciate it.'

They turned as the door opened once more, and a man in a dark grey suit appeared, his bald pate shining under the spotlights set into the ceiling.

'Lady Griffith, Mr Whittaker,' he said, shaking hands with them both, 'I'm sorry if I've kept you waiting.'

'Not at all, Henry – we've just arrived,' said Diane. She gestured to Kay. 'Detective Hunter, this is Henry Alderley, of Alderley and Sons.'

Kay shook hands with the funeral director and resisted letting out a sigh of relief. Until he appeared, it hadn't even crossed her mind that it could have been the same undertaker she and

Adam had turned to for guidance nearly a year ago.

However, the older man in front of her was a complete stranger, and she let the voices wash over her as he explained to the Whittakers the steps that would be required to release Sophie's body.

She jerked to attention as the funeral director turned to her.

'All the paperwork is here,' he said. 'We have the authority for removal of the deceased, and the coroner's burial order has been signed.' He took a document from the outstretched hand of one of the administrative staff and held it up.

Kay nodded. She knew Debbie had tried to persuade the Whittakers to let the funeral director meet Kay at the hospital, assuring them that there was no need for them to attend.

However, Diane Whittaker had been adamant that she would be there to collect her daughter, something which Kay could understand. She turned to the woman, who held on to her husband's arm, her eyes wide.

'I believe there's some paperwork that needs to be signed, and then Mr Alderley will take care of Sophie from there,' she said.

Matthew Whittaker stepped forward. 'What do I need to sign?' he said, his voice shaking.

'It's all been taken care of,' said Alderley, his hands clasped in front of him. 'I've signed all the documentation to release Sophie's body into my care. There's nothing you need to do.'

'I want to see her.'

Kay's heart sank. Diane Whittaker's words were what she feared to hear.

'Lady Griffith, I realise that you would like to see Sophie one last time,' said Alderley before Kay could speak. 'However, if I may respectfully suggest, it would probably be best if you didn't.' His face softened. 'Please understand, it will help you to grieve if you remember how she always was, not like this.'

Diane whimpered.

'He's right,' said Matthew. 'I want to remember my beautiful girl as she looked that afternoon. I couldn't bear it. I don't want to be reminded of what that monster did to her.'

Diane murmured her agreement, and Kay breathed a sigh of relief. Her eyes met Alderley's, and he gave her a slight nod.

'Will you make the necessary arrangements?' she asked.

'Of course,' he said. 'If you'd like to escort the Whittakers out, I'll take care of everything from here.'

As Kay led Sophie's parents along the corridor away from the mortuary, Diane dabbed at her eyes with a handkerchief, Matthew's hand clasped around hers.

They left the building in silence, not speaking until they reached the car park.

'Detective, your superior phoned us this morning.'

'Inspector Sharp?'

'No,' said Matthew. 'Chief Inspector Larch. He said he wanted us to invite some of his officers to Sophie's funeral.'

'Oh?'

'Yes, he said he felt it might be prudent, in case anyone there wanted to speak to you, in case anyone had remembered anything.'

Diane sighed loudly, and flapped her hand. 'Of course, we told him that wasn't necessary. It's going to be bad enough as it is with the local media being there, but when he heard that he was most insistent – said at least you would be able to keep them from approaching us.'

'Local media?'

'Somehow, they found out about the funeral arrangements,' said Matthew. His face flushed with anger. 'I don't know how, but they did.'

'Well, I suppose when one's family has been in the area for centuries, it is a bit of a shock for the locals to take in,' said Diane. 'I would imagine as they can't all go to Sophie's funeral, at least they'll be able to see it on the television.'

Kay bit her lip. She didn't trust herself to speak, despite the words that had immediately formed in her head. No doubt Diane Whittaker had tipped off the media – anything to draw attention to herself.

'We had best be off,' said Matthew.

Kay watched as the couple walked across the car park away from her, and then waited as the car pulled away from the hospital grounds before turning towards her own vehicle.

The last thing she wanted to do was attend another funeral, but it seemed Larch had his own plans for her and the team.

Plans he hadn't seen fit to share with her that morning.

She sighed, and turned the key in the ignition.

It was going to be a long week.

CHAPTER THIRTY-SEVEN

When Kay returned to the incident room, a sullen atmosphere hung in the air, and the door to Sharp's office was closed.

'What's going on?' she said to Barnes as she typed in her password for her computer.

'Jude Martin from the CPS has been over,' he said. 'They've recommended we drop all charges against Peter Evans. Larch went ballistic.'

'I'll bet.'

Kay could well imagine the DCI's wrath at the turn the investigation had taken. She had little sympathy for his motives though – all Larch would be concerned about was his performance targets and his political standing within the community. He tended to show none of the dedication the investigating team had, despite the frustration at the twists and turns it had taken.

'Next steps?' she asked.

'Sharp's got us going through the financials for Matthew Whittaker's business again, to see if that sheds any light.' Barnes sighed. 'Although why a bloke would kill his daughter, just because his business is going down the shitter is anyone's guess. We're going around in circles, Kay.'

'Hmm. You've got that right. You know, considering she was taking a purity pledge, Sophie didn't seem the most chaste of teenagers, did she?'

'You think she was stringing someone else along?'

'Apart from Peter Evans and Josh Hamilton?' She shrugged. 'Who knows? Gavin and Carys spent two days at the school interviewing her classmates – they didn't even know about Peter so I'm guessing if there was anyone else, she wasn't telling anyone.'

'What made Eva Shepparton so different, then?' said Barnes. 'Why tell her?'

'Desperation? Eva told Carys that Sophie had only found out she was pregnant the day before the party – maybe Sophie blurted it out, when she didn't mean to.'

'And her killer overheard her and acted on impulse?'

Kay rubbed at her eye. 'We're going to have to go through all the statements from the guests at the party again, aren't we?'

'I'll get the coffee.'

'Thanks.' Kay glanced as Gavin approached her desk. 'What's up?'

The probationary detective constable held up a printout from the HOLMES2 database. 'I was going through the list of items the crime scene investigators compiled from this search of the Whitaker's house. There was a small key found in the bedside table in Sophie's bedroom.'

Kay frowned and took the pages from him. 'Any idea what it's for?'

'No. I think everybody's been so busy with other aspects of this case, it hasn't been properly looked into yet.'

'Right, send out descriptions and photographs to all the local banks, check with the school to see if it's a match for her locker there, and phone the local post offices, too. Might be for a post office box or something like that.'

'I hope so. We could really use a breakthrough.'

———

'Duncan? What are you doing here?'

Courtney Hamilton held on to the front door, blinking in the bright sunlight.

'Is Blake here?'

He tried to peer around the door, but she remained standing in the way. 'What do you want?'

'I need to speak to Blake. It's urgent.'

'He's only just got home,' she said. 'Can't it wait?'

'No.'

'Who is it?'

She glanced over her shoulder, and then the door opened fully. 'Duncan.'

Blake stood at the bottom of the staircase, his hair dishevelled, and his shirt untucked from his trousers.

'We're not due to meet again until next week, are we?' The American frowned and ran his hand through his hair, tried to flatten a tuft that stuck out from behind his ear, and then gave up. 'I've got this, honey – go and make yourself busy in the kitchen.'

'Are you sure? I—'

'Go.'

Duncan waited until she'd disappeared from view,

and then turned back to Blake. 'Where the hell have you been?'

'The police took me and Josh in for questioning.'

'Questioning? Why?'

'They found something. Here. They thought it was the murder weapon.'

'Did – did you—'

'Of course not.' Blake studied a fingernail. 'It simply took a while to convince them of that.' His eyes met Duncan's as he dropped his hand. 'What're you doing here, anyway?'

'I need to speak to you.'

'About?'

In reply, Duncan withdrew the white envelope from his shirt pocket and held it up to the other man.

Blake ignored it, refusing to take it from him, and so Duncan opened the envelope and withdrew the single page it held, waving it in front of the other man's eyes.

'It didn't stop. You killed her, and it hasn't stopped!'

'I didn't kill her,' Blake hissed. He checked over his shoulder, and then pushed Duncan into the room he used as an office at the front of the house.

Sunlight bathed the space, the vertical window blinds creating a striped silhouette across the opposite wall, which was home to a large collection of certificates and awards, interspersed with photographs of Blake smiling at the camera while shaking hands with various dignitaries, politicians, and the occasional B-list celebrity.

Duncan ignored all of it. 'Who else knew about the letters, Blake?'

The American shook his head. 'No-one. Only you and I, and whoever this is.'

'You said it was Sophie Whittaker.'

'No, I said I thought it *might* be Sophie Whittaker.' His eyebrows shot up. 'Jesus Christ, you didn't kill her, did you?'

Duncan shot him a pained expression. 'Blake, please – don't take His name in vain. Of course it wasn't me! How could you even ask that?'

'Well, you sure as hell have motive.'

Duncan swallowed. Hamilton didn't know the half of it, and he certainly wasn't going to provide enlightenment. 'That's not true.'

'Oh, come on, Duncan – you'd think the same if you were in my shoes.'

'You know, if you changed your mind and wanted your money back, you could've asked. You didn't have to do this.'

'It's not me.' Blake shrugged. 'I'd written that

money off, anyway. I know it didn't turn out the way we planned, but there's nothing we can do about it now. Water under the bridge.'

'I wish it had never happened.'

'It's a bit late for that.'

'It could damage my career if this gets out!'

'It can't be about us. Otherwise, why haven't I been targeted this time?'

Duncan pinched the bridge of his nose and tried to concentrate, fighting down the sense of panic that was threatening to overcome common sense. 'Maybe whoever it is doesn't know about you.'

Blake moved to the desk at the far end of the room, and trailed his fingers over the polished surface. 'Then, how did they find out about you?'

Duncan sank into one of the armchairs that faced the desk and ran his eyes over the single slice of tree trunk that Blake had ordered especially from a Canadian lumber yard, the whorls and gaping eyes of the natural surface left in place and polished to a high sheen.

He tore his gaze away. 'I don't know.'

'Well, I suggest you have a long think about what it might be,' said Hamilton. 'I haven't got a clue.'

Duncan shoved the page back into the envelope and shoved it into his pocket. 'It didn't stop. She's dead, and it hasn't stopped. She must've been working with someone else, Blake!'

'Or it was never Sophie Whittaker that was blackmailing us in the first place.'

Duncan leaned forward, his head in his hands.

'What have I done?'

CHAPTER THIRTY-EIGHT

Kay bit the skin around her thumbnail and tried to concentrate on what was being said on the television news.

Instead, her thoughts turned to recent events at work and the fact that she wasn't sure who she could trust anymore. She felt let down, especially as the small team had gelled so well over the past months.

She couldn't understand how news of her miscarriage had come to light if it wasn't Carys gossiping. She didn't want to believe that Carys was the source of the leak, but how else would anyone find out about it?

And then there was the business with the newspaper article. She knew full well that Barnes would never speak to the press – after an incident involving his daughter the previous year, he avoided the media wherever possible, often delegating phone calls to and from the local newspaper to Gavin or one of the administrative staff rather than speak to them himself.

It was almost as if someone was spying on her.

She leaned forward, picked the television remote control off the coffee table and muted the newsreader's voice.

A thought crossed her mind, a fleeting moment that she tried to grasp at, a frown on her face.

Upstairs, Adam's footsteps moved from the bathroom to their bedroom as he used the toilet and then changed into the old jeans and sweatshirt he used for outcalls to farms.

After what seemed an age, he returned downstairs, sat on one of the bottom treads to pull on his work boots and called through the open door.

'Don't wait up for me. Higgins is notorious for talking and he'll probably insist I stay for a cup of tea before I leave, so God knows what time I'll get back.'

Kay pushed herself up from the sofa as he straightened and joined him in the hallway. 'Do you think everything will be all right?'

'I expect so. This mare of his had a foal eighteen months ago, so she's used to it now. He probably wants me there as a precaution more than anything else.' He smiled. 'I don't mind. He knows his horses better than I do. I'd much rather he was paranoid and it turns out he doesn't need me.'

He moved to the cupboard under the stairs and pulled out his go-bag containing everything he might need for a visit to the stables, and checked his pockets. 'Okay, I think I've got everything.'

'I'll leave the porch light on for you. Can't have you stumbling about in the dark and waking me up.'

'Very funny. You in early tomorrow?'

'Yeah. Half seven start. Fancy a Chinese takeaway tomorrow night?'

He kissed her. 'Sounds perfect. Behave yourself.'

'Will do.'

She waited while he disappeared out the front door, shut it behind him and then made her way to the living room. She hovered next to the coffee table until she heard his four-wheel drive start and creep down the driveway to the lane before it roared off into the night.

She checked her watch.

Half past ten.

She would need to get some sleep before leaving to attend the briefing in the morning, but calculated the least she'd need would be five or six hours. Adam wouldn't be back until at least one or two in the morning.

She dropped her arm.

That left her with a space of two hours to get done what she needed to do.

She turned up the volume on the television and then, heart hammering, she set off for the kitchen and crouched beside the drawer next to the kitchen sink where Adam kept a small selection of tools for emergencies.

In the living room, the news ended and the theme music for a late night chat show began.

She rummaged through the drawer until she found a screwdriver and a small torch. She twisted the end of it until a pinprick of light shone across the worktop, then clutching both items in one hand she hurried through the hallway and up the stairs.

She stopped on the landing, and then raised her gaze to the covered hatch that led up into the attic. She wiped the back of her hand across her forehead before reaching up and pulling the hatch open.

She tugged at the end of the ladder until it began to slide downwards towards her. Checking it was secure, she climbed up halfway and then felt around the edges of the square hole until she found the plug socket Adam had fixed there. She pressed the button, and the lights they had installed the length of the attic flickered to life.

She gripped the sides of the ladder and made her way to the top of it, clambered over the lip of the hatch and stood on the bare boards that lined the attic space.

She made her way along the attic until she was standing above their bedroom.

To her right, the light fittings lay amongst the insulation – an ugly electrical setup left over from some minor renovations she and Adam had undertaken a few years ago when he'd inherited the house.

They'd been so busy in the intervening years that they'd never found time to finish boarding up the rest of the flooring space.

Kay crouched down and shone the torch a little to the left of the electrical work, and frowned.

At the time, and because they knew they had a lot of work to undertake, they had bought extra wiring from the hardware shop. In fact, they had bought so much, at least half the reel still lay untouched in the garden shed. It had been a running joke at the time that Kay's enthusiasm for red coloured wiring knew no bounds. Adam was still using the leftovers for tying back the tomato vines in the back garden.

Now, however, a length of blue wiring could be seen in the torchlight.

Kay held her breath and moved closer, careful not to lean on the insulation for fear of falling through the ceiling.

A black object sat above the light fitting, the end of the blue wire disappearing into the back of it, beneath which a green LED light flickered.

Kay sat back on her heels and swallowed.

She raised herself on shaking legs and squeezed past some old packing boxes until she reached the area above the room she used as a home office.

Once again, a blue wire had been added to the familiar red cabling.

Kay rose from the floor and hurried back to the hatch, climbed down the ladder and sank onto the carpet, her heart racing and an urge to be sick twisting her gut.

She'd worked in a support role on a number of observation postings and knew exactly what she'd discovered. It was why the thought had first crept into her mind.

Her thoughts spun as she tried to recall the conversations she and her colleagues had had in her house, the intimacy she'd shared with Adam, and the images the cameras had no doubt recorded.

Bile rose in her throat and, shaking, she staggered to the bathroom and vomited.

Flushing the toilet, she moved to the basin and turned on the tap, scooping cold water past her lips before she turned and sat on the edge of the bath, her head in her hands.

Her house had been fitted with miniature spy cameras and listening devices.

But, by whom?

And, why?

CHAPTER THIRTY-NINE

Kay jumped in her seat at a tap on the car window, and then lowered it.

'Are you coming, or what?'

'Yeah, sorry – daydreaming.'

'They'll be here in a minute.'

She raised the window, ripped the keys from the ignition and then joined Barnes beside the vehicle. Her hands shook as she shoved the keys into her bag, and she turned slightly, so he wouldn't see.

The occasion brought back too many painful memories that hadn't yet had a chance to soften over time; a short ceremony, and then a small casket that disappeared behind a curtain while only she, Adam, and the nondenominational minister looked on.

'Sarge?'

She blinked, and tried to concentrate.

'You okay?'

'I'm fine. Let's go.'

The police rarely encroached upon a family's grief to the extent of attending a funeral, but with a murderer still unpunished and a pressing need to serve justice, Larch had insisted that Sharp send his dwindling team there. Almost a week had passed since Sophie's body had been released to her mother and father, and in that time, the investigation had slowed to a crawl. Administrative staff had been reassigned to other, more pressing matters, and the remaining team had been spending their days revisiting witness statements, trawling through Sophie's history, while all the time fighting off a growing sense of desperation.

Sharp had made it clear to them behind closed doors that Larch saw the funeral as a way to assure the public that the police wouldn't give up on the case. Sharp himself had other ideas. 'Watch the congregation closely,' he'd said at the morning briefing once the detective chief inspector had left the room. 'Everyone is still a suspect. Someone at that funeral must know something.'

Kay followed Barnes across the road and through a narrow lych-gate, and tried to ignore the moss-covered gravestones that littered the long grass either side of the path.

Once, she had enjoyed exploring graveyards, seeking out the oldest dates, the most interesting histories, despite her lack of faith.

All that was in the past, and she couldn't imagine ever returning to such a place by choice.

She glanced over her shoulder at the sound of other vehicles approaching the church, and saw the elongated sleek black outline of a hearse, followed by a dark-coloured courtesy vehicle.

Matthew Whittaker climbed from the back seat a few moments after it drew to a standstill, and held open the door. Diane emerged, her face pale, eyes hidden behind sunglasses despite the overcast sky.

Neither of them noticed Kay and Barnes under the shaded canopy of trees.

'Come on.'

'No, wait.'

Kay put her hand on his arm and frowned as Matthew slammed the car door shut and Diane's voice carried on the breeze.

Kay couldn't hear what was being said, but the woman's tone was laced with acid as she stood on the pavement and berated her husband.

The undertaker and his assistants kept a respectful

distance, until Matthew held up his hands to Diane, managed to pacify her, and then nodded to them.

He led Diane across the car park towards the church door, and Kay watched with interest as Diane shrugged off her husband's arm from her shoulders and stormed through the open door ahead of him.

'Okay, let's go.'

'What was all that about?'

'No idea. Listen, I'm going to try to grab a seat at the back. See if you can find somewhere to sit halfway down.'

'You want to make a run for it afterwards?'

Her lips thinned. 'As much as I would like to, no. I want to be able to watch everybody from there, and not make it obvious by twisting around in my seat all the time.'

'Okay.'

They hurried up the path, and Kay waited a moment upon entering the cool building to allow her eyesight to adjust to the gloom, and then made her way over to the middle pew in the back row. It was empty, save for her, and the next four pews were empty as well. Most of the congregation had bunched together towards the altar end of the church, and she ran her gaze over the gathering of people.

Some girls that looked to be the same age as

Sophie took up two pews on the left hand side, and appeared to have been allowed out of school early to attend, evidenced by their school uniforms. Eva Shepparton was amongst them, and her eyes opened wide when she saw Barnes and Piper.

Barnes kept walking until he reached a half-full pew on the right-hand side, which placed him two thirds of the way back from the busier middle section and able to hear what was being said amongst the people gathered there.

She couldn't see Gavin or Carys, and presumed they were spread somewhere within the building, also watching the congregation.

She settled into her seat and peered over the heads in front of her to the front row, where Matthew and Diane sat, their heads bowed. Across from them, on the right-hand side, were the Hamiltons. Blake appeared to be lost in thought, staring up at the stained glass window behind the altar. Courtney's attention was directed at her son, and the pair appeared to be talking in hushed tones.

A door opened behind Kay, and she glanced over her shoulder as Duncan Saddleworth emerged from the vestry, and crossed to the main door to the church as the funeral director led his colleagues who carried Sophie's coffin.

The two men conferred for a moment, last minute instructions were issued, and then Duncan led the short procession down the aisle towards the altar.

Sniffing and soft sobs trailed in Sophie's wake, and Kay dug her fingernails into her palms, determined to steel herself against the emotions of the next few hours.

She knew she would be emotionally and physically drained by the time the day finished, and tuned out the dulcet tones of the pastor as he began to guide the congregation through the ceremony.

She stood when the people in the pews ahead of her raised themselves from their pew, mimed singing words to hymns she vaguely recognised from school, and checked her watch during the eulogy.

Her head snapped up as Duncan introduced Matthew Whittaker.

Sophie's father walked towards the pulpit as if he wished time could slow down, and Kay began to take deep breaths.

She fully understood the pain he was in; it was in the way his shoulders sagged, how his hands gripped his notes before he placed them on the wooden frame that surrounded him, and how he took a deep breath before leaning down to the small microphone.

Kay blinked and tried to fight down the urge to

join in with the wailing that began from the front row and travelled through the congregation as the gathered people lost their resolve at a broken-hearted father's words.

She sniffed, and then turned at the sound of the door to the church being edged open.

'Crap,' she muttered under her breath.

On the threshold, his eyes wide, stood Peter Evans.

Tears streaked down his face, and he wore a cheap suit that hung off his skinny frame, accentuating his hollow cheekbones.

Kay launched herself out of the pew and crossed the aisle.

It took him a few seconds to notice her, but she didn't give him a chance to speak. Instead, she grabbed his arm and shoved him, hard.

'Outside. Now.'

CHAPTER FORTY

'I didn't know you smoked.'

Evans grimaced. 'I gave it up. Sophie didn't like it.' He tapped the end of the cigarette, but didn't take another drag. 'Why haven't you found out who killed her?'

'We're doing our best, Peter. It's a complicated case.'

He snorted. 'Too many suspects to choose from?'

Kay narrowed her eyes at him. 'Care to elaborate?'

'Oh, come on – she fooled them all, didn't she? The Hamiltons, and her own family. None of them had a clue about me.' He raised the cigarette to his lips and inhaled deeply before blowing a smoke ring to one side. 'So, you have to ask yourself – which one of them was more pissed off about it, and who else wanted to kill her?'

Kay folded her arms across her chest. 'And I suppose you have a theory about which one of them is the murderer.'

'It doesn't matter if I have a theory, Detective. The question is – do you?' He dropped the cigarette butt to the ground and squashed it under his foot.

'I could fine you for that.'

'Yeah, but you won't. Mitigating circumstances.'

'What?'

In response, he jutted his chin towards the church behind her.

The double doors had been opened wide, and the sound of the piped music from the church organ filtered through the opening, moments before Duncan appeared, his attention taken by the funeral director who began to lead the procession back to the hearse.

Kay turned back to Peter. 'All right, go. Don't turn up at the burial though, okay?'

His bottom lip quivered.

'Peter, please. Visit her grave tomorrow, when it's quieter.'

'Okay.'

He turned and hurried away across the graveyard,

weaving between the ancient stones, and then left through the lych-gate.

Kay made sure he kept walking down the lane where she assumed he'd parked his van, and then wandered back to the church and stood at a respectful distance as the congregation filed past.

Barnes joined her.

'Where did you go?'

'Peter Evans turned up.'

'When?'

'Halfway through the last hymn. I managed to get him out the door before anyone saw him.'

Barnes snorted. 'Yeah, that wouldn't have gone down well. What did he have to say for himself?'

'He suggested there might be a number of people responsible for Sophie's death.'

'Not a great help.' Barnes nudged her arm and pointed. 'We need to make a move. Everyone else is heading off.'

They hurried back to the car, and Kay let Barnes take the keys from her.

Lost in thought, she clipped her seatbelt into place as he manoeuvred the vehicle out into the lane and began to follow the funeral procession towards the cemetery south of the town.

Peter's words echoed in her mind.

Both Blake and Josh Hamilton had been cleared of any wrongdoing – for the moment. Unless new evidence came to light, it was unlikely that charges could be brought against either of them.

Kay rubbed at her right eye as she considered the other options.

Courtney Hamilton had made it clear that she hadn't agreed with Josh marrying Sophie, but how far would she be prepared to go to stop an engagement going ahead? Was she desperate enough to kill?

As for Matthew and Diane Whittaker, the pair had seemed distraught – in fact, Kay wouldn't have been surprised if Diane had been prescribed some sort of tranquilliser. The woman certainly seemed distant when Kay had spoken to her since the night of Sophie's murder.

'We're here.'

Barnes's voice jolted her from her thoughts, and she resolved to go back over the Hamiltons and Whittakers' witness statements in the morning and start again.

Maybe Peter was right.

Maybe they had missed something.

CHAPTER FORTY-ONE

As the group dispersed back to their desks following the afternoon briefing, Carys beckoned to Kay and then called out to Sharp as he headed back to his office.

'Guv? Could I have a word?'

Sharp peered over her head, and then gestured towards his office. 'It's bedlam out here. Sit down, and tell me what's going on.'

He shut the door behind them, muting the hum of noise from the incident room.

Carys waited until they'd all sat. 'I got a call via the hotline. A man phoned and said he couldn't speak for long as he was at work, but said that he went to university at Oxford and recognised Duncan

Saddleworth on the news footage of the church service on the lunchtime news.'

'What did he have to say about him?'

'He was very cagey. Said he didn't want to speak over the phone. I've offered to drive over to his house at Tonbridge in the morning. All he told me was that he had some information about Duncan Saddleworth that might prove useful.'

Sharp sighed and ran a hand over his close-cropped hair. 'Are you sure he's not wasting your time?'

Carys shook her head. 'He sounded genuine. A bit afraid, too, to be honest.'

'All right. Take Hunter with you and see what he's got to say for himself – what's his name?'

'Felix Ashgrove. Lives in Tonbridge.'

'Okay. God knows we could use all the help we can get at the moment. Let's hope Mr Ashgrove can shed some light on what the bloody hell has been going on around here.'

'Guv.'

As Kay moved towards the door, she let Carys go out ahead of her, then turned to Sharp.

'Guv? Could I have a word in private?'

His brow creased. 'Of course.'

'Not here.' She forced a thin smile. 'Meet you outside in ten minutes?'

'What's going on, Hunter?'

'You'll find out.'

———

Kay glanced up as Sharp appeared at the back door to the police station and, seeing her leaning next to her car, wandered over to join her.

'What's this all about?'

Kay took a shuddering breath.

On the drive into work that morning, she had rehearsed the conversation over and over in her mind, choosing her words carefully and trying not to let anger cloud her thoughts. Now, faced with sharing her findings, fear writhed its way through her veins.

She was taking a gamble, and there would be no turning back.

She reached into her pocket and withdrew her mobile phone, opened the photo album, and held it up to Sharp.

He blinked before taking the phone from her and cupped his hand around the screen, sheltering it from the bright sunlight. He frowned. 'This looks like a listening device with a tiny camera attached.'

'It is.'

'Where is it?'

'In the ceiling above my living room.'

His head snapped up, his eyes locking with hers. 'What?'

'There's another one in my kitchen, one in my bedroom, and one in my office.'

'Who put them there?'

'I don't know.'

'Any idea why they're there?'

'No.'

'Does Adam know?'

She shook her head.

'You've left them there?'

'I was too scared to move them, guv. I don't know who's put them there, and I don't know what they'll do to me or, worse, to Adam if I remove them.'

He handed the phone back to her and exhaled as he leaned back against her car beside her, his gaze roaming the straggly tree line beyond their position.

She pushed her phone into her pocket. 'I need your help. I don't know what to do.'

'Any idea how long they've been there?'

'Since the burglary. I think that's what it was – a smokescreen they used to plant the microphones.'

'Are you sure?'

'There were a few things like the television that were smashed that had to be replaced. I had some jewellery that went missing, but nothing of great value. Most of it was left to me by my grandmother – it hadn't been valued at much. Whoever did this made sure they only did enough damage to make it look like a genuine burglary.' She shifted to face Sharp, although his eyes remained fixed on the horizon. 'It explains why I thought Carys was the one who told everyone about my miscarriage. When she stayed behind to clear up after the burglary, she and I spoke about it briefly – I keep the baby clothes and things in our home office. It was going to be the nursery…'

She wiped at her eyes and fell silent.

'What else?'

'I was chatting to Barnes on my phone after we'd been to the Hamiltons'. He gave me an update about some information we had about Hamilton so I asked him to go in first thing and get his notes entered onto the database before the morning briefing.'

'You don't suspect Barnes?'

She shook her head. 'Definitely not. Not his style,

for a start and if he didn't like something I did, he'd tell me to my face.'

'True. What made you suspect someone's been spying on you?'

'That business with the media finding out we were looking into Blake Hamilton's finances. Barnes and I have worked together for ages. He'd never gossip, let alone speak to Larch. If Barnes ever had a problem with me or anyone else, he'd talk to you. I couldn't work it out, especially as Barnes was blamed as much as me for what happened. Same with Carys. She's never gossiped about anything the entire time she's been with us. There had to be another reason.'

'But listening devices? That's a leap in thinking.'

She shrugged. 'I was up late watching a spy film. It crossed my mind.'

Sharp blinked and turned to her. 'Why trust me?'

'I didn't know who else to trust.'

He snorted. 'Last choice, was I?'

'Okay, and you've got an army background. I figured if anyone could corroborate what these things were, it'd be you.'

'It was a long time ago.'

'And you've never told anyone what you used to do in the army, have you?'

His lips thinned and he fell silent for a moment,

his brow furrowed. Eventually he straightened and turned to face her. 'Anything else you want to tell me?'

She swallowed. 'I think Gavin was beaten up because of me back in the spring.'

He raised an eyebrow.

Kay sighed. 'I stayed late and used his computer to check something on HOLMES2 about the Demiri investigation. The same night, Gavin is beaten up and his attackers are never caught.' She rubbed at her right eye. 'I can't help but think that wasn't coincidence. There's information missing from the database, too. All to do with the case that fell apart. Someone's been covering their tracks and making sure I don't ruin whatever it is they've got planned.'

He straightened his jacket and pushed himself away from the car. 'All right. Don't tell anyone else. Leave this with me.'

Kay watched him stroll back towards the police station and bit her lip.

Had she made the right choice?

―――――

That night, Kay stepped from the shower in the en

suite, swiped her towel from the rail next to the sink and scrubbed at her skin until it was red.

Beyond the closed door, she could hear Adam pacing the bedroom as he stripped down to his boxer shorts, threw his clothes in the laundry basket and switched on his bedside light.

As she entered the bedroom, she slipped under the duvet and switched off her light after making sure her alarm was set for the morning.

Adam rolled over and nuzzled her neck, before she felt him push up against her.

She rolled over, a smile forming, and then froze.

Her eyes locked onto the light fitting above the bed.

Were they watching?

She placed a hand on his chest. 'I'm sorry. I can't.'

His brow creased. 'Everything alright?'

'I don't feel well, that's all. There's something doing the rounds at work.'

He pulled her into his arms. 'That's no good. You should've said. I wondered why you didn't eat much tonight.'

'Sorry,' she mumbled into his chest.

She could hear the disappointment in his voice, but she wasn't lying about not feeling well. Bile threatened to rise, and she held her breath, forcing the sensation away.

Sickness gathered in the pit of her stomach and she resisted the temptation to stare up at the ceiling again.

She couldn't let them know that she'd discovered their dirty secret.

CHAPTER FORTY-TWO

'Here it is, coming up on the left. Number seventy-two.'

Kay slowed the car to a crawl and drove past the house until she could find a parking space.

They walked back to the property at a slow pace to give them a chance to get their bearings.

'How long has Felix Ashgrove lived here?'

'Records show that he's always lived in Oxford, but he moved to this house seven years ago. From the title deeds, it looks like it was his mother's house prior to that.'

They reached a tall privet hedge with a wooden gate halfway along its length, two chrome numbers nailed to the front of it.

'Number seventy-two. Alright, let's see what Mr Ashgrove can tell us.'

Kay let the gate swing back into place behind them and led Carys up the path to the front door.

It opened before she could raise her hand to press the doorbell, and a middle-aged man half a head shorter than her appeared, a pair of reading glasses pushed up into his thinning black hair.

'You're the detectives?'

Kay smiled. 'Are we that obvious?'

He blushed, then cleared his throat. 'I don't get too many visitors during the day. Come in.'

Kay stepped into the hallway and formally introduced herself and Carys.

'You've come a long way,' he said. 'I'll put the kettle on, shall I?'

'That would be great, thanks.'

'Go through to the living room. I'll be there in a minute.'

Kay walked through the door he indicated and checked over her shoulder.

While Carys waited by the door, she carried out a quick look around the room, but found nothing untoward.

The man appeared to live alone, and the decor didn't look like it had been updated since his mother had died. However, the room remained fresh, and she noticed at the far end that a patio door led out to a well-tended garden.

'It's quite a sun-trap on the right day,' he said, entering through a second door near the back of the room with three steaming mugs. 'But a bit too cold today.'

'How long have you been here?'

'I grew up here.' He handed her and Carys a mug each. 'I've moved around a bit since, but when my mother died seven years ago, I thought I'd move in rather than sell. The housing market wasn't brilliant at the time, so I figured it wouldn't hurt to wait.' He took a sip of his drink. 'But you didn't come here to talk about houses, did you?'

'I understand from DC Miles that you spoke to her yesterday about Duncan Saddleworth.'

'Yes, that's right. Shall we sit?'

He gestured to the two generously stuffed sofas near the front window, and sat in one.

Kay and Carys took the other, and Carys retrieved her notebook and pen from her bag.

'Oh. I didn't know this was a formal interview.'

'It doesn't have to be,' said Kay. 'But we do need to have a record of what we've discussed. There's a lot to recall when conducting an investigation like this. If you prefer, I can let you have your rights, and we can go from there.'

He held up his hand. 'Don't worry. I've got nothing to hide.'

'Okay, great. So, to start us off, tell me what led you to phone us.'

'I saw the news the night before last – the teenager's funeral. Must've been a slow news day in Oxfordshire.'

Kay nodded, but said nothing. It was more likely that Sharp and the media officer had requested the regional news stations within a certain radius of Maidstone broadcast the footage in case it jogged anyone's memory. It didn't always work, but when it did, it often offered a breakthrough or another lead to follow up that they wouldn't have otherwise got.

'Go on.'

'Well, I was taken aback when I saw Duncan Saddleworth, to be honest. I thought he was still in America. I'm surprised he wasn't keeping a low profile though.'

'Oh? Why?'

Ashgrove leaned forward and placed his half-empty mug on the coffee table between them. 'Because he's being blackmailed.'

Kay's eyes narrowed. 'What?'

'I know. You'd think the last thing he'd be doing is appearing on television, right?'

'How do you know that Duncan is being blackmailed?'

In response, he got up, walked over to an antique-looking writing bureau near the window and opened the top drawer. His hand shook as he plucked out an envelope and handed it to Kay.

'Because the same person was trying to blackmail me.'

In the silence that followed, Kay cast her eyes around the room, taking in the sparse decoration compared to the collection of photographs that took up one corner of a sagging bookshelf.

Carys's pen dropped to the floor, and Kay's thoughts snapped back to the task at hand.

'Sorry,' said Carys, and scrambled for the ballpoint pen.

Kay sat further forward on the sofa. 'If you only saw Duncan on the news yesterday, how do you know he's being blackmailed?'

'We've spoken. He phoned me out of the blue when he received the first letter.'

Kay changed tack. 'How many letters have you received?'

'Eight in total.'

'Do you have them?'

She waited while he returned to the desk, rummaged through the top drawer and retrieved a handful of similarly-coloured envelopes. She took them from him, and pulled out each letter before reading it and then placing it back.

'How often have you received these?'

'One a month. The day they arrive differs, but it's usually around the third week of the month.'

'There are no postmarks. Were these delivered in an outer packaging?'

'No. I'm presuming they were hand-delivered.'

'When did you find them? In the morning? When you returned from work?'

'Both. Sometimes I'd be upstairs getting ready to go to work. Sometimes there'd be one waiting for me on the mat when I got back.'

'These are all asking for money.'

'I haven't paid any.'

'Why not?'

'I don't care if people find out about my past. I've never hidden from it.' He sighed, and joined her on the sofa. 'I suppose someone of Duncan's calling might not see it that way. He might be desperate to stop the blackmailer.' He shrugged. 'It's only a thought.'

'So, let me make sure I understand this. You haven't paid any money, but the letters kept arriving, and you haven't been exposed?'

'No. I wondered perhaps whether I was being used as leverage somehow. The fact I've stayed silent might have been helping not hindering the blackmailer. I didn't know how to contact Duncan, and even if I did, why would I? He might not be receiving letters like this, so why would I draw attention to the fact that I was? I wanted to pretend it wasn't happening, until I saw the story about that young girl. And then Duncan phoned me. I don't know – I'm sorry, maybe I'm wasting your time—'

'Not at all. We'd rather you spoke to us than not. What can you tell us about Duncan Saddleworth?'

He smiled. 'He was a charmer. Everyone that met him fell for him. The girls, and the boys. He loved the attention – couldn't get enough of it. Walked around like he was a rock star or something.'

'Were you jealous of him?'

'Not really. It might sound strange, but it was enough to be accepted into his circle of friends. Everyone adored him.'

'What did you get up to?'

He leaned back in his chair, his face wistful. 'It was the 1990s in Oxford, Detective. Bands from here were going global. Everyone got caught up in the scene – the music was incredible. So, we hung out in pubs, watched bands, and probably drank a bit too much.'

'Drugs?'

He smiled. 'Maybe. Just fun.'

'And yet you lost touch with him. How long has it been since you last saw him?'

'I haven't seen him since the end of the third semester. I'd never spoken to him until he phoned about the first blackmail letter.'

'Why?'

'It all changed. He fell in love with someone else.'

'Who else was around at that time? Can you recall any names?'

The smile faded. 'I-I'd rather not say. I don't want to get sued for slander or something.'

'If you know something that would help our enquiries, you should tell us. I'm trying to find the killer of a sixteen year old girl.'

'I'm sorry. I know.'

'Who did he break your heart for?'

His head snapped up, his eyes wary. 'How did you know?'

'There are only photos in here of your time at university. There's no-one else in your life, is there?'

His Adam's apple bobbed in his throat. 'You're very perceptive, Detective.'

He got up and wandered over to the collection of carefully framed photographs on the shelves. He pulled out a cotton handkerchief and dabbed at the glass of one of them, before turning back to Kay, tears in his eyes.

'You're right, Detective. He did break my heart.'

'So, who was Duncan Saddleworth involved with after you?'

'An American. Blake Hamilton.'

CHAPTER FORTY-THREE

Kay left Carys to park the car on their return to the police station, and wandered into the incident room.

Her mind spun with the information Felix Ashgrove had provided.

The probability that Sophie Whittaker was blackmailing three people was a serious allegation – and opened up more possibilities as to who murdered her.

The problem was, who?

She slumped into her chair and wiggled her mouse to wake up her computer screen, then looked up as a shadow passed her desk.

Gavin held a plastic evidence bag in his hand, a broad grin on his face.

'Come on, let's have it,' said Kay. 'What've you

found? It must be good – you look like you've been bursting to tell me.'

His grin widened. 'Remember that key Harriet's lot found in Sophie's bedside drawers?'

'Yeah. You managed to trace it?'

'Eventually. It's from a safe deposit box – the sort you can rent from a bank.'

Kay held out her hand for the bag and turned it in her hand.

A nondescript steel key lay in one corner, bare except for the manufacturer's stamp and a row of letters and numbers stamped into one side of the bow.

'Do you know which one?'

Gavin held up a piece of paper. 'This one. It's here in Maidstone. I spoke to the manager – it's held in Sophie Whittaker's name.'

Kay handed back the bag and checked her watch. 'Well, they're going to be closed now. Grab your jacket though – let's go and talk to Sophie's mother to see what she has to say about this. I've got some more questions I want to ask her anyway.'

―――――

Grace Jamieson led Kay and Gavin to the library of Crossways Hall and announced their arrival to Diane

Whittaker, before stepping to one side and gesturing to them to enter the room.

'Thank you, Grace, that will be all,' said Diane.

The housekeeper nodded deferentially, and left the room leaving the door open behind her.

'I'm surprised you have any questions left,' said Diane, turning back to the bookcase next to her and running her fingers over the spines. 'I thought you must have exhausted all your avenues of investigation by now.'

Kay ignored the barb. 'When was Sophie's engagement to Josh first announced?'

'As soon as she reached her sixteenth birthday. That's what we'd all agreed,' said Diane.

'No plans to continue her education beyond college?'

'Good grief, no. What for? Josh will be taking over his father's business one day and Sophie would have had her hands full coping with a young family and running the house.'

'Here, you mean?'

'Of course. Where else?'

Diane turned from the bookcase and Kay peered over the top of her head to where Gavin stared at her, stony faced.

She managed a small smile, to let her colleague

know she probably shared the same sentiment about Diane, and a moment later was struck by the fact her own mother would get on well with the irritating woman.

'Did Sophie share your love of books?

'Not as much, no. I tried to encourage her as much as possible – she was more interested in clothes shopping and listening to that horrible pop music the girls at her school listened to, but I was starting to instil a better appreciation of the finer arts in her. You've got to keep an eye on these girls, you see. They're too easily led astray.'

'You didn't contemplate sending her to boarding school?'

Diane's lips thinned. 'She went to boarding school, when she was younger. Unfortunately, my husband's business hasn't been doing as well as it could have been these past few years, and so we had to find an alternative. Not an ideal situation, as I'm sure you'll appreciate.'

Kay made a noncommittal sound at the back of her throat. 'Was Sophie someone that would keep secrets from you, do you think?'

'Whatever do you mean?'

'All teenage girls rebel at some point. Do you know if Sophie had anywhere she might hide stuff she didn't want you to see? It seems strange that we didn't find a diary or anything in her room, that's all.'

Diane frowned, opened her mouth to say something, then clamped it shut.

Kay pulled out the evidence bag containing the safe deposit box key. 'This was found in Sophie's possessions by our crime scene team. It's for a safe deposit box at a bank in Maidstone. You didn't think to mention anything about a safe deposit box to us all this time?'

'I didn't think of it before, with everything else going on. I arranged for her to have a safe deposit box at our bank in Maidstone, so she could keep some of the jewellery left to her by her grandmother there.'

'Do you have a key?'

'No. Sophie had the only one. I lost mine years ago, but I didn't worry about it as Sophie had the other. When I couldn't find it the other day, I realised your people must've taken it when they were in Sophie's room. I thought I'd simply fetch my mother's jewellery once your people had returned the key.'

'We need to see what's in that box, Mrs Whittaker – as a matter of urgency.'

'Oh, right. Of course. I'll need to check my diary first.'

The woman wandered over to a small table beside one of the armchairs and picked up a silver bell. She waggled it between her fingers. A soft ring filled the room before she placed it back on the table surface and clasped her hands in front of her, a benign smile on her face.

The housekeeper appeared at the door. 'You rang, Lady Griffith?'

'Yes. Fetch my handbag from my bedroom, please.'

Kay turned away, and concentrated on staring out the patio doors to the terrace beyond. She knew if she caught Gavin's eye now, she'd burst out laughing at the woman's snobbery.

The housekeeper returned shortly with the handbag, and Diane moved across to where Kay stood while she rummaged through the contents.

'Here it is,' she said triumphantly, and held up a leather diary. 'When did you want to go?'

'We've spoken to the manager. He'll meet us there at nine o'clock tomorrow morning.'

Diane's eyebrows knitted together. 'Why so soon?'

Kay resisted the urge to sigh. 'Because, Mrs Whittaker, I'm trying to find out why your daughter was murdered. I thought you might want to accompany me, anyway – to collect your late mother's jewellery?'

'Oh. Very well, then.'

'Great – see you tomorrow. Please make sure your husband is there, too.'

Kay managed to keep her frustration in check until she and Gavin were back in the car.

'She's living in a time warp,' Gavin grumbled. 'I almost raised my hand in the air to get permission to speak a couple of times.'

Kay laughed. 'She's all right, I suppose. Lives in her own little world.'

'She's mad.'

'Ah, see that's where you're wrong – people with money like that, we call them "eccentric", not "mad".'

Gavin snorted, and turned the car back towards Maidstone. 'I don't know whether to feel sorry for her, or be infuriated by her.'

'Different world, isn't it? Her whole life has revolved around keeping the house in the family, and now with Sophie gone, she's got no-one—'

Kay broke off, and held up her hand to stop Gavin from interrupting. 'Hang on. Who benefits from Diane selling the house?'

'I can't imagine the National Trust going to such extreme measures to get their hands on it, Sarge.'

'Very funny. Come on – who else?'

Gavin leaned forward and turned down the radio. 'It's of no use to Blake Hamilton – he was only interested in Sophie's social position Why would he buy a house that's in desperate need of some work when he's got a much better one of his own?'

'Exactly.' Kay peered out the window, the scent of honeysuckle reaching her through the gap where she'd wound it down to let in fresh air. 'We'll have to get some details from the council regarding property valuation. That place must be worth a fortune with the land it takes up.'

CHAPTER FORTY-FOUR

The next morning, Kay and Gavin stood on the pavement outside the Whittakers' bank, waiting for the front doors to open.

There was no sign of Sophie's parents yet, and Kay wondered what was going on between the two of them. It had been evident at the funeral that all was not well with their relationship, and despite knowing the strain they had been under since Sophie's death, she couldn't help wonder if the rot had set in well before.

The sound of bolts being drawn back across the heavy-set wooden door roused her from her thoughts, and she turned as a member of staff swung it open and secured it against the far wall before smiling at them.

'Morning. Would you like to come in?'

'Thanks.'

Kay admired the art deco ceilings as she moved into the cool space of the building. The original panelling had been retained too, with the cashiers' windows set to one side, four in total.

A secured door at the end of room displayed a "Staff Only" sign, warning of dire consequences if any member of the public tried to pass.

She checked her watch.

'Nine on the dot.'

'How long do you think Lady Griffith will keep us waiting?'

'God knows.'

The member of staff who had ushered them through the front door returned, a quizzical look crossing her features.

'Can I help you with something?'

Kay fished out her warrant card. 'We're waiting for someone to join us.'

'Oh.' Flustered, the staff member went to walk away, then rocked back on her heel. 'Would you like tea or coffee while you're waiting?'

'That'd be great, thanks.'

Half an hour later, the two coffees dispatched, Kay was beginning to wonder where the hell the

Whittakers had got to, when Gavin murmured under his breath.

'About bloody time.'

Diane and Matthew Whittaker walked towards them, Diane a little ahead of her husband as if she wanted to reach the detectives first.

'Detective Hunter, sorry to keep you waiting,' she said. 'Have you been here long?'

Kay's eyes rested upon the empty coffee cups before she raised an eyebrow. 'Shall we get on with it?'

She caught the attention of the staff member who had provided the hot drinks and asked her to fetch the manager.

'Is everything okay?'

'Yes. Please tell him that Lady Griffith needs to speak to him.'

Kay turned on her heel and faced Sophie's mother. 'I'm presuming we'll be taken to a private room to open the safe deposit box?'

'Y-yes. That's normally what happens.' She forced a smile. 'Couldn't have one's private things in view of the staff, after all.'

The secure door at the end of the room opened, and a short man with carefully coiffed black hair hurried towards them, his expression a mix of delight and terror.

He wrung his hands as he approached.

'Lady Griffith, Mr Whittaker. Terrible news about Sophie. Terrible.'

'Thank you, Mr Parsons.' Diane introduced Kay and Gavin. 'We'd like to open Sophie's safe deposit box, please.'

'Of course. You have the key?'

'I do,' said Kay.

'As the counter-signatory to the safe deposit box, Lady Griffith, I must ask if you're happy for the detectives and your husband to accompany you?'

Diane opened her mouth to speak, but Kay held up her hand.

'She is.'

Diane clamped her mouth shut, glared at her, and then seemed to recover. 'Of course, that's fine.'

'Well, if you'd like to follow me.'

He led them through the secure door, which opened out into a carpeted corridor with three offices leading off from it, before swiping his access card and holding a second secure door open while they filed through.

He gestured to a table and six chairs. 'If you'd like to wait here, I'll retrieve the box for you.'

An awkward silence filled the room when he disappeared, and Kay let it do so. She had no wish to make unnecessary conversation, and it was sometimes better to simply observe other people rather than try to draw them out with words.

Matthew Whittaker appeared confused, as if he didn't know why his wife had summoned him to their bank, whereas Diane wore a defiant look upon her face and twisted the wedding band on her finger.

Relief washed over her features as the bank manager reappeared, a long black metal box in his hands.

He elbowed the door shut and then set the box upon the table, and stood there, apparently unsure whether to defer to Kay or to Diane.

Kay saved him the bother.

'We'll let you know when we're finished, Mr Parsons.'

He bowed his head slightly, and Kay realised it was more in deference to Diane than her.

She waited until he'd disappeared from the room, before reaching into her jacket pocket and extracting three pairs of gloves, holding one set out to Diane and passing the other to Matthew.

He wiggled his fingers into them, his face pale. 'I didn't know she had anything to hide.'

Kay paused, the key in her hand. 'You didn't know about this safe deposit box?'

He shook his head, and glanced at his wife. 'They didn't tell me.'

Diane flapped her hand. 'You didn't need to know. I simply wanted to ensure Sophie had somewhere to keep her heirlooms.' She shot a thin smile at Kay. 'We don't have those ugly "safe" things in the house. It'd spoil the decor, for a start.'

'Put your gloves on please, Lady Griffith.'

Bewildered, the woman stared at the gloves in her grasp. 'W-why?'

'We need to preserve the contents of this for evidence. Our CSI won't be pleased if we contaminate everything with our own fingerprints.'

Gavin withdrew his notebook and a pack of plastic bags from his jacket and set them down on the table, ready to record everything and label it accordingly.

Kay twisted the key in the lock and lifted the lid off the box.

CHAPTER FORTY-FIVE

Diane Whittaker gasped.

Bank notes – fifties, twenties and tens, had been bundled together and secured with elastic bands before being stacked in neat rows that ran the length of the box.

'How much is there?' Gavin murmured, his eyes wide.

Kay picked up a bundle and flipped through it, then dropped her gaze to the remaining notes. 'Thousands.'

'What's it all doing there?' said Diane. 'What's going on?'

Kay kept her suspicions to herself for the time being, and instead lifted each bundle before sliding them across the table to Gavin. 'Log it by denomination.'

'Sarge.'

As Kay pulled out each bundle of notes, she began to understand what Sophie Whittaker had really been using the secret box for.

'You never thought to order a new spare key to check the contents of this?' she said to Diane.

'Never! These are my daughter's private things.'

'If I hadn't mentioned that Sophie might have somewhere she could hide secrets, would you have brought this to our attention?'

'Detective, I know you have a job to do, but I find your questioning insulting.'

'Just answer the question, Diane,' said Matthew.

Kay met his eyes and sent a silent "thanks" in his direction.

Whether the marriage was failing before Sophie's death, or had manifested itself within the past weeks, she had no idea. However, it was evident all was not well within Lady Griffith's household.

'Well, of course I would!' Diane's eyes shot from her husband's to Kay. 'Yes, I would have told you.'

Kay turned her attention back to the box. Underneath the bank notes, she found the jewellery

Diane had alluded to. Each piece had its own velvet box, and when she opened them, the ceiling lights glinted off sapphires, rubies and other precious stones.

Kay removed each one and passed them to Gavin. 'Log these as well.'

'But—'

'You'll get a receipt for it all, Lady Griffith, don't worry. Do you recognise all of these items?'

'They were my late mother's.' Diane waved her hand dismissively and turned away.

Kay cleared her throat and pointed at the open boxes before repeating her question. 'Do you recognise *all* these items? Are there any here that didn't belong to your mother?'

Diane clenched her jaw, then dropped her gaze and ran her eyes over the jewellery. A small gasp escaped her lips, and she pointed a shaking hand at one piece.

'I haven't seen that before.'

Kay picked up a light blue-coloured box and plucked out the simple diamond ring that had been nestled within its lining. Compared to the other pieces, it appeared newer and less worn.

'Are you sure?'

'Positive.' Diane's top lip curled. 'My mother

would have never worn a diamond of such low grade.'

'Note that, Gavin.'

'Sarge.'

A piece of patterned cloth had been laid beneath the jewellery boxes and as Kay passed those across to Gavin, she realised it was a tea towel. Lifting the last jewellery box out, she tugged at the cloth and peered underneath.

'Bingo,' she murmured.

She dumped the tea towel on the table and plucked out the pad of writing paper, a glue stick and an exercise book and held them up to Diane.

'Ever seen these before?'

'No. What's going on?'

Kay held the notebook up to the light, but could see no indentations on the pages. She rolled the tube of glue towards Gavin.

'Pop that in an evidence bag and put in a request for Harriet to test it for any fingerprints against what was used on the blackmail notes.'

'Will do.'

'Blackmail notes?' Voice shaking, Diane looked from Matthew to Kay, her eyes wide. 'What's going on?'

'We've had our suspicions that Sophie was

blackmailing people. Each person received letters demanding money in exchange for the blackmailer's silence on a regular basis. The letters comprised words cut from newspapers or printed out articles that were then glued to notepaper. The same as this. This notebook contains a record of each letter sent, the amount of money received, and her victims.'

'Who are they?'

'I'm not at liberty to say. As you'll appreciate, the people she targeted would rather keep that private.' Kay closed the notebook and passed it to Gavin.

Diane covered her mouth with a trembling hand. 'How could she?'

'It takes all sorts, Lady Griffith.'

'Does – does anyone else know it was her?'

'I'll be speaking to her victims as soon as we're finished here to confirm our suspicions were correct.'

She didn't say that she'd also be speaking to Sharp about re-interviewing Blake Hamilton and Duncan Saddleworth, given that both now had a clear motive for killing Sophie.

Diane was pacing the room, wringing her hands. 'Oh my Lord. We have to keep this secret, Detective. We can't let anyone find out. My family's reputation—'

'Lady Griffith, I'm in the middle of an

investigation to find out who killed your daughter. We will be speaking to everyone we've interviewed to date to find out if they knew about her little scheme.'

'You can't. I'll never be able to show my face in public again!'

'Is that more important than finding your daughter's killer?'

The woman fell silent, her mouth working as her eyes darted to the notebook in Gavin's hand. 'Give it to me.'

'That's not going to happen, Lady Griffith.' Kay gestured to the contents of the box. 'This is all going to be lodged as evidence.'

She reached out and pressed a button set into the surface of the table, a soft ringing sounding in the corridor outside.

Within moments, the bank manager appeared, his face hopeful.

Kay pointed at the empty box. 'We'll be taking the contents with us, Mr Parsons. In the circumstances, I'd suggest you arrange for Lady Griffith to close the account so she no longer has to pay for this service.'

'I'll wait in the car,' said Matthew, and stormed from the room.

Flustered, the bank manager hurried after him,

promising to bring the necessary forms for Diane to sign on his return, and Kay busied herself helping Gavin log and bag up the jewellery, notebook and cash.

When he returned, the bank manager placed the forms on the table and handed Diane a fountain pen, indicating where she should sign.

Grumbling under her breath, she snatched it from his hand and scrawled her signature across the bottom of the page, her hand curling round on itself at an awkward angle as she signed one form after the other.

'My husband normally deals with this sort of thing.'

'I'm afraid that as you opened the account with your daughter, we require your signature to close it,' said Parsons. 'I do apologise.'

The formalities complete, he led them back along the corridor and out into the bank's main room, the cashiers now busy with a steady stream of customers who filed through the doors.

'If that's all, Detective?'

Kay nodded. 'Thank you, Lady Griffith. We'll be in touch.'

'I've no doubt you will be.' Diane glared at Gavin and jabbed her finger at him. 'Just you make sure all that jewellery is returned intact. I know exactly what my late mother gifted to my daughter.'

She spun on her heel and stalked from the bank without a backward glance.

'Bloody charming,' said Gavin.

CHAPTER FORTY-SIX

Kay stood to one side on a bare brick doorstep while Barnes rang the bell and peered through the frosted glass of the front door.

'They should be in,' he said. 'I phoned her mother to let her know you wanted to talk to Eva.'

After going through the statement Eva Shepparton had given to Barnes and Gavin, and the subsequent events since the discovery Sophie Whittaker had been pregnant when she'd been murdered, Kay wanted to speak to the teenager herself.

Barnes had said at the time he'd felt the girl was hiding something from them, and Kay was inclined to agree.

She knew she was missing something, something

that tied everything together, but she couldn't fathom what, and it bothered her.

She roused herself from her thoughts as the front door was opened and a woman in her late forties peered out.

'Mrs Shepparton?'

The woman's face softened a little when she recognised Barnes. 'Detective. Sorry to keep you waiting. Will you come in?'

'Thanks. This is my colleague, Detective Sergeant Kay Hunter.'

'Hello.'

The woman shook hands with Kay and then gestured towards the end of the hall. 'I thought we'd chat in the kitchen, Detective Barnes. Do you want to go through?'

'Thanks.'

Kay followed Barnes along a brightly decorated hallway, a staircase off to the left against the wall where the house adjoined the one next door. The front door slammed shut in their wake and Eva's mother called over their shoulders.

'I've just put the kettle on. Take a seat and I'll sort you out with a hot drink. Detective Hunter, this is my daughter, Eva.'

As Kay entered the kitchen, her eyes fell upon the

scrawny teenage girl sitting at the worktop, her brown eyes wide at the sight of the two police officers.

'Hi, Eva. Do you remember me? Detective Ian Barnes.'

'Hello.'

'This is Detective Kay Hunter. She's my boss. Would you mind answering a few questions for her?' He held up his hands apologetically and glanced at Mrs Shepparton. 'It's about girl stuff, so if it's all right with you, I might take my cup of tea and step out into the garden, if that'd make you more comfortable?'

'Thanks, Ian,' said Kay. She smiled at Eva. 'It's all right. I wasn't here when he spoke to you last, so I just want to go over a few things in your original statement to clarify them – I'm hoping it might help me find out who's responsible for Sophie's murder. Okay?'

The girl peered over her shoulder at her mother, who gave her a reassuring nod, and then turned back to Kay and Barnes.

'Okay.'

'Great.'

Barnes took the mug of steaming tea from the girl's mother and moved across the kitchen to the back door. 'See you in a bit.'

Kay waited until the door closed behind him, then took the stool Mrs Shepparton indicated to her, nodded her thanks, and opened up her notebook.

'Eva, when my colleagues spoke to you, you indicated to them that Sophie was pregnant.'

'She was, it's the truth.'

'We know. The thing is, we need to find out who else knew. Obviously, Sophie told you because you were a good friend to her and she could confide in you, but do you know if she told anyone else?'

Eva shook her head. 'She'd only found out the day before. I think she was still in shock.'

'Can you remember her exact words that day when she told you?'

The girl's brow furrowed. 'She said that she was scared, and I asked her why. I thought she was nervous about taking the purity pledge, but then she said she'd taken a pregnancy test the day before and it was positive. She said "they'll kill me when they find out", and I figured she meant her mum and dad because, like, they'd spent so much money on the ceremony and everything. I mean, I know her mum can be a silly old cow—'

'Eva!'

Kay held up her hand to Eva's mother and gestured to the teenager to continue.

'Well,' she said, and shrugged. 'She is. But I told Sophie it didn't matter – by then, she'd already told me she was planning to run away with Peter.'

'You knew about that?'

The girl nodded, and then blushed. 'I helped her move some of her clothes from Crossways Hall to his place.'

Kay paused and made a note on a clean page. Already, the girl had told her more than she'd ventured to Barnes and Gavin.

'Do you know who the father was, Eva?'

Her eyes locked with Eva's as the girl rocked back on her stool, her mouth open.

Kay waited.

Eventually, the teenager's shoulders sagged.

'It's okay, darling, you can tell the detective,' said Mrs Shepparton. She reached out and clasped her daughter's hand in hers. 'Just tell the truth. You want to help Sophie, don't you?

A fat tear escaped Eva's left eye and trickled down her cheek. She withdrew her hand from her mother's and wiped at her face before a shudder wracked her body and she lifted her gaze to Kay.

'She said she thought Duncan was the father.'

'The priest?'

Mrs Shepparton's shocked outburst echoed the thought that ricocheted in Kay's head.

'Do you mean Duncan Saddleworth?'

'Yes.' The girl's voice trembled. 'I knew Sophie fancied him – she said when we'd passed him in the town one afternoon that he was good looking. "One to watch", she said.' Eva snorted. 'I didn't think for one minute she meant she was going to have sex with him as well.'

She shook her head, and then burst into tears.

Kay waited while the girl's mother pulled her into a hug and settled her down before picking up her pen once more.

'After she told you who the father was, what else did Sophie say?'

Eva shook her head. 'Nothing. Her mum appeared on the terrace wanting to know where Mrs Jamieson was. We were frightened, I can tell you – we thought she'd overheard us, but she didn't say anything. The housekeeper came along a few seconds later anyway, and they both disappeared. By then, Sophie had clammed up. She didn't tell me anything else.'

And didn't get a chance to, thought Kay.

'Eva, you've been a great help today.' She raised herself from the kitchen stool and signalled to Barnes through the window to return.

As Mrs Shepparton showed them to the front door, Kay lowered her voice.

'How's your daughter coping in the circumstances?'

The woman's lips pursed. 'As best she can. You find out who did that to her best friend, Detective. That'll help her. She wants to see Sophie's killer caught.'

'So do we.'

CHAPTER FORTY-SEVEN

Kay leaned against the car door and took a moment to breathe in the fresh morning air.

Duncan Saddleworth's car had been parked to the side of the church, and she'd spotted two of the women who had been tending to the flower arrangements the first time she'd been to the church, although they hadn't seen her. They'd walked out the doors, busy chattering while carrying brooms before disappearing around the corner of the building.

She'd parked away from the place of worship, along the lane and at an angle that she could see the main doors to the building as well as a smaller door that she presumed led from the vestry where she'd spoken with Saddleworth at the beginning of the investigation.

'How do you want to do this, Sarge?'

Carys locked the vehicle and wandered round to join her, her neck craning up at the bell tower that cast a shadow over the front apron of the church grounds.

'We'll ask him down to the station. He hasn't been interviewed formally yet, and I'd rather not have to repeat myself.'

'Sounds good. Ours or his?'

Kay cast her eyes over the blue hatchback at the side of the church. 'He can meet us there. I don't get the impression he's going to do a runner. Not when we know where he lives, and where he works.'

'Do you think he killed her?'

'I don't think so, no. I *do* want to get to the bottom of whatever Sophie was playing at, though.'

'You think her blackmailing the three of them was what got her killed?'

'Not sure.' She pushed off the car. 'One way to find out.'

She strode towards the church as the doors opened once more, and Duncan Saddleworth appeared, a harried expression on his face.

His shoulders slumped when he noticed the two detectives approaching.

'DS Hunter.'

'Morning, Mr Saddleworth.'

He held up the briefcase in his hand and gestured towards his car. 'I was about to go home and do my paperwork there. Did you want something?'

'Actually, we'd like you to come to the police station.'

'What? Why?'

'We've obtained some more evidence in relation to the murder of Sophie Whittaker.' Kay lowered her voice at the sight of the two women reappearing, their eyes agog at the presence of the police. 'We'd like to speak with you as a matter of some urgency. Away from prying eyes – and eavesdroppers.'

Duncan glanced over his shoulder at the two cleaners, who scurried through the doors to the church, guilty expressions on their faces.

He sighed. 'That's not a bad idea, Detective.'

―――――

Duncan took the steaming cup of coffee from Carys, and then set it on the table between them while Kay pressed the "record" button and recited the formal caution for the interview to begin.

She'd draped her jacket over the back of her chair, silently cursing the temperamental air conditioning that was evidently going to start going on the blink as the summer began, and opened up the folder in front of her.

'When did you first start receiving the letters from the blackmailer, Mr Saddleworth?'

He rocked back in his seat, stunned. 'How do you know about that?'

'Please answer the question.'

He ran a hand over his mouth, and then leaned forward and cradled the coffee mug between his hands, his gaze downcast.

'It started about two months ago, maybe a bit longer.'

'Were you aware that there were others being blackmailed?'

He nodded.

'I'll need to know who.'

'Blake Hamilton.'

'Anyone else?'

He shook his head.

'Mr Saddleworth—'

'Call me Duncan.'

'Thank you. Duncan – we were alerted to your being blackmailed by a Mr Felix Ashgrove, a resident of Tonbridge.'

A gasp escaped his lips. 'Felix?'

'Can you confirm you know him?'

'Yes.'

'What was your relationship to Mr Ashgrove?'

His Adam's apple bobbed, before he blushed. 'We – we had a bit of a fling while I was studying at Oxford.'

'When was the last time you saw him?'

'Late Nineties.'

'But you've spoken to him recently?'

Saddleworth lowered his eyes. 'Yes. He told you?'

'He saw your face on the news report about Sophie's funeral, and telephoned us. Is Blake Hamilton the reason you went to Connecticut after you finished your volunteer stint?'

'Yes.'

'Did you know he was married at the time?'

'Yes.' His lifted his head, his face miserable. 'It only happened once after we left Oxford. He'd already gone months before I left for South America. His leaving was partly the reason I made the decision I had to get on with my life. Then I heard a rumour he was in Bridgeport, so I went there. It only happened the once, Detective – you have to believe me. It was when I first arrived in the USA. After that, it never happened again and we never spoke of it. Neither of us could afford the damage to our reputations.'

'Do you know who was blackmailing you?'

'I thought I did.'

'Who?'

'Sophie Whittaker.'

'Why?'

He shrugged. 'I can only imagine she found an old picture I kept from our Oxford days in my desk drawer in the vestry. It shows the three of us together at a party – I was kissing Blake. I always keep it locked – you've seen what the cleaners are like. One day, around the time she first started asking about the purity pledge, I had to take a phone call and I left her in the vestry on her own. When I got back, she had a smug look on her face. I knew something was wrong, but it wasn't until she'd left that I realised I'd left the key in the lock. Nothing was missing, but after I received the first letter, I realised what she'd done.'

'Did you kill Sophie Whittaker?'

His eyes widened. 'No!'

'We've gone through the statements taken on the night of her murder, Duncan. You were nowhere to be found after the ceremony.'

'That's because I made my excuses and left. I had to be up early for the next day's service.'

Kay nodded to Carys, who slid across the notebook they'd found in the safe deposit box.

'We found out about a safe deposit box held in Sophie's name. The entries in this notebook suggest that Sophie was blackmailing all of you on a regular basis, yet you were the only one to pay up.'

'What?'

'I can only presume that the thought of being blackmailed didn't bother Blake Hamilton. Felix Ashgrove certainly wasn't worried about his reputation. Why did you pay?'

'I was scared.' He ran a shaking hand over his face. 'There was... there was a minor indiscretion a year or so ago and, if anything else happened, I would've been kicked out of my church.' His eyes became pleading. 'I have nowhere else to go, Detective.'

'What sort of "minor indiscretion", Mr Saddleworth?'

He blushed. 'I had a relationship with a younger member of my congregation. Female.'

'Was she under age?'

'No!'

'Have there been any other indiscretions like that?'

'Only one,' he mumbled.

'Who?'

He lifted his gaze, his eyes miserable. 'Sophie Whittaker.'

'When?'

'I didn't mean to.'

'When?'

'About four months ago. She stayed late one Saturday night – supposedly to ask me about her purity pledge. She seduced me, Detective.'

'Did it happen again?'

'No – only the once. I-I realised she was probably using me. For one of such a young age, she certainly had a reputation.'

Kay fought down her anger, and instead wrote a note on the inside of the folder. If Duncan Saddleworth slept with Sophie Whittaker four months ago, then he definitely wasn't the father of her child, despite what Sophie thought.

Kay's mind went back to what Carys had mentioned in passing weeks ago – that girls who took a purity pledge were often ignorant about safe sex or any other family planning issues. It simply wasn't spoken about within those closed church communities.

'How did you manage to afford to keep up with the blackmail payments? I can't imagine the church pays that much of a salary?'

Saddleworth tapped his fingers on the desk for a moment, and then slouched in his chair. 'You might as well know. Blake Hamilton paid me to make sure Sophie's purity pledge ceremony and engagement to Josh went ahead. He was worried she'd change her mind.'

'How much?'

'Enough that I didn't have to worry about meeting the blackmailer's demands.'

'How much money did you pay in response to the letters?'

'Up to the night Sophie died, nine thousand six hundred pounds.'

Kay caught Carys's eye. The sum tallied with what they'd found in the safe deposit box.

'I paid another fifteen hundred pounds nine days ago.'

Kay frowned. 'Nine days ago?'

'Yes.' His top lip curled. 'You see, Detective, I *thought* it was Sophie Whittaker blackmailing me because she found out about Blake Hamilton and Felix Ashgrove. I thought it was because she seduced me. Evidently, I was wrong. I'm still being blackmailed.'

'Do you have the letter?'

In response, he reached into his jacket pocket and

withdrew a crumpled envelope before sliding it across the table.

Carys caught Kay's eyes and slipped a pair of gloves on before picking up the envelope and extracting the page from within.

Again, the note had been constructed from words cut out from printed out newspaper articles, demanding money in exchange for secrecy about Duncan's affairs.

'Is this the letter that arrived after Sophie's death?'

He nodded, his eyes full of misery. 'Yes.'

'We'll need to hang on to this, Mr Saddleworth.' Kay reached over to the recording machine, her finger hovering over the "stop" button.

'Interview terminated.'

CHAPTER FORTY-EIGHT

'Are you going to ask him to come down to the station?'

Barnes peered through the windscreen as Blake Hamilton's house came into view, and flipped the indicator stalk on the steering column.

'No. I don't think there's any need for that. It wouldn't go down well with Larch, for a start.'

Kay fidgeted in her seat until she could reach the notebook in her bag and flipped through the pages once more. 'What I do want to find out is if Hamilton's been receiving letters since Sophie died, like Duncan Saddleworth has.' She paused on the last page of the notebook to include Sophie's handwriting. 'Whoever it is didn't know about Sophie's record keeping habits. She was meticulous.'

'So, someone found out about the blackmailing and when Sophie died, decided it'd be a good way to make some money.'

'Yeah. When we're finished here, can you go and speak to Peter Evans again? I've got a feeling we still haven't had the whole story from him. Take it easy – he's likely trying to protect Sophie's reputation. I think he really did love her.'

'Will do. What are you thinking?'

Kay tapped her thumb against the side of the notebook. 'One of them isn't telling us everything.' She sighed. 'It's like they've all got secrets, and we're only chipping away at the surface. I mean, why would Duncan Saddleworth be the only one to pay her? Having a gay relationship when he was at university doesn't seem a strong enough reason. There's got to be something else going on.'

Barnes grunted in response, then braked outside the house and climbed from the car, reaching into the backseat for his jacket before shrugging it over his shoulders.

Kay tucked the notebook back into her bag and joined him as he stalked across the gravel towards the front door.

Blake Hamilton's face broke into a sneer when he

opened it and found the two detectives on his doorstep.

'This is becoming tiresome, Detective Hunter.'

'We won't keep you long, Mr Hamilton. We've had some developments in our investigation we'd like to speak with you about.' She smiled. 'We can either do that here, or at the police station. Your choice.'

He stepped back and held the door open. 'Come in.'

'Thank you.'

'My wife isn't in. She's taken Josh out for the day. Shopping, or something.' He led the way through to the vast living area, but stopped short of offering them a seat.

'I won't take up too much of your time, Mr Hamilton.' Kay withdrew Sophie's notebook from her bag. 'I'd like to ask you about the blackmail letters you've been receiving for the past two months.'

Blake took a step back, his face flushing. 'How the hell do you know about that?'

'Have you any idea who was blackmailing you?'

'I had my suspicions.'

'Were you aware of anyone else being blackmailed at the same time?'

'I presume the only reason you're here is because

Duncan Saddleworth told you I was also being blackmailed.'

'That's correct. There was also a third man being blackmailed. Did you know Felix Ashgrove?'

'Christ, a long time ago. He was a guy that Duncan was involved with in Oxford. Haven't heard his name mentioned in years.' He pointed to the notebook in the plastic bag in Kay's hand. 'What's that?'

'We were informed about a safe deposit box yesterday that was previously overlooked. This notebook was inside it, together with a lot of money. And notepaper that Duncan Saddleworth confirms matches that of the letters he had been receiving until recently. This notebook contains a record of letters sent to you, Felix, and Duncan.'

'You never said who it was, Detective. The blackmailer?'

'Sophie Whittaker.'

He snorted, an explosive sound that ended in a bitter laugh. 'Wow, and I thought her mother was a conniving bitch.'

'The problem is, Mr Hamilton, that although the entries in this notebook finish the day before Sophie was killed, the letters to Mr Saddleworth haven't stopped. Were you aware of this?'

He bowed his head. 'Duncan did mention to me that he'd received another letter. He seemed convinced that when Sophie died the letters would stop, too.' He raised his gaze to hers. 'I have no idea who is blackmailing Duncan now.'

'You've not received any other letters?'

'No.'

'What did you do with the ones you received before Sophie died?'

'I destroyed them. I had no intention of paying up, but neither did I want my wife finding out.'

'Why did you pay Saddleworth to ensure the purity pledge went ahead?'

Hamilton had the decency to blush, although he recovered quickly. 'I viewed it as a business investment,' he said. 'I knew Duncan needed the money. The arrangement suited us both well.'

Kay's eyes narrowed. 'And what if Sophie decided she didn't want to go ahead?'

'Well, she didn't, did she? She took the pledge.' His lips thinned. 'I'd appreciate it, Detective, if this conversation was kept between us. Courtney doesn't know about me and Duncan. I'd prefer to keep it that way.'

'If this conversation has no bearing on the murder

of Sophie Whittaker, then I'll consider it. I'm not making promises though.'

'Thank you, Detective. I owe you.'

CHAPTER FORTY-NINE

As Kay left the police station and headed towards the river, she pulled out her mobile phone and scrolled through the contact list before hitting the call button.

Peter Evans answered before the third ring, his voice weary.

'Detective Hunter.'

Kay didn't pause for niceties. 'Did you give Sophie Whittaker a ring?'

'Yes. She refused to wear it though. She said she had to keep it a secret.'

'Can you describe it for me?'

'It was a gold band with a single diamond. It took me four weeks to save up for it. I even worked some overtime. I know she was probably used to more expensive jewellery, but it was everything I could afford. I wanted her to have it now, and we were going to get married in France.'

'We found it in a safe deposit box that Sophie had at a bank here in Maidstone.'

He exhaled, his relief apparent. 'I wondered where it had gone. I thought maybe her mother had found it.'

'Her mother didn't know anything about it,' said Kay. 'She was quite surprised to see it. I'll arrange for it to be returned to you as soon as possible.'

'Thank you.'

Kay finished the call, then picked up her pace and wound her way past the stone-clad walls of the Bishops Palace and down towards the footpath that ran alongside the river. She stood for a moment, and watched a pair of ducks paddle their way across the water, four diagonal lines following in their wake, before she turned right and back in the direction of town.

A woman with a toddler in tow appeared in front of her, and Kay stood to one side to let them pass on the narrow path.

The woman smiled and murmured her thanks, before her attention was taken up by a happy chortle from her daughter as she spotted the waterfowl on the other side of the river.

Kay thought back to Matthew and Diane Whittaker, having to collect their daughter from the morgue and organise a funeral, and realised that despite her own loss, she couldn't imagine what it must have been like for the sixteen-year-old's parents to have to endure such a tragedy.

She was jolted from her reverie at the sound of her mobile phone ringing. Pulling it from her pocket, she frowned as she saw Sharp's number displayed on the screen.

'Guv?'

'I need you back at the station. Where are you?'

'Down by the river getting some fresh air. What's wrong?'

'Matthew Whittaker just turned up here demanding to speak to us. Says he thinks his wife murdered their daughter.'

'I'll be right there.'

Kay stuffed her phone back into her pocket and took off at a sprint.

Reaching the police station, she swiped her card and burst through the doors, took the stairs two at a time and launched herself into the incident room.

Sharp's conversation with Carys died on the air as he saw her approach.

'What's going on?' she said, trying to catch her

breath.

'We've got him in interview room one,' he said as she shrugged off her jacket and draped it over the back of her chair. 'You'll do the interview with me. We haven't been able to locate Larch at the moment so Carys left a message for him.'

'How do you want to do this?'

'We'll let him talk, see what he has to say for himself.'

Kay nodded and followed him from the room. 'I have a feeling the marriage is in trouble, guv.'

'Okay, so this might just be vindictive, is that what you're saying?'

'It's something we have to bear in mind, yes.'

'All right, good point.'

He led the way down the stairs to the interview suite and swiped his card over the security panel. 'He didn't nominate his own solicitor, so I've got one of the duty solicitors to attend. I want this done properly, Kay. If he's telling the truth, then I don't want Larch breathing down our necks for not following procedure.'

'Understood.'

He placed his hand on the door to the interview room and raised an eyebrow. 'Ready?'

'Ready.'

CHAPTER FIFTY

Matthew Whittaker sat, arms folded across his chest, his eyes downcast as Kay and Sharp entered the interview room.

Kay remained silent as she took the chair next to Sharp, and waited until he'd pressed the record button and formally cautioned Whittaker.

Sharp gave a curt nod to the solicitor and then clasped his hands together on the table and leaned forward.

'Now, Mr Whittaker, when you arrived at the reception desk forty minutes ago, you told our desk sergeant that you wished to make a statement, is that correct?'

'That's right. I think my wife murdered our daughter.'

'That's a very serious accusation, Mr Whittaker.'

The man blinked.

Kay spread out the annual accounts Carys had compiled for Matthew Whittaker's business on the table in front of her, turning them so the rows of numbers faced Sophie's father.

'You've had some business ups and downs, Mr Whittaker.' She stabbed her finger on one document that was several years old. 'You were nearly bankrupted by the dot-com bubble, yet you've always managed to fight your way back.'

'I'm good at what I do.'

'I don't doubt that. The question is – are you good enough?' She tapped the latest reports. 'Seems to me you're doing little more than treading water these days. How is that affecting your relationship with Diane?'

'What? What's that got to do with it?'

'Answer the question, Mr Whittaker,' said Sharp.

Matthew sighed. 'All right, well, I guess Diane will probably tell you. Our marriage is over.' He ran a hand over his head. 'It wasn't brilliant before we lost Sophie, but since then it's deteriorated.'

'That can happen with families of victims,' said Sharp. 'Are you seeking help?'

The man shook his head. 'Honestly, unless it

involved financial help, Diane wouldn't be interested.' He leaned back in his chair. 'No, I think she's come to the conclusion that she's managed to suck me dry of everything I'm worth to her – my business is struggling, you're right there, Detective – and she's looking elsewhere for help.'

'What about her inheritance?' said Kay. 'When the Earl died, didn't he provide for you?'

'Him?' Whittaker emitted a bitter laugh. 'Not a hope in hell. You should've seen Diane's face when the will was read out – the man had racked up so many gambling debts he'd had to re-mortgage the house to pay them off. She was lucky she had a roof over her head at all.' He clasped his hands together on the table. 'Sometimes I wish she *had* lost the house.'

'What about her mother?'

'Diane's mother died within a week of the Earl. Diane always maintained it was due to a broken heart, but it was more likely the gin consumption that finished off the old bitch.'

'Was Sophie aware of your marriage problems?'

Tears welled up in his eyes and he angrily brushed them away. 'It was never about Sophie. It was always about trying to save Diane's bloody house. You know it's falling down? I spent every penny I earned trying to renovate the place, but it's rotting from the inside out.' He snorted, his gaze falling to the table between them. 'Just like the woman I married.'

'Mr Whittaker, the fact that your marriage is breaking down isn't the reason you're accusing your wife of murder, is it? What proof do you have?'

Whittaker shrugged, but said nothing.

'What's your relationship with the Hamiltons like, Mr Whittaker?'

'Relationship?'

'Yes. Did you socialise with them outside of your church obligations?'

'Well, yes, we met at different functions to do with mine and Blake's businesses, and occasionally we'd have dinner with each other.'

'It went further than that, though, didn't it? Blake Hamilton was going to help bail out your business once Sophie got engaged to his son.'

Whittaker's eyes fell to his lap. 'I only found out about that after Sophie died. It was something he and Diane had arranged.'

'How did that make you feel?'

'Feel?' His head shot up, his expression incredulous. 'How the hell do *you* think it made me feel? She'd sold our daughter! My little girl. I hated her for it. I still hate her for it. Do you know what we did this morning, Detective?'

Kay shook her head, but remained silent.

'We were discussing our divorce. I filed for bankruptcy this morning, and apparently that's too embarrassing for Diane and her bloody airs and graces.'

He wiped at his eyes and sank into his seat, exhaustion sweeping his features.

'What makes you think Diane killed your daughter?'

'She must've found out she was sleeping with Peter, and that she was pregnant.'

'Yet, she seemed as surprised as you to find out about Sophie's pregnancy,' said Sharp.

Whittaker snorted. 'She's a great actress, Diane. Very convincing. I've already told your colleague here,' he said waving a hand in Kay's direction, 'Diane went to drama school in London. Trust me, I've seen how she can convince people.'

Sharp sighed, and leaned towards the recording equipment. 'Interview suspended at three-fifteen,' he said.

CHAPTER FIFTY-ONE

'What the hell is going on, Sharp?'

Larch's voice echoed off the walls of the corridor as he strode towards the team gathered outside the interview rooms.

Kay paused, her hand against the doorframe of the observation suite where Barnes and Gavin sat, having watched the interview with Matthew Whittaker in order to provide feedback.

Carys hovered at the threshold, her eyes wide.

'We've reasonable suspicion to bring Diane Whittaker in for formal questioning,' said Sharp, his voice calm as the DCI glared at him. 'Her husband has suggested she killed Sophie.'

'Why on earth would Lady Griffith kill her own daughter?' said Larch.

'We don't know that she did,' said Kay. 'But she's certainly been a busy woman, that much is for sure.'

'Explain yourself, Hunter,' said Larch. 'And make it quick.' He glared at Kay before turning his attention back to the interview room monitors, his hands thrust into his pockets and his jaw clenched.

Kay took a deep breath. 'Okay, well this is how I see it. Somehow, Diane comes to an arrangement with Blake Hamilton that he'll help her out with the ongoing upkeep of Crossways Hall, if she agrees to make Sophie marry Josh. That way, she gets to keep her family home, and Blake gets his son the aristocratic kudos he's so desperate to cultivate.'

'And everyone lives happily ever after.'

'Yeah, but Sophie gets pregnant. She panics – suddenly she's faced with the reality that she's in way over her head. She's due to take a purity pledge to remain chaste until she marries, she's making that pledge on the same day she's getting engaged to Josh Hamilton, and she can't talk to anyone about it.' Kay paused in an attempt to fight down the adrenalin enough so she could explain herself to her senior officer. 'What if Sophie wasn't the one blackmailing Duncan Saddleworth?'

'But we already know it was – we found the cash in her possession in the safe deposit box.'

Kay rubbed at her eye. 'Sophie was the blackmailer to start off with,' she said patiently, 'but after she was killed, Saddleworth received another letter, but Blake Hamilton and Felix Ashgrove didn't. Someone else knew Sophie was blackmailing him, and decided to do the same to make some money, but didn't know about the others – that's why they haven't received any.'

'Has it occurred to you Sophie could've arranged for the letters to be delivered before she died?'

'It was hand-delivered. That means there was someone else involved. Peter Evans denies all knowledge of the safe deposit box, and he seemed genuinely surprised when I told him. Seems to me Sophie found a way to make some money in anticipation of them leaving the country.'

'Hunter, there wasn't enough money in that safe deposit box to warrant killing someone – there was only a few thousand pounds.'

'But what if Sophie's killer found out about it, and figured they needed the money more?'

'What's that got to do with the Whittakers?'

'Matthew Whittaker has admitted their house is falling down around their ears, and his business is about to go into voluntary administration within weeks – you've seen the state of the financial records.'

Larch sighed and turned away from the monitor. 'Still too tenuous, Hunter.'

'Wait, let me finish. Sir.'

'Go on,' said Sharp, and held up a hand to stop Larch interrupting again.

'When Barnes and I first spoke to the Whittakers, Diane told us that they overheard Sophie talking to Eva about Peter Evans – that's when Barnes had Diane show him where she was standing on the terrace. It got me thinking while we were interviewing Matthew Whittaker – if Diane knew she could eavesdrop underneath Sophie's bedroom window, what else did she hear?'

'You think Diane found out Sophie was pregnant and killed her because she'd spoiled her plans to marry her off?' said Barnes.

'That's what Matthew alleges. In the circumstances, we've got no choice but to interview Diane Whittaker.'

'Bloody hell, Hunter. You'd better be right about this,' said Sharp.

'I agree,' said Larch. 'The political ramifications if we're wrong could end our careers.'

Kay caught Sharp's eye, but he shook his head.

The only one worrying about his career being ruined by Diane Whittaker's links to local people of influence was the DCI.

Sharp cleared his throat and followed Larch's gaze to the interview room monitors, then sighed. 'It's a long shot. However, I agree we should question her under caution – to eliminate her, at least.'

'I'll head over there now,' said Kay and headed towards the door. 'Come on, Barnes. House visit.'

CHAPTER FIFTY-TWO

Kay yanked the handbrake and released her seatbelt.

'This place looks more rundown every time I come here,' said Barnes, straining his neck to view the house through the passenger window. 'I don't know why people insist on living in houses like this if they can't afford to keep it looking nice. I mean, what's the point?'

'I guess it's partly to do with keeping up appearances.'

'That's not going to last long,' said Barnes. 'You heard they dismissed the gardener the other week as well?'

'Finances must have been bad for a long time.' Kay stared out the window, a frown creasing her brow at Barnes's comment, and a thought crossed her mind.

It would mean changing her tactics slightly, but she knew Sharp would support her, if it came to that.

The question was, would Larch?

'Come on,' said Barnes. 'Let's do this. The sooner we get her down the station, the closer we are to finding out what the bloody hell has been going on around here.'

'Couldn't agree more,' said Kay, and reached out for the door handle before climbing out.

She raised her gaze over the roof of the vehicle as a marked car pulled up beside them, and two uniformed officers joined her on the gravel driveway, their bright fluorescent waistcoats painfully bright under the sun's glare.

'Round the back, you two,' she said. 'We'll be bringing the housekeeper in for formal questioning as well, so make sure no-one leaves through the tradesman's entrance, got it?'

'Sarge.'

The elder of the two placed his cap on his head and led his colleague across the driveway and down the side of the building, the crunch of their boots on gravel subsiding as they disappeared from sight.

In the distance, Kay could hear a tractor negotiating the narrow lane, its engine revving as it climbed the slight incline at the end of the driveway. Above, a hawk fluttered on the breeze and she was struck by the sense that the house seemed to be in a vacuum, waiting for her to tear down the façade its owners had created.

'How do you want to do this?' said Barnes.

'Formally,' she said. 'Larch will have my warrant card for this if I don't. I don't know what's been going on in this house, but none of it's good.'

They walked side by side towards the front door, and Kay frowned. The front door was ajar, and raised voices could be heard from within.

'After you.'

'Thanks.'

She pushed the door open and entered the dark hallway. Straight away, she noticed the bare walls, and a gap where once an oak-panelled dresser had taken up one wall.

'Moving out?' murmured Barnes.

'Or selling to stay.'

Footsteps carried from the far end of the hall, beyond the curve in the staircase before fading away and Kay realised the housekeeper would be returning to the kitchen as the two uniformed officers appeared at the back door.

She headed towards the formal conservatory

where she'd first questioned Sophie's parents, and knocked on the door.

Diane's face appeared at the gap, and she reared back, startled to see them standing there.

'The front door was open,' said Kay. 'We tried to knock, but—'

'I didn't hear you,' she said. She swung the door open and peered out. 'Where's Grace?'

'Mrs Jamieson?'

'Yes – didn't she meet you at the door?'

'I don't think she heard us.'

'Oh. Will you come in?'

Diane remained poker-faced, but her whole stance exuded defiance as she hovered near one of the chairs.

'What do you want?'

Kay's eyes met those of Barnes, and he gave a slight nod. There would be no easy way to do this, and so she may as well get on with it. 'Caution her, please, Barnes.'

'Diane Whittaker, I'm arresting you on suspicion of causing the murder of Sophie Whittaker...'

Kay studied the woman's face as Barnes spoke, and noted that she appeared flustered.

Good, she thought.

She glanced over her shoulder as the younger of

the uniformed officers appeared, the housekeeper behind him while the older officer brought up the rear.

'Have you cautioned her?'

'Yes, Sarge.'

'Put Mrs Jamieson in your vehicle. Mrs Whittaker will be coming with us.'

'I want to speak to my husband,' said Diane, her voice shaking as the housekeeper was led away. 'This is preposterous. I demand to know what's going on.'

'We'll explain at the station,' said Kay.

'I want to call my solicitor.'

'Again, you can do that at the station.' She stepped to one side and gestured towards the waiting cars. 'After you.'

CHAPTER FIFTY-THREE

'What's going on?'

Diane Whittaker's biting tone cut through the cold air of the second interview room the moment Kay and Sharp opened the door.

'A moment, please, Mrs Whittaker,' said Kay. She pressed the record button and formally cautioned the woman, including the charges that had been laid against her.

'I'd prefer to be called by my proper title,' said the woman officiously.

'And we prefer to call you Mrs Whittaker,' said Sharp.

Kay didn't wait for her to respond. 'Tell me about your arrangement with Blake Hamilton.'

'That was a business transaction between Mr

Hamilton and me,' sniffed Diane. She waved her hand. 'I don't have to discuss private business matters with the likes of you.'

'Mrs Whittaker,' said Sharp. 'At the present time, you're under arrest. I'll remind you of the caution that was just read out to you.'

'What was the arrangement you had with Hamilton?' Kay repeated.

'Blake Hamilton was our saviour,' said Diane. 'He was only trying to help us.'

'Did your husband know his daughter was entering into an arranged marriage?'

'It's all his fault we're in this position in the first place!'

'Tell us about that.' Kay opened the folder under her arm and peeled back the pages until she found the financial statements. 'From what I can see, when your father died he left a considerable number of gambling debts. Substantial losses that resulted in him remortgaging the house prior to his illness. Your husband has been using every spare penny from his business to maintain the upkeep of Crossways Hall, is that correct?'

Diane scowled. 'Yes.'

'Right. So perhaps you could enlighten me as to why you believe this is his fault?'

The woman sighed, tried to cross her legs and then realised the table was too low for her to do so. She shifted in her seat. 'He's never amounted to anything, Matthew. He tries to be an entrepreneur, but he's not really cut out for it. Not like Blake.'

'So, I'll ask you again. What was the arrangement you had with Mr Hamilton?'

Diane tutted, before clasping her hands in front of her as if in prayer. 'Blake noticed that his son had taken a liking to Sophie at one of our church meetings. He happened to mention to me that it had always been his dream to be part of the English aristocracy.'

'Josh's dream?'

'No.' Diane waved her hand as if a bad smell had wafted in front of her. 'Boy wouldn't have a clue. *Blake*. Blake loved his history – had done since he was at university here, apparently. Well, as soon as I heard that, I thought perhaps I could turn it to our advantage.'

'In what way?'

Diane leaned forward, warming to her story. 'It was delightfully simple. After the engagement, Blake was to hand over a sum of money that Matthew and I could then use to get some of the more urgent work done to the house. Once Josh and Sophie were married, we wouldn't have to worry – they would live at the Hall, and Blake would provide us with a stipend. He was even going to pay us a bonus when we had our first grandchild,' she beamed.

Kay fought down the anger and frustration that was boiling inside her.

'How much?'

'Well, I'd only received part of the dowry of course.'

'How much?'

'Six thousand pounds.'

'Why did you decide to blackmail Duncan Saddleworth?'

Diane's jaw dropped open at the sudden change of direction to Kay's questioning, but didn't answer.

Kay shrugged. 'It's because you overheard Sophie telling Eva she thought he was the father of her baby, wasn't it?'

Sharp stiffened next to her, but she ignored him and continued. 'I figured you were going to keep quiet about it until after the engagement and purity pledge ceremony before you confronted Sophie, but you couldn't help yourself, could you? That's what Josh Hamilton saw the two of you arguing about on the terrace, wasn't it?'

Diane sighed. 'The stupid girl. Couldn't keep her

legs closed by the sounds of it. Of course, I'd already made some discreet enquiries that day with a doctor regarding a termination.'

'Is that what you were arguing about?'

'Yes.'

'Except, with her death, you'd have forfeited any money due to you by Blake Hamilton. Instead, you thought you'd blackmail Mr Saddleworth to make up the cash deficit, isn't that so?'

The woman's mouth dropped open. 'How did you—'

'Saddleworth received a letter after Sophie's death. The other two people Sophie was blackmailing didn't receive any correspondence. It was because the blackmailer – you – didn't know about them. You only knew Saddleworth was being blackmailed by Sophie because you heard her tell Eva about her plans to run away, didn't you?'

'Don't be ridiculous.'

'On the contrary, Mrs Whittaker. You told your husband that you'd been shopping in Tunbridge Wells recently, and he mentioned you'd bought new diamond earrings. Given the state of your finances, how on earth could you have afforded those otherwise?'

Diane glared at her.

Kay turned the page and held up a document so Diane could read it. 'This is the inventory for the safe deposit box we emptied at the bank. Duncan Saddleworth was ordered to pay an additional fifteen hundred dollars by cash to a post office box in Tunbridge Wells. None of Sophie's entries in her notebook tally with that amount, and all of the cash she received went to a post office box in Maidstone town centre.'

'The bitch deserved to die,' Diane suddenly spat. 'Dirty little whore, sleeping around like that. I hope she rots in hell.'

The solicitor beside her choked and spluttered, his eyes wide.

Kay folded her arms across her chest and sat back in her chair, before turning to face Sharp.

He raised an eyebrow, but remained silent.

She nodded, and faced the woman in front of her once more.

'Diane Whittaker, we'll be seeking authority from the Crown Prosecution Service to charge you with blackmailing Duncan Saddleworth...'

CHAPTER FIFTY-FOUR

DCI Larch paced the corridor outside the interview room but stopped as Kay and Sharp emerged and closed the door behind them.

Kay ignored him for a moment and handed an envelope to Carys. 'We need to speak to the housekeeper. Can you take this in and show Diane Whittaker? I didn't want to use it during the interview.'

'Will do.'

Kay turned to Larch.

'What the hell?' he began. He stabbed a finger towards the interview room. 'I thought you said she killed her daughter?'

Kay brushed past him and knocked on the door to

the next interview room, then winked. 'No, I didn't. Matthew Whittaker did.'

'Excuse me, guv.' Sharp edged round the DCI and followed Kay into the room, quickly straightening his face as he settled into the chair next to hers.

Kay closed the door behind him as a loud wailing began from the room next door.

Grace Jamieson sat next to the young duty solicitor who had been appointed for her.

'What's going on?' She rose from her chair, her eyes wide. The duty solicitor reached out and placed his hand on her arm, but she shrugged it off. 'What's all that noise? Is that Lady Griffith? What have you done to her?'

'Sit down please, Mrs Jamieson,' said Sharp.

She sank into her seat, kneading her hands together. 'She sounds distressed. Are you sure I can't see her?'

Kay leaned over, switched on the recording machine, and then formally cautioned the housekeeper whose eyes widened as the charges were read out to her.

'What's going on?'

'Please roll up the sleeves of your cardigan.'

'Why?' Jamieson turned to the solicitor. 'Why she asking me to do that?'

The solicitor's eyes found Kay's. 'My client has a point.'

'Every time we met, you've worn long sleeves, Mrs Jamieson. At first, I put it down to the fact that the Whittakers' house seems to be cold all year round. However, when I last saw you, and despite it being a warm morning, you still wore long sleeves. I'd like to know why.'

The woman jutted her chin. 'I fail to see what that's got to do with anything.'

'Mrs Jamieson,' said Sharp, and leaned forward in his chair. 'This interview is going to go faster if you help us with our enquiries. Roll up your sleeves.'

She glared at them both then wrapped her fingers around her sleeves one after the other and tugged them up to her elbows.

'There.'

Kay's eyes fell to the woman's forearms. Faint scratches could be seen above her wrists, with one large scratch on her left arm.

'How did you hurt yourself?'

'I was gardening. Until recently, we had George to help, but Lady Griffith had to let him go.'

'When did he leave?'

'About a week ago.'

'Why?'

'Lady Griffith's husband has made a mess of his business and she's in danger of losing the house. Mr Whittaker decided we couldn't afford a gardener full-time anymore.' She pulled a tissue from the box on the table and dabbed at her eyes. 'It's the end of an era, Detective – do you realise that? Lady Griffith's house has been in the family for years. My mother was employed by her mother.'

'How did that make you feel, when your husband lost his job?'

The woman recoiled. 'I didn't say he was my husband.'

'No, but he is, isn't he?'

'It's all Mr Whittaker's fault.' The woman pouted. 'We'd never be in this mess if he ran his business properly.'

'You have a knack for eavesdropping don't you, Mrs Jamieson?'

The woman dropped her hand to the table, the tissue scrunched up in her fist. 'Whatever do you mean by that?'

'You have a tendency to hover at closed doors, hoping to hear gossip,' said Kay. 'When my colleagues and I have visited the Whittakers at home, you've been close by, listening in, haven't you?'

The woman's cheeks coloured and she jutted her

chin at Kay. 'It's a housekeeper's business to know what's going on in the household.'

'When did you find out about Mrs Whittaker's arrangement with Blake Hamilton?'

'It was a good arrangement.'

'Answer the question.'

The woman glared at her, then lowered her gaze and plucked an imaginary piece of fluff from the thin gold band of her wristwatch.

'He came to the house when Mr Whittaker was out at a meeting with his bank,' she said eventually. 'Lady Griffith met with him in the conservatory and they spoke about the purity pledge then. Sophie had already mentioned it to her parents, and Lady Griffith knew she'd taken a shine to Josh, so she proposed the arrangement to Mr Hamilton and he agreed. It suited them both very well.'

'How did you find out Sophie was pregnant?'

The woman sneered. 'She always looked down her nose at me. The years I've tidied up after her, ironed her clothes, cooked for her. She was insolent, disrespectful. She ignored me most of the time unless she wanted me to do something for her. I was invisible to her. She and that trollop of a friend of hers were talking on the terrace outside the dining room after breakfast the day of her engagement party – it was easy to hear what they were saying. I was shocked to hear she was pregnant. I didn't take her for the type.'

Kay pushed her chair back at a knock on the interview room door.

Carys stood in the corridor, and handed a plastic evidence bag to Kay. Kay thanked her, and closed the door before returning to the desk and placing the evidence bag on it.

'While you were waiting for us to speak with you, one of my colleagues has been speaking to our crime scene investigators.' Kay pushed the bag towards Jamieson. 'Luckily, on the night of Sophie's murder the first responders at the scene had the sense to smother the flames of the braziers around the terrace. The remains are all that are left of a rolling pin.'

Jamieson paled, and lifted a shaking hand to her mouth.

'The reason why old rolling pins like this are passed down through families is because they're made of a hard wood,' said Kay. 'It makes them difficult to destroy.'

'I-I don't know what you mean.'

'You were expecting caterers the morning of the party. While they were busy working in the kitchen, you took the rolling pin from the kitchen drawer and hid it amongst the rhododendron bushes beyond the terrace. That's how you got scratches on your arms. You heard Sophie talking to Eva Shepparton earlier that day. You heard her tell Eva she was pregnant and who she thought the father was. As far as you were concerned, it ruined your plans to help Mrs Whittaker keep her ancestral home, and put your position in the household at risk. There's not much of a requirement for housekeepers these days, is there?'

Jamieson made a small noise at the back of her throat.

Kay ignored her and continued. 'Later that day, after the speeches finished and the disco started, you lured Sophie into the darkness beyond the terrace and you struck her so hard with the rolling pin, she was killed instantly. You must have been covered in blood.'

Jamieson whimpered.

'You removed the cardigan you were wearing, wrapped the rolling pin in it, and on your way back up to the terrace you threw the two items into the first brazier you came to. The problem was, unknown to you, the wind had picked up and the brazier wasn't burning as hot as it could have been. It was blowing mostly smoke at that point, stinking out the disco.' Kay pointed at the burnt remains in the plastic evidence bag. 'We have another one of those bags with the remains of your cardigan in.'

'Don't be ridiculous.'

'You've been employed by Mrs Whittaker all your adult life, haven't you Mrs Jamieson?'

'Yes, and I've been proud to serve Lady Griffith.'

'Except of late, you've had to stand and watch as, one by one, all the other staff have been made redundant, ending with your husband, George Jamieson.'

The woman glared at Kay. 'If that stupid runt of a child of hers hadn't got herself pregnant by that godawful priest, then none of this would have happened,' she snapped. 'She ruined everything.'

'No, Mrs Jamieson, you did. You killed Sophie Whittaker, and you killed the baby she was carrying at the time. A baby whose father was Josh Hamilton.'

Kay sat back in her chair, her palms on the table and watched as a look of absolute horror stole across the woman's features.

'No – no, that's not right. Josh isn't the father. It's the priest. Or that Evans fellow. Not – not Josh.'

'We've received the paternity results a moment ago,' said Kay. 'And *that's* why you could hear Mrs Whittaker. One of our colleagues broke the news to her while we came to speak with you.'

Jamieson's eyes widened as realisation sunk in.

'Grace Jamieson, we are now going to seek authority from the Crown Prosecution Service to charge you for the murder of Sophie Whittaker...' Sharp edged forward on his seat and read out Grace Jamieson's rights before setting out the formal procedures that would now take place.

His final words were lost on Kay as she pushed her chair back, slipped through the door into the corridor, and walked out of the building.

CHAPTER FIFTY-FIVE

Kay turned the key in the ignition and released her seatbelt as the car engine died.

She leaned forward, resting her chin against her hands on the steering wheel while her eyes traced the line of gravestones beyond the car park.

An emptiness clawed at her gut, a familiar sensation that she knew would never leave her, not completely.

She leaned over, grabbed her handbag from the foot well and eased herself from the car, waving the key fob over her shoulder until she heard the *thunk* of the internal locking mechanism.

Picking up her pace, she meandered between the headstones, breathing in the fresh summer air.

A bumblebee hovered close to her face before

sweeping away towards a patch of dandelions in the grass to her right while a wood pigeon cooed in the trees that lined the site to her left.

She blinked, and glanced up as the breeze carried the sound of a distant siren towards her, before pulling her mobile phone from her handbag and switching it off.

Someone else could be dragged from their late afternoon sabbatical.

She tossed it back into her bag and slowed as she reached the next row of stones. Turning right, away from the grassy aisle she'd been following, she made her way halfway along the row, then stopped and placed her hand on top of the cool grey granite headstone, her eyes tracing the simple inscription.

Elizabeth Hunter-Turner. Beloved daughter, taken too soon.

'Hello, Elizabeth.'

She dropped her bag to the floor and began to tug at the long grass that had already begun to encroach around the base of the stone despite Adam's attendance to it only a couple of weeks ago.

The light summer rains and bright days had caused the whole countryside to burst with life, and here among the monuments to the dead, it was no different.

Lost in her work, she didn't hear anyone approaching, and jumped at the sound of a man clearing his throat.

She spun round on her toes and shielded her eyes from the sun at the figure towering above her.

'Thought I'd give you a few moments to yourself before joining you.'

Sharp shoved his hands in his trouser pockets and turned to survey the cemetery. He squinted in the afternoon light as his eyes roamed the landscape. 'It's a peaceful spot up here.'

'Yeah.' Kay straightened, threw the weeds to one side and brushed her hands together to lose the remaining leaves.

'Do you visit often?'

'We try to get here a couple of times a month. Adam will be here in a bit – he wanted to pick up some fresh flowers first.'

'I won't hang around. I've got something for you that I didn't want to give to you at the station.' He reached into his pocket and handed her the spare key to her front door. 'I had someone go to your house while you were both out. He took a look at the equipment you found. Whoever put the cameras and microphones in there, they're professionals.

Especially given the limited timeframe they had to do it in.'

'More than one of them, then?'

He nodded. 'Probably. Two to trash your house, and maybe two or three to fit all the equipment. My contact removed all the cameras and microphones so you won't have anything to worry about in that respect now. They won't be able to see or hear anything.'

'Won't they suspect something?'

'My contact ran white noise for a bit and then increased the frequency – that killed the equipment. They'll probably assume that mice, rodents, equipment giving out or a power surge wrecked the microphones. Happens all the time.'

'Okay.'

He passed her a set of four miniature cameras and microphones that had been sealed within a plastic evidence bag. 'There were no fingerprints – we checked.'

Kay let out a shaking breath and turned the bag between her fingers. 'Thanks, guv.' Kay's hand trembled as she held up the bag to the light and inspected its contents. As she remembered what the equipment had been used for, it seemed to exude a malevolent quality and it was all she could do not to throw it to the floor and grind it under her heel. Instead she raised her eyes at Sharp's voice.

'Are you going to tell me who you suspect is behind all this?'

She blinked, and rubbed at her right eye. 'It wouldn't be very professional of me, would it? Spreading rumours?' She dropped her hand. 'No – I need more evidence, or a breakthrough or something.'

'You'll hang on to the cameras and microphones for evidence though?'

'Yeah. I went back to the Whittakers' bank and opened a safe deposit box of my own.' She clutched the evidence bag in one hand and pulled out a small key from her trouser pocket. 'I want you to have the spare. In case anything happens to me.'

His eyes met hers as he plucked the key from her fingers. 'Are you sure?'

'I don't know who else to trust, guv. And I'm trying not to get Adam involved. Can I trust you?'

He tested the weight of the key in his hand. 'Yes. And I'm not going to open that box, all right?'

'You might have to. If anything happens to me.'

He sighed. 'Adam doesn't know you're still hunting for whoever did this to you, does he?'

She bit her lip. 'He knows.'

'Be careful, Kay. I'd hate for anything to happen

to you two. He's a nice bloke.' Sharp checked his watch. 'I would imagine he'll be here any minute. I'd best be going.'

He patted her arm as he passed, and she watched as he stalked back to his car, his head bowed.

As he climbed in and powered the vehicle away, she turned her attention back to her daughter's headstone.

A groan escaped her lips.

Eighteen months ago, her life had been normal.

She'd had a job she loved, colleagues she could trust and have a laugh with, and a safe home life.

Now, she could feel it all slipping away from her. She couldn't let them do that to her.

Wouldn't.

She turned her attention back to the car park at the sound of another vehicle approaching, and then relaxed as she recognised Adam's four-wheel drive.

He braked to a halt and climbed from the driver's seat, and she held her breath.

He caught her eye and raised his hand before reaching into the passenger side of the car and extracting a bunch of fresh flowers. He ran a hand through his hair, then aimed his key fob at the car and began to walk up the slight rise towards where she stood.

As he drew nearer, Kay shoved the collection of cameras and microphones into her handbag before swearing an oath she had every intention of keeping.

She'd do anything to protect Adam from those that were trying to harm her.

Anything.

<< THE END >>

FROM THE AUTHOR

Dear Reader,

First of all, I wanted to say a huge thank you for choosing to read *One to Watch*. I hope you enjoyed the story.

If you did enjoy it, I'd be grateful if you could write a review. It doesn't have to be long, just a few words, but it is the best way for me to help new readers discover one of my books for the first time.

If you'd like to stay up to date with my new releases, as well as exclusive competitions and giveaways, you're welcome to join my Reader Group at my website, www.rachelamphlett.com.

I will never share your email address, and you can unsubscribe at any time.

You can also contact me via Facebook, Twitter, or by email.

I love hearing from readers – I read every message and will always reply.

Thanks again for your support.

Best wishes,

Rachel Amphlett